But Never Hate

D1611618

But Never Hate

My
Gym Crush!.

Your So amazing!!.

your bitch

DeAna Nelson

Copyright © 2015 by DeAna Nelson.

ISBN: Softcover   978-1-5035-9417-3
               eBook   978-1-5035-9416-6

All rights reserved. No part of this book may be reproduced or
transmitted in any form or by any means, electronic or mechanical,
including photocopying, recording, or by any information storage and
retrieval system, without permission in writing from the copyright
owner.

This is a work of fiction. Names, characters, places and incidents
either are the product of the author's imagination or are used
fictitiously, and any resemblance to any actual persons, living or dead,
events, or locales is entirely coincidental.

Any people depicted in stock imagery provided by Thinkstock are
models, and such images are being used for illustrative purposes only.
Certain stock imagery © Thinkstock.

Print information available on the last page.

Rev. date: 08/10/2015

To order additional copies of this book, contact:
Xlibris
1-888-795-4274
www.Xlibris.com
Orders@Xlibris.com
713410

This book is dedicated
to the loving memory of my grandfather,
James Bundy

I love you, Papa

For me, writing comes naturally,
and I thank God for giving me the talent, the strength,
and the unspeakable insight to do so.

Attract to you that which is yours.
Call on the universe to fulfill your dreams.
Be positive and stay inspired.
Show love, affection, and undying gratitude.
Then . . . Sit back and let God handle the rest!

Acknowledgments

I thank my mom, Olivia Bundy, who taught me never to give up on anything that was important to me. Thanks to my husband, Everton Nelson, for helping me to grow and learn commitment. You keep me young. Thanks to my aunt, Norma Lindo, for telling me I would be good at anything I tried to do. Those words will stay with me for all eternity. Thanks to my wonderfully loyal little sister, Cossandra Vann, for reading each and every page of my book with great interest and enthusiasm. Thanks to my spiritual mother, Harriet Braswell, for listening, in the wee hours of the morning, to all my crazy ideas regarding the book and for watching it take shape. I really don't mind you being you thirty years younger. Thanks to one of my best friends and the godmother to all four of my children, Dhita Ngy, for always believing in me and cheering me on from the stands; what a powerful little woman you are. Thanks to my cousin, Sophia Hendricks, for teaching me determination. You are truly one of the most determined women I've ever had the pleasure of knowing. Thanks to a longtime family friend of thirty-something years, Racquel Royal, for making me fly solo; the best of me came out when I was alone. Thanks to Carol Grant for telling me I could write and for getting me through my stage fright. Falling on your lap has changed my life forever. I have become aware of so much about myself with your help.

Turn of the Season

Peering from the open window it felt cooler now

I watch as a leaf departs from the tree it once called home and slowly falls to the ground.

They seem to glow as orange as the sun shining after a rainy day.

The wind is blowing this way and that way

Throwing the leaves around and filling the yard with fun and laughter.

Bare were the branches that connected to this glorious birch,

So big and full of wet weeping limbs.

Though bald of its beautiful summer glow,

It was still a sheer delight to see one of God's ultimate creations coming ahead.

It was fall . . .

Chapter 1

OK . . . so here we go again. I am being forced to attend another breakdown, ghetto charade of Labor Day, with the family from hell.

"Sasha. We're gonna be late!"

"I'm coming, Tray," I said in a very unwilling tone. "I was just getting my jacket!"

Shit, doesn't he realize we're already late? I can't stand these family picnics! Every year we have to celebrate Labor Day with these people. Why can't we do something by ourselves? It takes so much out of me. It's a "labor" day, all right. We go way out to Hartford and get together with the hood rats and the hoochies of the family. All damn day long, you have to hear a bunch of criticisms, cussing, and gossip, and since

I'm an artist, they kill me with artist jokes. That would make anyone wanna run away, move to another country or something, but instead, I chose to come to this ratched event year after year. Obviously, I got out of the line and got into the "put up with bullshit" line. I thought that by moving out to East Lyme, I could get away from them, but no, they just keep coming. My cousin, Tiffany, lives in Providence, Rhode Island, which is closer to the family than we are, and she somehow seems to keep them distant, as if she lived somewhere in Peru.

"Tray, where's TJ?" I screamed downstairs, from my son's bedroom.

"He's down here with me, Sasha! We're waitin' on you!"

That boy's always ready to go somewhere.

"Does he have his asthma pump?" I said, thinking of a reason to stay upstairs.

"Yeah, I think so."

"Well, could you ask him?"

"We won't be having any episodes out there in the middle of Keney Park today."

"Yeah, Sasha, I'll ask him," he said, sounding annoyed with me.

Last year, TJ had an attack while they were playing volleyball. I almost lost my mind. I thought we'd have to rush him to Saint Francis Hospital, and even though it was just down the street from the park, I wasn't trying to be in nobody's emergency room all night. Finally, I got him calm and made him sit his behind down on a bench for the rest of the day and play board games. He was so mad with me, and to add insult to injury, my bigmouth Aunt Trudy, gotta have something to say.

"If you didn't hang out in the clubs all the time with your cousins when you were pregnant, your son wouldn't have asthma now. All that damn smoke ain't good for a fetus." She gets on my last nerve.

"Sasha, he got the pump Tray said. "Now keep it moving and stop playing like you don't wanna go."

My husband sure does know me well. If it weren't for that son of mine be going. He's so attached to the family, especially my cousin, Tiffany, it's ridiculous. He adores her more than anyone else in the family. If it weren't for that, I would not still be coming to these sad-ass events every year.

"Sasha, did you bring the cups and plates that were on the kitchen table?" Tray yelled from the garage.

"Yes, Tray, I put everything in the car last night so we wouldn't forget them."

"All right then, let's hit the road."

"I can't wait to see Aunt Tiff," TJ said, happily getting into the backseat of the car. "She always has something special just for me."

Tiffany is the cool one of the family. Even though she kept her distance, she got along with everyone in the family, except her mother, Trudy, and her sister, Melony. When Tiff came around, everyone knew they would be getting something. She would bring candy for everyone. Even when her mother gave her dirty looks as she offered up our favorite treats, it didn't stop her from coming. Tiffany and her mother never got along. Aunt Trudy said Tiff disrespected her wishes by opening a damn candy store.

"You can't make no money off a candy store!" she told Tiff.

The only problem with that statement is that Tiff was making money off her store—and good money too. What burned Aunt Trudy most is that Tiff didn't do things the way she wanted her to. Aunt Trudy told her to go to college, become a lawyer or something. But Tiff went to business school and opened a candy store. She told her to get a nice condo in Bloomfield or Simsbury; Tiff bought a house in Rhode Island. She was gonna do what she damn well pleased, and who didn't like it didn't have to watch. Her lifestyle was the biggest family secret. It was the secret of the century. If Aunt Trudy knew the truth, she'd probably disown her. You see, the truth of the matter is that Tiffany is a lesbian. And despite her mother's hatred for lesbians, Tiffany is happily dating a female.

What I couldn't figure out is how she kept it from certain family members for so long. I mean, I can understand some of us not knowing— like Uncle Peety, Aunt Trudy's brother, who's always drunk; and my cousins, Tony and Lee, who were always wrapped up in their own shit; and maybe even Aunt Trudy, who doesn't really care what's going on with Tiffany and my cousins, Nathan and noisy-ass Melony. Now keeping secrets from those two is a hard thing to do. Nathan hung out with the Jamaicans and sold marijuana out of his home. He likes to keep to himself, but he was always up on the latest news. He may not hang with his family, but he usually knew what was going on.

Now my cousin, Melony, she's another story. She is the digger of all information to be known. She is so damn nosy. She wanna know where it came from, when you got it, and how much you paid for it. I call her the private investigator of the family. She should have been a news reporter instead of an accountant. I don't understand why other people's business was so important to her. Maybe she defines her life by what others have. I don't know. What I do know is that somehow, Tiff has managed to pull the wool over their eyes.

I mean, maybe if Tiff and Mel were closer, she would have found out, but Tiff stays clear of Melony's path. Ever since they were little, they just didn't mesh. They never were on the same wavelength. Tiffany had no respect for Melony as an adult either. She couldn't understand why everything Mel did had to be based on what other people were doing.

She never really stopped to try to figure out what she liked for herself. It was always, "Hey, did you see what so-and-so bought?" or "Did you hear where so-and-so is going?" Nothing was based on herself. I don't even think Mel knows who she really is.

She was always constantly selling herself short, like staying with her cheating husband, even after he's been caught twice with other women. He was caught once by my cousin, Simone, and once by Nathan. She told us she stayed with him because they bought a house, and she wanted the girls to grow up with their father; meanwhile, she is so unhappy. You can hear the doubt in her voice. Doesn't she realize she's only hurting herself and teaching all three of her girls to settle for less than they're worth, for the sake of commitment? What about being committed to yourself? Someday, she'll get it. You have to love yourself in order to love others.

My cousin, Simone, told me that Mel is scared to be alone, but I don't believe that. All you got to do is give Mel a couple of drinks, and you'll see the real person come out. She'll tell you how she could've had a great life if things were different. She blames everything that is going on now on her past. When she's tipsy, she is so much more fun and relaxed too.

I don't know what to say about her; all I know is that I'm glad Aunt Trudy didn't raise me. She really did a number on those folks, starting with her little brother, Peety. Shoot! He started out wrong from birth. His mom named him after a dog she had that died. She said that when Pettaris died while she was pregnant, it was a sign. That dog's spirit was in her newborn baby. She had some shit going on with her too. It's no wonder he's a drunk. He still borrows money from Trudy to buy his booze. I mean, the damn man is, like, what, fifty-two. Trudy raised him when their mother died. She was only nineteen, and he was eleven.

Then there are her three sons, Lee, Tony, and Nathan. They were the product of her three now-dead husbands: Lee, who is the oldest, is raising his daughter by himself since her mother went to jail; Tony, who sells crack cocaine and owns a strip club; and Nathan, who thinks he's a Rasta—not dreadlocks, but a full-on Rasta. Speaks like one and everything. He walks around town, selling incense and preaching the Bible to people with a spliff in his mouth.

Aunt Trudy didn't spend nearly enough time with those boys growing up. She always thought that was a man's job. The problem with that is there wasn't a man around long enough. Aunt Trudy killed them off faster than you knew it.

Then you got her four girls: Tiffany, who is the oldest, is a secret lesbian; Melony, always tryin' to keep up with the Jones' so confused; Maggie, who chose to move to New York right out of high school; and Simone, who is still in college and is basically living off her mother. Simone, although she's my girl and all, lives in a beautiful condo in the suburbs of Bloomfield, drives an Explorer, and gets regular manis and pedis. Mind you, she's been in college for the last seven years because she only goes part-time.

Trudy wants so bad to have a professional in the family to brag about she'll do whatever it takes to make that dream come true—even if she has to take care of Simone with the inheritance money her three dead husbands left behind.

Oh, and did I mention she worked for her brother, Tony? She had a lot going on in her life. I thought she had everything then. Then comes this guy named Richie, also a drug dealer, like Tony. They met at the strip club, and if you know her, you know you gotta keep her in luxury. I like to call him Richie Rich. But you know what? I feel like this: If you can get away with having anything you want, without having to work hard for it and without lowering your self-esteem, go for it. You only got one life to live. Live it to your fullest.

"TJ, are you all right back there?" I said, suddenly remembering my child in the backseat. "Are you hungry yet?"

"Yeah, I'm hungry," TJ said from the backseat.

"Dad, how much longer before we get there?"

"Boy, we just got on the road. You got at least a good forty-five minutes to go," Tray said, surprised, since he just made the boy breakfast about an hour ago.

"Look in the little cooler back there on the floor," I told TJ, ignoring his father. "There are some tuna-fish sandwiches in there," I said, grinning.

By the time we get to the picnic, he's gonna be full. That gets right up under Melony's skin. She always says, "That's why Tramaine Jr. is so skinny." Little does she know, he eats all day! I guess she would prefer for him to look like her, a fat big heffa. She makes me so sick. She is the only one that won't call my son TJ, 'cause she feels it's too ghetto. She thinks nicknames are stupid. She has a conniption fit when we call her Mel.

"My mother named me Melony," she says with an attitude.

She is so funny. She turns her nose up at anything she thinks is ghetto, but she won't turn her nose up at all the food she shovels down her throat. She's probably bigger than the last time I saw her, which was on the Fourth of July.

Her husband, Alexander, is always feeding her. I mean, by right, he should be feeding her, if it weren't for her working two jobs to put him through culinary school, he wouldn't have that restaurant now. Well, he wouldn't be a partner in the business, I should say. He's never fully owned anything a day in his life, except his own bottle of liquor and his own crack pipe.

"Sasha, do you hear me talking to you?" Tray said, sounding annoyed.

"What!" I said sharply, interrupting my thoughts. "What did you say?"

"I said, pass me a bottle of water out of the cooler."

"Oh," I said, dazed. "Why can't you ask your son to pass it? He's there in the back with the cooler."

"What, you're sleeping?"

"No, Tray, I'm not sleeping. I was just thinking."

"Thinking about what?" He said curiously.

"Oh, you know, this and that," I said, not wanting to tell him my thoughts.

"Oh, I get it. You don't want to tell me. That's cool. I should be used to it by now. You don't talk to me anyhow."

"Tray, that's not true. I'm talking to you right now."

"You know exactly what I mean, smart-ass."

Tray was always complaining about me not sharing my thoughts with him. He just doesn't understand. I've been with him my whole young-adult and adult years of my life. He tends to be very controlling. There's got to be a point when I take control of just how much of me I give to him and how much I keep. My mother, God rest her soul, always told me, "Never let a man know everything that's going on in your mind. They'll use it against you if they have to." And it's the damn truth. There are plenty of times I've told my husband things, and when he gets upset with me, there he goes, bringing it up.

Anyway, back to my thoughts. Now where was I? Oh yeah, let's see. I think I left off with my Uncle Peety. He is the slow one in the family. He went out with this crazy woman named Brittany. She hit him in the head with a baseball bat one day during a fight they had. Ever since then, he has never been the same. We all told him to stay away from her, but he didn't listen. I could see straight through her. All Uncle Peety could see was that big old ass she had. Well, you see where that got him. She took him for everything he had. I mean, it wasn't much, but it was his. His father left him a Mercedes-Benz sold to pay her rent. He didn't even live with her. She had all sorts of guys coming in and out of that place like you wouldn't believe. Uncle Nathan sold weed to two of the men she was seeing. When she got pregnant, he worked full-time and part-time to try to provide for her. We still don't know if his daughter, Shari, is his biological child. I mean, we all love her like she's one of us, but she looks nothing like us. Brittany went to jail a couple of months after Shari was born, for selling drugs. That was the last we saw of her. Ever since then, Uncle Peety hasn't been the same. All he does now is sit around, drunk as a skunk. I don't think he'll ever get over that woman.

Shari now lives with Aunt Trudy. She hates living with her, but there's no one else that will take care of her, including me. Occasionally, she'll call me and ask if she can come and spend some time with TJ. They both enjoy writing poetry, so a lot of their time is spent doing that. She is really good too. I mean, so is TJ, but Shari has something special. I think all the pain she has experienced has made her a really intense writer. When I read her poems, I forget it's a child's work I am reading.

Of course, Aunt Trudy thinks she's wasting her time. "You're fifteen years old now. You need to go and do some volunteer work at the hospital. Get a good start on life. Maybe you can become a doctor or something." She is always trying to control what we do. She didn't learn from Tiff.

Then there's gangster Tony. He's got the most money and the longest rap sheet. You name it, he's done it, from selling drugs to selling women and everything in between. He has always said he would buy his mother a big house on the hill, with a white picket fence and a dog, even though she's scared of dogs. He has lived up to that, in a manner of speaking. The first house he bought was big, on a hill and had a picket fence, but after he lived in it for a couple of months, it was seized by the feds. After that happened, he decided to put everything he owned in his mother's name. It was the best thing he could have ever done. Aunt Trudy had a little money coming in from so many sources, so the police never suspected a thing.

I must say, Aunt Trudy is good about attracting money to her. Although she takes care of Uncle Peety, Simone, and Shari, she has never really wanted for anything, as far as any of us can see. The last child is Maggie. She moved away right out of high school. No one has seen her in years. She doesn't keep in touch with anyone. We only know she lived somewhere in New York, and she is a dancer.

"Sasha! What the hell is wrong with you?" Tray said angrily. "What the hell are you thinking about? You planning to leave me or something?"

"Why would you say that?"

"You're sitting right next to me, and you can't hear me calling you?"

"Sorry, Tray," I said, kind of amused. "What can I do for you, honey?"

"What can you do for me? You can tell me why you haven't said more than two words to me since we got in the car and why I have to be talking to myself. You in your own little world, TJ stuck in that video game. I mean, damn, I'm so sick of this shit. It ain't funny."

"Baby, you don't have the curse, and just so you know, I dozed off for a minute. That's all." I tried to lie.

"Yeah, with your eyes open. I bet you dozed off. That's all right, Sasha. Don't do me no favors. That's all right. I got you."

My husband tends to over-react at times. Since he opened his barbershop ten years ago, he is hardly ever home; he is always off, taking care of some sort of business. When I ask him what he's been doing, he doesn't go into every detail of his business with me. He just says, "I've been taking care of business."

Now you let me sell a painting—or even try to. He wants to know how much I sold it for, whom I sold it to, where they live, how they heard about me, and what brought them to the shop. You name it, he'll ask it, as if I were having an affair with my clients or something.

He feels that because we've been together for the last fifteen years, I am somehow bored with him. But I'm not bored. I'm just fine. I paint my pictures at the studio, teach my art classes at the university, take care of my son, and hang out with my cousins. I don't want for anything else. I am very content with my life. I like it that Tray is the only man I've ever been with, and I like the fact that I've been married since I was nineteen. It doesn't bother me or make me feel like I'm missing out on anything.

"Finally, we're here!" TJ screamed as we pulled into the park.

As usual, who do you think is the first person to notice we're here? Yes, that would be Ms. Melony, with a piece of chicken in her mouth. Oh the fourth. Wonder what she's been doing. I'm sure she has a mouthful to say about me. As soon as Tray parked the car, TJ opens the door and runs to Tiffany.

"I knew she'd be here already," TJ said anxiously. "She's always early for everything."

She doesn't have any children to worry about; that's why.

"Tray, don't take that cooler out. Leave it in the backseat for the ride home," I told him while he was unloading the forty-pound box of chicken I seasoned last night.

"Sasha, don't forget the cups and plates," he said, struggling with the box of chicken.

"Yes, sir," I said sarcastically.

He's always trying to tell me what to do. The truth is, I did forget about the cups and plates. Who cares anyway? I'm sure Melony brought enough cups and plates for all of Hartford.

"Hey, girl, what's up?" Mel said, walking toward me. "Oh, you cut your hair?" she said, looking me up and down.

"Yeah, a little. I needed a change."

"You always cut your hair anyway. It grows so fast. It must be that Indian blood in you," Mel said sarcastically.

"Yeah, I guess so," I said, not really wanting to make conversation with her.

"Did you see what Simone got?" Melony said with her eyes opened wide.

"No, what did she get?"

"Girl, she got a three-karat diamond from Richie. They are officially engaged. I had to show Alexander, 'cause, you know, it's time for me to get a new one. Shoot, we've been married for what, fourteen years now. It's time for a new ring. I'm tired of wearing this one."

Mel never knew that Simone and I knew her ring wasn't real. Alexander didn't have any money to get her one at that time, so she settled for a large cubic.

"Where is Simone?" I said, cutting her off.

"She went for a walk with Richie. You know, they probably went to smoke some weed," Melony said, laughing. "They ain't nothing but a bunch of potheads."

I couldn't take it anymore. I started walking toward the table to see what was on it.

"Hi, Aunt Trudy," I said, looking over her head to the street.

"Hi, Sasha baby," she said, with her phony self.

Seeing that I'm almost two hours late, I'm sure she was talking about me like a dog before I got here. The way I see it is, the later I get here, the less time I have to spend with these people. Tiffany sees it the other way. The earlier she comes, the earlier she can leave.

"Hi, Ms. Harriet. Hi, Mr. Carter," I said, looking over at my aunt's friends.

"Hi, Sasha," they both answer.

"How've you been?" Ms. Harriet said.

"Oh, hanging in there."

"Sold any new paintings lately?" Mr. Carter said.

"Oh yeah, I sell paintings all the time."

"Hmm," said Aunt Trudy under her breath.

"I just sold one for four thousand to this man from New York," I said, making sure that Mel heard me.

"That's the way to do them," Mr. Carter said, flipping hamburgers over on the grill; he was so Jamaican. "Oh yeah, make that money," he said, laughing.

"You are such a good girl, you know that, Sasha?" Ms. Harriet said, smiling at me.

"Yes, Ms. Harriet," I said, grinning.

They have so much confidence in me. Too bad all of what I just told them is a lie. I can't possibly tell them that all I am is an art teacher at the local university and that I haven't sold a painting in almost two years, especially with Aunt Trudy standing there, listening. She is ready to find something wrong with my life. I will never allow her to be right. Not even for a second. I mean, I've been working on paintings, but somehow, I just feel stuck. I just can't find the right energy. All I know is, I'm doing the very best I can, and I am so sure that it won't be enough for Aunt Know-It-All. Well, I guess I better go see what all the commotion is over there at the volleyball net.

"Just serve the damn ball!" Uncle Peety yelled out to Tony across the net.

I was shocked to see Tony here. He usually comes after dark, when we're packing up everything to leave. Tony, Alexander, Mel's girls, Diana and Liz, and someone I didn't know were on one side of the net, and Uncle Peety, his two friends, Albert and Chancy, along with Tiffany and Jade, were on the other side.

"Hey, guys!" I yelled out.

"I'm out," Tiffany said, coming over to me.

"I'll play!" Tray yelled.

"Hi, Aunt Tiff!" TJ screamed happily when he saw her.

"Hey, handsome, what's up?"

"Nothing," TJ said, looking to see if she was gonna pull anything out of her khaki jean pocket.

"I got something for you. It's in my car."

"You do? What is it?"

"I don't know. You're gonna have to come with me to find out."

"Well, well, well," I said, watching Simone walking toward me with her scrawny little boyfriend.

"Hey, girl!" she screamed from halfway across the park.

I walked toward her with a big smile on my face. I love her so much. If there's one thing I can say about Simone, she is not fake—at least not fake with me. She always tells me how it is, whether I like it or not, and God knows I need it sometimes.

"Girl, I know you heard," she said, getting closer.

"Heard what?" I said, pretended Big mouth didn't already tell me.

"Don't lie to me, Sasha. I know Mel already done told half of Hartford."

"OK, OK, let me see! Damn! Damn! Now that's a ring!" I said, holding her hand up to the light. "I am so proud of you. You got what you wanted. Give me a hug!"

"I know, right?" Sasha said, sighing in relief.

"So why didn't you call me when you got it?" I said, with a little attitude.

"Oh, girl, your hair is getting so long," Simone said, changing the subject.

"Yeah, OK," I said, rolling my eyes at her. "Didn't you just see me last month? It's no longer than it was then. Anyway," I said, changing the subject again.

"No, I don't think so. I don't have sex enough to do that. Plus, I just got off my period, like, three days ago. I think it's my vitamins."

"Well, girl, I need to take some of them."

"For what? You don't even like your hair? Oh, please, Moni. You know you're the weave queen. You wouldn't wear your own hair even if it was long."

"I know. That's right. I got to have different colors. You know me. Today, I want it straight. Tomorrow, I may want it curly. Next day, I might just want it short."

"Yeah, she changes her hairstyles like she does her draws," Richie said, interrupting.

"Hey, Richie," I said, smiling at him.

"Hey, Sash," he replied back, looking me up and down.

"What's up with you lately? You looking real good, with you fine ass."

"Richie, you better stop flirting with that man's wife before he do you in," Simone said, laughing. She knew how Tray was about me. He would have a fit if he heard anyone talking to me like that.

"I've been fine, Richie. I heard the great news. It's official. You are now a part of the family."

"Thanks, Sasha," he said, grinning at me. "Does this mean we can be kissing cousins?"

"Um, I don't think so, Richie," I said, grinning back. He was the biggest flirt.

Now you would think Simone would be jealous, hearing her now fiancé speak to me like that, but the fact of the matter was, she didn't have an insecure bone in her body. She was fine, and she knew it. Everyone around her knew it too. She carried herself like a million bucks and demanded that everyone around her live up to her standard of care. Even Tray can't help himself when he's around her. He stares at her.

You know what's so funny though? He wouldn't want me to be like that—I mean, I don't anyway. I am much more conservative, but he is so attracted to women who look like that. I don't feel comfortable dressing like that. I still can't get rid of my baby pouch from TJ. When Tray and I first started dating, I was a size 4. Of course, I was only seventeen. If I didn't have TJ, I would probably still look like that now. Here I am, thirty-one and still fighting the bulge. I must admit, I don't work out, and I don't eat right. I don't overeat, 'cause I don't wanna look like Mel, but I don't eat the way I should.

"Hey, Sasha, does Mel look like she lost weight to you?"

"I don't know, Simone. Did she lose weight?"

"Yeah, she started that no-carb diet. The only problem is that since she lost, what, fifteen pounds now, it's gone straight to her head. You should see how she walks now."

"So that brings her down to what? Like, one ninety or so."

"Yeah, girl, something like that, but you would think she lost a hundred pounds the way she's been acting."

"Ma, look what Tiff got me!" TJ said, all excited about the mini motorcycle Tiff bought him.

"Tiff, I can't believe you spent that kind of money on that. You know he can't ride that out where we live. They don't allow it."

"It's all right. It can stay at Aunt Trudy's house. You can ride anything in the ghetto," Tiff said, laughing.

"So, Tiff," Simone whispered, "when's your woman gonna put on some clothes?"

"Would you hush? I don't care what she puts on, as long as when we get home, she takes it off for me."

"Oh lord, I don't wanna hear about you and your woman," I said with a chuckle.

"You know you do. Shoot, if it weren't for me and Simone sharing our lives with you, you wouldn't have anything to fantasize about, 'cause Tray sure ain't doing it for you."

"Well, you got that right. He hasn't even been sleeping in the bedroom lately. All he does is watch that damn big screen TV downstairs until he falls asleep."

"Girl, I'm telling you something ain't right with that, Sasha."

"Simone, why are you always saying stuff like that? We've been married for a long time. It happens. I hear about it all the time. Couples get comfortable with each other."

"Nah, that's not what it is. I'm telling you, you better look into that. All them late nights at the barbershop. Who stays at the barbershop till twelve o'clock almost every night? How much hair do they cut anyway?" Simone said sarcastically.

"Oh, boy, look who's back," Tiff said, looking out to the parking lot. "It's Ms. Mel, with them old-school Janet braids down her back," Tiff said, laughing.

"Girl, ain't it time she took them braids out now? Those damn things are so played out," Simone said, laughing.

"You know she's old-school," Tiff said, looking at me.

"Don't put me in it. You know her ears are really big, and she got radar up for anything that comes out of my mouth."

"All I know is, she's been sportin' them for as long as I can remember."

"Simone, you know you ain't right. Leave that woman and her braids alone," I said, with another chuckle.

"Who is that Big Bertha with her? Oh lord, she's gonna finish all the chicken and burgers. Y'all better get a plate now."

"Simone, you are so bad," I said.

"That's one of her co-workers," Tiff said.

"She sure is big. How does she fit in that car?"

"Tiff, I can't believe you got something to say about somebody being big. Remember Carol?"

"Carol who, Sash? What are you talkin' 'bout?"

"Yeah, you know who I'm talking about. You were after that woman for the longest. You used to say she had the prettiest biggest legs you ever saw."

"Girl, she did," Tiff said, grinning.

"Yeah, I thought you didn't remember any Carol," Simone said, laughing.

"You know what, Tiff? You've been gay for a long time now. Don't you think one day, you might want to give a man a try?" Simone said playfully.

"Me? Be with a man? Never again. Not after Walter's ass. He turned me gay in the first place."

"Oh, please, I don't think someone can turn you gay. It's either you are, or you're not."

"No, Simone, that's not true," I said. "Some people go through so much with men that it makes them want to be with a woman."

"Sasha, please! I have gone through a whole lot with the men I've dated, and not once since I've been working in the strip club did I ever think about being with one of those women. If anyone should be attracted to a woman, it would be me."

"Hey, y'all!" Mel shouted, walking over to us with her big friend. "This is Joyce and her son, Charles. She and I work together. Joyce, these are my sisters, Tiffany and Simone, and my cousin, Sasha."

"Hey," Simone said, looking away.

Hi," Tiff said, trying not to laugh.

"Nice to meet you, Joyce," I said politely. "Charles, you see that little boy with the dreads in the blue-and-black striped shirt?" I said to her son. "That's my son, TJ. Go over and tell him I sent you to play with him."

"Yes, ma'am," he said, with a smile.

Simone and Tiff are so funny. They act like they don't like Mel, but the minute Alexander starts acting up, they're the first ones over her house wanting to beat him down. I just can't believe them sometimes. I know she's as phony as can be at times. But that doesn't mean we should embarrass her in front of her friends. I sure wouldn't want anyone to do that to me.

"Mom, I got the ice you wanted," Mel said, walking over to Aunt Trudy.

"Thank you, baby," Aunt Trudy said, smiling at Mel.

"Mr. Carter, you need any help with that grill?"

"No, baby, I got this. You know this is my job every year," he said to Mel, cheesing from ear to ear, with his side teeth missing.

I don't know how or why he puts up with Aunt Trudy, but they've been friends for a long time now. He just keeps coming around. I think something is going on between the two of them. They've been hanging out together a lot lately.

Ms. Harriet has been friends with Aunt Trudy since they were little. She's married, but her husband never comes around, 'cause he can't stand Aunt Trudy. You only see him from the car, when he drops Ms. Harriet off and when he picks her up. No "hi"; no nothing. Ms. Harriet always makes sure she brings home at least two plates for him. Mr. Carter came to one of our cookouts a long time ago, and all hell broke loose. He and Aunt Trudy started arguing over something he said to Ms. Harriet, and that was it. He told her she needed to mind her own business and tend to hers. He said that was the reason why she was alone. That, of course, was before Mr. Carter started coming around. Aunt Trudy was so hurt she told Mr. Carter that he better not ever show his face around her again. And that was all she wrote. He never set foot at another function. We didn't see Ms. Harriet the year after that, but she and Aunt Trudy have been friends since they were kids, and she couldn't stay away.

Aunt Trudy—she's only ever had two real friends: Ms. Harriet and Ms. Grace Angelou, who moved to Georgia about seven years ago. She comes up once a year for Aunt Trudy's birthday. She's a nice lady. I remember, as a child, she would always call on the phone to speak to my mother. "Lydia," she'd say, "how is that beautiful daughter of yours? You know she's something special." My mom would laugh and say, "Yes, I know. That's why she's an only child. I wanted to give her the world." And that she did until the day she died.

"Sasha, what's up with the dance contest?" Simone said, laughing. "You wanna be the judge?"

"No, I don't want the pressure. You guys get too serious. Wanna beat people up for not choosing your child," I said, looking at Mel.

Tony went to his truck to get his portable CD player.

"I'm surprised you didn't have the music going already, Tony," Tiff said.

"Yeah, Mama didn't want to watch it while we were playing volleyball. She said it was too big and cost too much for her to be responsible for. You know how she is. All right now," Tony said, gathering all of us together. "Who's dancing today?"

We all got up and started to form a circle. Mel pushed Liz and Diana closer to the center. By this time, more of the extended family and friends had arrived: Tony's girlfriend, Emily, and her sister, Leslie, who came fiercely dressed; Richie's boys, Andre and Paul; Shari's little friends, Mary and Courtney; and Alexander's boy, Joe, and his son, Raymond.

We had a pretty good crowd of about fifty. There have been times when we've had around a hundred or so. Even people from the neighborhood came out to our Labor Day gathering, like they were part of the family. They've never caused any problem, so Aunt Trudy lets them stay.

"Now, who else is dancing? I know it can't just be these two. What do y'all wanna jam to?" Tony said.

Diana looked at her mother and then at Liz. They knew the kind of music they wanted to hear wasn't gonna be approved by their snobby white-wannabe mama.

"I wanna hear, um," Diana said, thinking out loud. "I wanna hear something fast." "No," Liz interrupted, "I wanna hear something funky."

"Better make up your mind soon, or I'mma pick it for you," Tony said, raising his eyebrows.

"I wanna be in the dance contest," a voice said from the parking lot. It was Melony's oldest daughter, Alezandria. She was supposed to be away on a trip with one of her girlfriends. She showed up in some shorts cutting off half her butt cheek, with one of them off-the-shoulder shirts. I know her mother was livid.

"Hey," she said aloud, walking over to us.

Aunt Trudy said nothing; she just looked at her. She didn't approve of the way she dressed or acted. She just never said anything about it because of her being in school and all. Zan, as we called her, wanted to be an architect. Aunt Trudy didn't know much about it, but she said at least it was a trade.

"Hey, Miss Zan, what are you doing here? I thought you were going to Georgia with your friend?" Simone said, smiling. "I like your outfit, girl."

"Thanks, Moni," Zan said, smiling at Alexander, who was just standing there next to Tony, staring at her like a piece of meat.

Mel never noticed the way he looked at that girl, but I did. You see, Alexander wasn't Alezandria's real father. Mel had her before they met. You see, Mel was raped when she was sixteen by this boy named Poppi that used to live in our neighborhood. She used to tell us that he would watch her all the time when she walked to the corner store and stuff, but no one ever took her seriously, till he did that. Tony and his boys went looking for him one night. The next day, the cops found him dead in a dumpster, with needles stuck in his arms. Mel never reported the rape to the police 'cause she was too embarrassed and because Tony told her he would take care of it. When we heard that the cops had found Poppi's dead body in a dumpster, we all knew what happened. Most of the others just thought it was a drug overdose since he was a known crack.

Anyway, Mel had the baby because Aunt Trudy told her she would go to hell if she had an abortion. Now Alexander came along when AleZandria was already one. After staying with her for a couple of months, like, six to be exact, she decided to change the baby's name from Allie to AleZandria. She figured since he has taken the responsibility for raising her, she may as well have his name. Poppi's family never knew he had fathered a child, and Mel never bothered to tell any of them.

One day, when Zan was about ten or eleven, Mel and Aunt Trudy sat her down and told her that Alex wasn't her father. They told her they thought it was only fair that she knew. But the truth of the matter is that Poppi was half-Hispanic, and AleZandria started to look more like him than us. She used to ask questions like why her skin and hair were so different from everyone else's and where she got her nose from, since it was kinda pointy, and everyone in our family had a, what you would call black nose—you know, a little on the flat side and kinda wide. Everyone was afraid to say anything about it. They would just say, "Oh, girl, your nose is just fine" or "Maybe we have some ancestors that look like that." Some lame old excuse. I knew she didn't go for it, 'cause she would ask different people in the family. Once she found out the truth, she started acting different.

Alex never really paid her any attention until she got older. All of a sudden, when she was about fifteen, they started hanging out together. He would pick her up in school and take her to the mall; they would even go to the movies together, without the other girls. Mel never questioned it 'cause she was just glad he finally started paying attention to her. Alex even went as far as to buy her a new car, with Mel's money, as soon as she got her license. When she graduated from high school, he wanted to send her to community college so she would live at home. He didn't want her away from him in some school far away. He said he didn't trust them boys on campus. Mel didn't care about anything they were doing together, as long as he gave Zan what she wanted.

Ever since Zan was told about Alex, she never wanted to come around us. She stayed mostly with her friends and hung out with Alex on the sneak.

Simone was the only one that she really spoke to. She said the rest of us were all phony liars.

See, Simone had never lied to her. Of course, she was never around enough to lie to her. She was always in the streets, doing her own thing, hanging out with her friends. Now she and Zan are best buddies.

She calls Simone and complains to her about her mother all the time. She tells her that all her mother cares about is her two prize daughters, Diana and Liz. Zan always thought her mother loved them more because they were Alex's biological daughters. They both came along back-to-back when AleZandria was about three.

If you ask me, I think Simone and Zan were way too close. Simone should have encouraged her to be closer to her mother instead of treating her like she was her little protégé. Simone told me and Tiff all of AleZandria's secrets. If Zan only knew that Simone couldn't hold water when it came to us, she wouldn't tell her anything. We never told anyone what Simone told us though; we had no reason to.

"All right, since you wanna dance, Zan, what do you wanna dance to?" Tony asked Zan, since she seemed like she would be able to make the decision.

"I don't care what. Just play something popping. I'm ready to get my party on."

Mel looked up at Zan and rolled her eyes. "You better not play any foolishness out here," she said, looking cross-eyed at Tony. "Having them children whining themselves up like they don't have any sense."

"You know what? I'm just gonna pick something myself," Tony said, grinning at Mel. "'Cause I see I can please none of y'all folks. Whatever I play, that's what it's gonna be. If you don't like it, go home." He popped in a CD, and Zan went wild.

"I'm bringing sexy back."

"Hey, that's what I'm talking about, Justin Timberlake!" Zan screamed out over the music.

They all started dancing. Aunt Trudy even started moving a little bit.

"Go, y'all, get busy. Go, Zan!" Simone screamed out.

Mel hated the way Zan danced. She had everything shaken up all over the place, and she wasn't such a small girl. I mean, she was about 180 pounds, and she's only five foot five. That's a lot going on. Hands and butt up in the air. Ms. Harriet sat back in her lawn chair and laughed. She loved to see the young kids being young. "Shake it while y'all can, 'cause one day, you're gonna wanna shake it, and not a damn thing is gonna happen."

Everyone seems to be enjoying themselves except Mel. Diana won the dance contest, of course, since Aunt Trudy ended up being the judge. She favored Diana over Liz and Zan any day 'cause she looked just like her. Mel said she should've named her True, but she named her Diana after that famous singer Diana Ross.

After everyone danced themselves into a coma, it was time to eat. Mr. Carter brought a big pan of rice and peas he made at home and made us some jerk chicken on the grill. You gotta love West Indians; they're always ready for the party. Ms. Harriet was famous for her banana pudding and those chicken-and-shrimp shish kebabs. She brought that along with some barbecue chicken and potato salad. We were in charge of all the tableware, and I made some macaroni salad. Tray brought a large cooler full of beer. Tiff brought about three of four different kinds of cakes and all the hot dog and hamburger buns. Tony brought the hot dogs, hamburgers, three cases of beer, a big cooler full of wine coolers, six cases of soda, three racks of beef ribs, and one of them big sheet cakes from the grocery store. He always spent a lot. After all, he did have it to spend. Uncle Peety brought the booze and himself, and Simone brought the chips and the ice.

By the end of the night, everybody's belly was busted wide open. We laughed, danced, played, and ate. Now it's time to go. It was almost eight o'clock, and the park was gonna be shut down soon 'cause it was getting dark. You didn't wanna be caught in the park after dark. Too many crackheads went out.

I didn't spend a single moment with Tray, which was fine with me. He spent half the night playing cards with the guys and some pregnant girl that I think Paul was dating, and then he left for a couple of hours with them. I thought she was dating Paul; I'd seen her at a lot of our events.

As usual, we are all getting ready to clean up, and who is missing? Simone, Richie, and Zan. They disappeared about an hour or so ago, as they always do. I and Tony's girlfriend, Emily, stay together most of the night. Tiff and Jade leave early as usual. They tell Aunt Trudy they have some business to take care of. Aunt Trudy doesn't care too much for Jade. She always complains about the way she dresses.

"That child never wears enough clothes. Is she trying to catch one of the men in this family, or is she selling her body? I just don't know why Tiffany would hang around someone like that."

If she only knew Jade was already in the family.

"Ma, I'm tired. Can we leave now?" TJ said, looking all sweaty and worn-out.

"Yeah, it is getting late. Go get your father."

"OK," he said, dragging his feet over to where Tray was talking to Andre, Paul, and that girl. They had been talking for a minute now. TJ should've been tired from riding that minibike all over the place all day.

Tony pulled his truck on the grass and loaded up the tables in it. He had about ten plates of food. Damn, that man could eat.

"Boy," I said to him, laughing, "you would think you were feeding ten people. All those plates for you, Tony?" I said, watching him load up.

"You know I'mma need my energy for them two later," he said, grinning.

"Them two? You know what? That's what's wrong with y'all now, always wanted to share."

"Shh, be quiet, or you'll mess up my game. You know one ain't enough for me. Never been and never will be."

"Yeah, whatever you say, player."

"That's right," he said, letting out a big laugh.

"Ma, what are we gonna do with my bike?" TJ said to me, walking back over toward me.

"Why don't you leave it at Uncle Peety's house? He only lives around the corner."

"I don't want to leave it at Uncle Peety's house. Somebody might steal it. You know how his apartment building is. He lives with all them crackheads. Can we take it home, Ma? Please?"

"We can't fit it in the truck. OK then, go ask your Uncle Lee to take it to his house, and we'll come down so you can ride it on the weekend, all right?"

As TJ walked over to where Lee was standing, I noticed that woman was still standing by Tray. She was all up in his face too.

"Tray!" I yelled out. Can you come here for a moment please?"

"I'll be there in a minute, Sash."

"Tray, I really need you now," I said, demanding him to come. I stood there, watching as he basically ignored me and kept right on talking. I wondered if she went with one of his friends. Why didn't they introduce me to her? I started to walk over to them, but TJ called me.

"Ma, Uncle Lee said it's OK if I leave the bike at his house."

"You sure it's all right if he leaves that bike at your house?" I said again to Lee. "I can bring him down on the weekend."

Lee was sitting down on the park bench, watching Leslie's butt roll, as she walked to Tony's truck.

"What? Sasha, did you say something? Yeah, that's fine. I mean, that's OK with me. He could leave it," Uncle Lee said, looking dazed. He was so horny.

Everybody said their good-nights, and we all drove off about the same time. Mel screamed out her window, "Take care of that scrawny boy of yours, Sasha!"

I just ignored her. On the way home, there was silence. TJ fell asleep in the backseat.

Tray and I did not speak. I wanted to say something about that girl in the park, but I didn't want it to start an argument, especially with TJ in the backseat. I decided to just lay back in my seat, turn and look out of the window, and fall asleep too.

Chapter 2

I woke up with a headache from all the wine coolers I had drunk last night. Tray had gone to the barbershop already, and TJ had already left for school. I looked over at the alarm clock.

"Oh, damn! It's nine thirty already, and my class starts at eleven. I better get my ass out of this bed. I have so much to do!" I screamed.

I pulled some dress pants and a button-up shirt out of the closet, threw it on the bed, and jumped in the shower. I got dressed, gathered up my art supplies, and headed out to work.

Tray had left about four ounces of coffee for me. He knows I need at least a sixteen-ounce cup to get me started in the morning.

I already dread going to work. I really don't want to be in this dead-end job. I mean, I know I'm helping others, but I am so sick of structure. I am an artist, and what I should be doing is painting for a living, not teaching some snotty college students how to pursue their dreams as an artist. I often feel like a failure at times, especially when I am not getting along with Tray. It doesn't take much for me to feel this way. That's why I had to lie to Mr. Carter and Ms. Harriet in front of know-it-all Trudy. I can't possibly allow her to know the truth about what is going on with me. She would only rub it in my face. I jump in the car and head for—"Oh, shoot, my phone is ringing," I say, digging in my pocketbook.

It was Tray calling me.

"Hello?" I said.

"Hey, I see you finally rolled out of bed."

"Yeah, why didn't you wake me up?"

"I tried to twice, but you wouldn't budge. That's why I set the clock to wake you up at ten!"

"You know my class starts at eleven. Why would you wake me up that late? Anyway, it doesn't really matter. I woke up at nine thirty."

"Well, I see then you're all set."

"Yeah, with no thanks to you," I said sarcastically.

"Look, I didn't call you to argue. I called to say good morning, if I can do that."

"Yeah, you can. I'm sorry, Tray," I said softly. "OK, let's start over," I said.

"Good morning, Tray," I said, trying to sound a little nicer.

"Good morning, Sasha," Tray responded softly. "Now, what time do you think you'll be getting home today?" he said, getting right to the point.

"Oh, I don't know," I said. "Why?"

"I was just wondering. You know I gotta keep tabs on you."

"I thought I might go out to see Tiffany for a while and then maybe stop at the mall in Providence."

"Didn't you just see Tiff yesterday? Damn, what, y'all joined at the hip? I guess that means no dinner tonight. That's all right. I guess I'll just go get something outside."

"Tray, are you forgetting we have all that food from the cookout yesterday? I don't think I should have to cook when there's all that food sitting in the fridge. Why don't you eat that first?"

"What food? I took that with me this morning. I had to have lunch, and you know if I eat in front of the guys, they're gonna be beggin' me for food."

"You took all of it, Tray? You didn't even leave a plate for TJ?"

"No, he didn't wanna eat that shit again. He had that yesterday. You're just too fuckin' lazy to cook. That's what your problem is."

"Tray, I cook all the time. What are you talking about?"

"Yeah, you cook when your cousins are coming over or for a staff meeting or something. But for us, you barely cook anything, and I'm sick and tired of this shit!" he said, screaming now. "You know what, I'll get TJ and take him to karate, and then I'mma take him out for dinner. You ain't thinking 'bout us. I ain't thinking 'bout your ass either."

"Tray, why are you acting like this? I don't understand how all of sudden, me cooking or not cooking affects you. It didn't before."

"Well, you know what, Sasha? It does now!"

"Oh, by the way, Tray, why are you calling me from your cell phone instead of the shop phone? Where are you? Are you even at the shop?"

I heard silence. He hung up on me. That bastard hung up on me.

What am I going to do with this man? He gets on my last nerve. I love him so much, but it seems like we're growing apart more and more every year. I don't wanna end up like Melony and just be married to prevent TJ from growing up in a broken home, but I don't wanna leave him either. He's the only man I ever slept with. I mean, I've dated other men when I was in high school, but he's the only man I've ever had sex with.

It's been fifteen years since I was sixteen years old in the eleventh grade. He had been trying to talk to me since our freshman year, and I wouldn't give him the time of day. My mother always told me that a man should look clean and neat, and he had dreads and always wore his clothes baggy like they were about to fall off him. The only reason why I talked to him was because he was into poetry, like me, back then anyway. I remember in our junior year, we had a poetry reading in the auditorium. He read the sweetest poem about pecans. I found out later that pecan was me.

My best friend then was a girl named Samantha. She would always tell me that Tray was looking at me, but I never looked back. I only had eyes for Greg Tyler. I thought he was the best-looking guy in the world. He was on the football team, and I swore one day, I would wear his letterman jacket. He was the only black guy I knew that only dated white girls. I always said I would be his first and last. I planned of being his wife. Instead, I ended up with Tray.

Sam took me to this party one night, and we got pissy drunk. Tray was there with some friends and kept flirting with me all night. The next thing I knew, Tray was walking my drunk ass into the bathroom. That was the night I lost my virginity, and that's the only man I've been with ever since.

After that night, I couldn't get rid of him. He wanted to go everywhere with me. We were so inseparable that we were voted as the most likely couple to stay together. What no one realized was that I really didn't want to be with him. What kept us together was that he was my first. I made a promise to myself that my first love would be my last.

When I got pregnant, Aunt Trudy took care of TJ so that I could finish college. Tray and I got an apartment together, and then he decided he wanted to be a barber. When he first opened that shop, I never saw him. He was always at work. He told me he had to build up his clientele. He went from one chair to six new barbers. Things got so good that he remodeled the shop and extended it. He took some of my paintings to display in his new sitting area.

After I finished school, I applied at the university near Tiff's house. I can't believe I am still working there. Don't get me wrong; I am so grateful, but there is a part of me that feels trapped. It feels like there is something missing. I envisioned my life very different from this.

The one thing I can say I have done right is with TJ. I have always seen the artist in him. I have tried to expose him to theater and art, even if Tray thought he should be out playing sports of some kind. Mind you, he knows he has asthma. After a while, TJ started performing himself. It made him feel so good when people snapped their fingers after he was finished. Once, he said to me, "Mommy, I think I want to be a famous poet one day."

I thought that was very sweet since that's what his father told me he wanted to be when we were younger. My son soon started looking more like the group I hung out with, more earthy, and he even wanted his hair dreaded up like his father's. To this day, he still has dreads, and he still wears Egyptian musk oil and beads around his neck. The kids in his school used to think he was weird, but I guess they just got used to the little black hippy. I thought he was cute.

"Oh, damn, it's ten forty-five! Where did the time go?"

I jumped out the car, slammed the door, and ran to go and sign in the office. I was always the last teacher to sign in. They've never said anything to me, but I know they will soon. I think it's because they have no one else to teach the class. I told them that I could teach the class but that I have my own business, so there will be times that I wouldn't be able to make it to all the morning staff meetings they had before classes started.

There was this one guy in my class. I think he was about twenty-six or so. He gives me these funny looks, like, "come take me" looks. He always smells really good too. When I address him, I call him Mr. Thompson instead of Guy, which is his first name. I mean, I address all the students by their last names, but I make his sound extra special. The kids laugh when I call his name because he likes to do things to catch my attention, which means I always have to reprimand him.

"Mr. Thompson, would you please explain to me what you think the artist was thinking when he painted this portrait?" He would answer something like, "Ah, what color should I use next?" And the class would laugh. He's so cute. I have to get my kicks somewhere.

Usually after my morning classes, I stop by Tiff's candy store for lunch. She'd always have something nice waiting for me from the deli next door. If not, she'd send Jade to go get us something. Sometimes, I feel like Jade is jealous of how close Tiff and I are. She tried to get close to me at one time, but I just wouldn't open up to her. She was too forward. She kept asking way too many questions about Tray. That bothered me, but I never told Tiff about it. I mean, if she's so happy with my cousin, why would she be asking about my man?

Simone told me about women like those. She doesn't trust Jade as far as she can see her. "Watch that bitch," she would say. "They'll take your man from right under your nose." I never really thought anything like that would happen to me. Tray and I have been together for so long; I don't think anyone could break us up, no matter what. I know he loves me and only me. We're just doing our own things right now. That's all. Everyone needs room to grow.

When I got to Tiff's store, Jade was the only one there.

"Hey, Jade," I said, walking through the back door.

"Ooh, you scared me," Jade said, startled.

"Oh, sorry, where's Tiff?"

"She went to the bank. She should be right back. She said she was bringing back some lunch from some bakery."

"That woman is gonna make me fat," she said, smiling.

Jade was so phony; she loved it, and anyway, she can't get fat. The only thing fat on her was her head and her big old ass she loved to show off. She had on these hip-hugger black jean capris, with a purple thong showing and a black half shirt that said, "Damn, I'm good." Oh, and don't forget her heels. She could never leave home without them, pointy black toe shoes, with the strap that comes up around the ankle. She had to look like she was going to the club 24-7.

"So how've you been, Sasha?" she said, grinning at me.

"I'm fine."

"That was some picnic yesterday, right?" Jade said.

"Yeah, it was all right. No big deal. Just the same old, same old."

"Yeah, we had to leave early. I was horny as hell, and you know I got to get my groove on."

Oh my lord, why do I have to hear this? Ever since I found out about Tiff and Jade, the two of them are so free around me. They tend to share a little bit too much with me. You see, five years ago, I found out that Jade and Tiff were a couple. One night, after having a fight with Tray, I went to Tiff's house. Whenever I needed someone to talk to, I always ran to Tiff. She was my rock. When I got to her house, I rang the bell. A woman answered the door in a long blue robe. The tie on the robe hung slightly open to reveal a black teddy garter belt. I just looked as if I were at the wrong house and politely asked her, stuttering, "Is . . . is Tiffany home?"

The woman turned around and yelled, "Tiff, Sasha's here!"

Funny she knew who I was, and I had never seen her before in my life.

Tiffany quickly replied, "Who is it? I'm not home. Um, I'm in the shower, damn!"

I kind of just stood there with my head bowed in shame. As the voice got closer to the door, I looked up to see Tiff coming to the door in a T-shirt and shorts.

OK, I said in my mind. *What is this?*

"Oh, it's you," Tiff said, trying to sound like she wasn't surprised to see me.

"Jade, this is my favorite cousin, Sasha. I told you about her. Sasha, this is Jade, my girlfriend," Tiff said, and then she was silent.

I stood there for a minute in the doorway, confused whether to turn around and act as if this wasn't happening, like Melony would have done, or go in and see what is going on in my cousin's life. Of course, being as bold as I can be at times, I went in. Tiffany sat me down on the couch and said, "Sasha, I wanted to tell you this before, but I didn't know how to. You know you're the closest one to me. I really didn't want to keep it from you. You know I love you," Tiff continued. "I hope that you will understand why I couldn't share this with you before. Things were not going good for me until Jade came into my life. You know I've dated a couple of guys, but there was no real attraction. I like girls," Tiff said with confidence.

"I know you used to experiment with the idea of being with another woman a long time ago," I said, trying to understand. "But I didn't know it had gone this far."

"Sasha, I met Jade about two years ago, and I've been with her ever since. We moved in together about six months ago when we decided we didn't want to be apart from each other anymore and because the commute was killing us. Going back and forth to New Haven was a lot. She really cares about me, and I care about her. We have more in common than a lot of straight couples I know. Present company excluded. Just let me explain how it all came about."

"Tiffany, Tiffany, just stop! I don't want to hear this. I don't care what you do or who you do it with, just as long as you're happy," I said, demanding her to listen. "Are you happy? Are you really happy with this woman?"

"Yes, Sasha, I am. I have never been happier in my life. Jade makes up for anything I could have ever missed with a man—except, of course, kids, and I don't plan on having any of those anyway. She also helps me through those family times I just can't bear, and you know what I'm talking about."

I looked at my cousin in silence for a long time. I wondered if a person could really be happy with a member of the same sex. I also wondered how they made love. How could they make each other happy sexually? I had so many questions for her, and before I could get another word out of my mouth, Tiff said, "We're going upstairs. Do you want to come?"

"Do I want to come?"

"Yeah, we got a piece upstairs we were about to light, and maybe drink a little something."

I hadn't been upstairs in a very long time. I usually stopped by to drop off TJ or to grab Tiff and go out somewhere. I felt so confused. I forgot how upset I was before I got there. I got up off the couch and followed them. I didn't know why I was going, but I followed them.

When I entered their bedroom, Jade sat me on the couch, which was across from their plush king-size bed. The room was filled with throw pillows in soft pink and peach that had an orange glow from the red lightbulb. The bed was made up with lace pillow shams and silk sheets. This was clearly Jade's taste, 'cause Tiff would have never picked these colors, much less lace pillow shams. It kinda reminded me of something out of one of those fancy magazines, cozy but sexy.

Jade immediately took off her robe, poured me a drink, and handed it to me. Tiff pulled a cigar box from underneath the bed and opened it. She pulled a really big joint out of it and put the box back under the bed.

"Get comfortable," Jade said, grinning widely at me.

She lay across the bed and watched me sip my drink. Tiff sat on the rug next to the bed and lit her joint. As she puffed, she watched the two of us. She took a couple of puffs before handing it to Jade. She puffed slowly, blowing the smoke up into the room. To my surprise, I found her very attractive. I sat back on the couch, swallowing my spit every time she took a puff. I wondered to myself, Why was I watching this woman? Am I gay?

"Sasha, you're gonna be all right?" Tiff said, noticing me staring at Jade. "You look a little dazed."

"Yeah, I'm fine," I said, trying not to make eye contact. "I was just thinking."

"Thinking about what?" Jade said eagerly.

"Oh ah, ah, just thinking," I replied nervously.

"You'll be fine, Sasha. Just relax and enjoy the ride," Jade said calmly.

I didn't know exactly what Jade meant by that, but at that very instant, I was so turned on by her voice; it shocked me. Tiffany got up off the rug and lay across the bed next to Jade. Jade got up and brought the joint to me and sat on the couch next to me.

"There's nothing wrong with being a little nervous, you know," Jade said, trying to relax me. I swallowed really hard. I couldn't believe this woman made me so nervous. She was beautiful, with her long black hair that shined in the red light. Her eyelashes were so long they looked fake, and her eyebrows were carved to perfection. She had the sexiest shape of lips I have ever seen on a woman, and her body had curves I only dreamed about having.

I didn't know what to expect next. I was used to seeing Simone having sex with other people back in the days when we used to share hotel rooms, but this was completely different. Tiffany got off the bed and came and sat down in front of Jade on the floor. They passed the joint back and forth and stared into each other's eyes. You could see they were both horny for each other. Jade put her hand on my leg.

"Why don't you get out of them jeans, Sasha? Aren't you hot?"

"Oh, ah . . . ah . . . oh, no, I'm . . . I'm fine," I said, stuttering.

"Well, how about you take off that top?" she said anxiously.

"Ah . . . ah . . . ah . . . ah, all right," I said, as if in a trance.

Slowly, I took off my top. Jade just sat there, staring at my body.

"Now, doesn't that feel better?" she said, as if I were a child whose boo-boo had just been bandaged by her.

"I . . . ah . . . I guess so," I said, nervous as hell. My heart was beating a mile a minute, and I couldn't understand how she could get me to do what she wanted me to do. All I knew is, she was gorgeous. I wanted to touch her face, just to see what her skin felt like. I couldn't believe I was lusting over a woman. I wanted to kiss her beautifully shaped lips to feel what they felt like. This was crazy. It felt very weird but so good. Why was I so intrigued by this whole thing? Did I want to be with a woman? I didn't think I would feel that way, but I did. I wanted Jade. I wanted to explore her whole body. I had never thought like this before for any woman. Was this a part of me that I didn't know was there? I didn't know. All I did know was that I was sitting about ten inches away from a very sexy woman that I wanted to get to know better.

Tiffany handed me the joint, stood up, and took Jade's hand. As she guided her to the bed, Jade looked back at me as if to invite me into her bed with her eyes, but I didn't dare move. They sat on the bed and began to kiss. I couldn't believe my cousin was doing this in front of me. She kissed Jade's cheeks and neck and gripped her breast with the palm of her hand. I was so excited. I puffed on the joint faster and took deeper pulls. I was sitting there three feet away from a bed where two women sat, entangled with each other and showing more passion than my husband has ever shown me.

Jade looked over at me with her big brown eyes and winked softly. She was beautiful. It was almost as if someone had airbrushed her imperfections away and left this masterful piece of eye candy.

I sat there for about thirty minutes as they moaned and cried out in sheer delight and licked all over each other. I couldn't believe it. My cousin was a lesbian—and a damn good one. I wanted to get up and leave them to their business, but I couldn't move from the seat. I was caught between amazement and delight. I found myself wanting to join them, but I didn't say a word.

Tiffany laid Jade down on her back, with her legs hanging off the bed, where I could see everything. She slowly took off her panties and got down on her knees in front of her. Jade looked over and saw me standing in the doorway and grinned. When Tiff began going down on her, she wiggled and moaned and held Tiff's head between her legs. It was the most exciting thing I ever felt inside of me. My heart was beating so hard I could feel it was about to jump out of my chest.

Tiffany acted as if I weren't even in the room, but Jade remembered I was there, staring into my eyes as each sensation moved throughout her body. When she was at her peak, she let out a scream and grinned at me. She kept motioning for me to come and join them, but I wouldn't move.

When Tiff was finished with her, she stood up and walked over to me. Jade looked at me with lust in her eyes. She kneeled down in front of me, reached up her hands, and began caressing my breasts. My heart almost jumped out of my chest. Tiff took the joint and the drink out of my hand. I couldn't believe how good it felt. She leaned me forward into her and reached behind me and unhooked my bra. I felt a gush of wetness in my panties. When her lips touched my nipple, I came instantly. She began to suck on my breast, rolling her tongue around my nipples. I'd never felt anything like it before.

I couldn't figure out if it was because she was a woman or because I haven't had sex in a couple of months. Tray was always gone, out of town for months at a time.

I didn't care anymore. I laid my head back on the couch and let her lick and suck all over my shoulders, neck, and cheeks as she stood up. Then she put her lips on mine; I thought I would die with passion. At that moment, she reached with her hand down between my legs and began rubbing my already wet crouch. I began to move my ass back and forth, squeezing her hand into my crotch more. The feeling was unbelievable. I never knew a woman could have so much passion.

Jade eased off my jeans and began licking and biting softly on my stomach. Inching her way back down, she put her mouth right between my legs, through my panties. Then she slid her fingers in my vagina.

"Ooh, you're so wet," she said, happy to see I was enjoying what she was doing to me.

Thinking of my cousin standing or sitting there, watching the whole thing, I refused to open my eyes. Jade rubbed her breast on my thighs and pulled me down onto the floor. With my eyes still closed, I just followed. She pulled off my panties and laid her body on top of mine and began to grind. I could feel her clit rubbing up against mine, and it made me explode with excitement. I came so hard I let out a scream. I didn't realize it came from me until after the fact. I fell asleep right there on the floor.

When I woke up the next morning, they were both still sleeping. They had given me a couple of pillows and thrown a blanket over me. I was so embarrassed I didn't even wake them when I left. I grabbed my clothes and flew out of there. I couldn't even believe what had happened. Some of it was a daze, but one thing was for sure: I had found a new part of my sexuality.

The next day, I couldn't get the scene out of my head. I could still hear Jade moaning, and I could still feel her body grinding on top of mine. The whole experience woke me up to something new. That night, when I went to bed, I couldn't help but relive the event over and over again in my mind. As I thought about Jade and how she moaned, I found my hand slowly caressing myself through my panty. It was the first time I ever had an orgasm. I never knew what it felt like before that. Tray never worried about my having an orgasm. I was intrigued and embarrassed at the same time. I didn't call Tiff for a couple of months after that night.

I didn't wanna talk about what had happened. I never wanted to mention it again. I saw Jade at the store once, and she kept staring at me and licking her lips. It made me feel so uncomfortable, but Jade thought it was funny.

When Tiff realized I was missing in action, she called me. She wanted to know why she hadn't seen me in so long. I told her that I didn't want to see Jade again. I explained what happened in the store and told her that I just wanted to put it all behind me now. Tiff must have spoken to Jade, because the next time we saw each other, she ignored me. I tried to stay clear of her. If I saw her, I went the other way. It was like that for about a year until Tiff called me to say all this shit was crazy and that she missed TJ. She knows I would never keep her from TJ. She was his favorite cousin. I would never come between them. I just didn't want to deal with Jade, but I suppose it was a package deal. Jade always had something to say about something. She didn't like things to be peaceful. Maybe that life was too boring for her. There are some people in the world that are only happy if there is some sort of drama going on.

"So, Sasha, how's Tray?" Jade said with a smirk on her face.

"He's fine. Why do you ask?"

"Oh, no particular reason. I was just making conversation. I didn't see that much of him yesterday at the picnic."

"No, you didn't. He had some things to take care of."

"Oh, OK. I did see him leaving with Paul and that other guy."

"Yeah, Paul and . . . what's his name? I don't remember their names," I said, trying to sound uninterested.

"So what time did you say Tiffany said she was coming back?" I said, changing the subject.

"I don't know what is keeping her so long. She said she was coming right back. Maybe the place she went to get the lunch from is crowded."

"Yeah, maybe, or she could've made another stop," I said, grinning.

"What's that grin for, Sasha? Don't start anything, and it won't be anything," Jade said, looking serious.

"What are you talking about? Girl, please. I wasn't trying to start anything. I'm just saying maybe she made another stop. That's all."

"She better not."

"Jade, if you gotta act like that, why don't you just call her on her phone?"

"I can't, 'cause she left it here."

I loved getting her all riled up. At least she stopped talking about my business.

Just as Jade began to say, "What the hell is taking her so—," Tiffany walked through the back door.

"I would really like to know what took you so damn long."

"Oh, baby, calm down," Tiff said. "I stopped and got this for you. Remember that blue top you said you wanted?"

Jade smiled and rolled her eyes at me.

"What's up, cuz?" Tiffany said to me, cheesing from ear to ear.

"Not a thing, cuz. What did you get to eat?"

"Oh, check this out," Tiff said, excited. "I went to a Greek restaurant and got us all salads with some garlic bread."

"And who told you I wanted to have stinking breath for the rest of the day?" Jade said, looking in the bags.

"My bad. I got mints. Just chill, Jade."

"You make me sound like a child sometimes," Jade said as she took her salad and went to eat at the sales counter in the front of the store.

"She always got something smart to say," Tiff said, shaking her head.

"Then why are you still messing with her, Tiff? Just get rid of her."

"Jade? I can't do that. Have you seen the ass on that woman? I got that shit on lockdown. She is never going anywhere."

"Never say never, Tiff. Suppose she goes back to sleepin' with men?"

"That'll never happen. I eat too nice," Tiff said, laughing.

"You know what, Tiff. TMI! That is way too much information," I said, taking a fork full of my salad. "You sound worse than a man. You need to get yourself together, you pussy whooped."

"Sasha, look who's talking about whooped. You and that fool husband of yours should've broken up."

"Whatever, Tiff. You need to leave my husband alone. We've been together for fifteen years."

"Yeah, fifteen long years."

"Mmm, this salad is good," I said.

"You change the subject if you want, but I know the deal."

"Tiff, leave it alone. Anyway, Mr. Thompson was in class today, smelling all good and stuff. You know he gotta make sure I notice him. He is always asking questions he already knows the answer to. Boy, I would turn that man out. He makes me wet."

"Oh, please. You wouldn't turn anybody out. You're all talk and no action."

"You think so. Just watch. You'll see. One day, I'mma surprise you."

"Yeah, yeah. Anyway, Sasha, I got to go into Hartford. You wanna come with me?"

"Girl, you must want my man to kill me. I have to go home. Besides, he's already mad 'cause I came to see you instead of going home, seeing that today is my early day." "You and your Tray. If he tells you to bark, you gonna do that too?"

"You know what, I got to get going. You are not gonna be my problem today, Tiff," I said, packing up the rest of my salad.

"Run, girl. Run on home to Daddy."

"Shut up, Tiff. I'll talk to you later. Bye, Jade!" I screamed in the front of the store, but she didn't respond.

When I got in my car, I noticed I had one missed call on my phone. It was an unknown number. They didn't leave a message. Oh well, they'll call back if they really want me. I stopped at the mall and got some new sneakers for TJ and a new pair of jeans for myself. I didn't realize how late it was getting. When I got home, Tray and TJ weren't home yet. All the better, I have the house to myself. I love being home alone. I can take a shower and go to bed early.

Chapter 3

The next morning, I rolled over to find Tray already gone. I'm sure he went to open the shop for the guys. I know some of them have early clients. We haven't really been speaking. Today is Saturday, and he's still mad at me for not cooking last week, Tuesday. He can be so foolish at times. I love him though.

It sounded so quiet with TJ gone to Lee's house for the weekend. He won't be back until tomorrow night. I guess I'll take my time rolling out of bed. I plan on spending this day doing absolutely nothing. Maybe I'll go get my hair done if Marlene can fit me in. I do know, anyway, first things first. I need some coffee. By the time I got downstairs, the phone rang.

"Hello," I said in a very passive voice.

"Hello," the person said on the other end, who was clearly a female.

"Yes, can I help you?" I said calmly.

"Yeah, leave my fuckin' man alone!" the voice said and hung up the phone.

OK, she must have the wrong number, 'cause I'm not messing with anybody's man. Anyway, I can't handle anything like that this early, not without my coffee.

"Let's see what's in here to eat," I said, walking into the kitchen.

Ten minutes later, my phone rang again.

"Hello," I said, sipping on my freshly brewed coffee.

"Bitch, you need to know a couple of things."

"Bitch?" I said, surprised. "Um, you must have the wrong number," I said and hung up the phone.

It was the same person again. She had a thick Hispanic accent. She must be tripping this morning. My phone rang again.

"Again?" I said out loud. "Hello," I said, amused.

"OK, look, don't hang up me," she said.

"Who is this? What is your problem?"

"My name's Maritza, and I'll tell you what my damn problem is."

"All right, I'll listen. Maritza, is it? What can I do for you?" I said, treating her like a juvenile, since that's what she sounded like.

"You can start by telling me why you're so damn blind," she said, with a bit of a chip on her shoulder.

"Blind about what, exactly?" I said, a little confused.

"Blind to the fact that I got your man!" she said, almost screaming.

"You have my man?" I said, amused.

"Yes, I have your man," she said.

"And what exactly is this man's name?"

"Oh, bitch, don't act like you don't know."

"Look, if we're going to have this conversation, I'm not gonna be too many more bitches. Now get to your point," I said, starting to get angry. "What do you want?"

"I want you to know that Tray is tired of your old ass," she said and laughed.

My heart dropped down in my stomach. I put my coffee cup on the counter.

"Tray? My Tray?" I said in disbelief.

"No, my Tray. He ain't been your Tray for years now."

"Years," I said, puzzled.

"Did you know we've been seeing each other for almost five years now?"

"Almost five years?" I said, questioning what she was saying to me. "Look! I don't have time for this," I said and hung up the phone.

Instantly, tears started rolling down my face. Who was this woman, and what was she talking about? Oh, I know; I'm still sleeping. Let me pinch myself. Who the hell is Maritza, and what did she mean she's been with my man for almost five years? How could she be going with my man for that many years? Somebody must be playing a game with me. I bet Simone got one of her little friends to play on the phone. I dialed Simone's number; while it was ringing, my other line began to ring again. I clicked over. "Hello."

"Why'd you hang up? You can't take the truth?" she said. "Look, I'm trying to be a woman about this."

"Well, you could have fooled me," I said with an attitude. "You called me cursing at me. Really, you think that's acting like a woman?"

"I just thought it was time you know what's been going on, seeing that I'm pregnant and all."

"You're what? Where do you know my husband from?" I said curiously.

"I met your husband five years ago in the club, through one of my friends."

"One of your friends, and what is your friend's name?"

"You know her," she said, sounding like a child. "Her name's Jade. She goes with your cousin."

"Jade?" I said in shock. "OK, and why would you go with a married man? Don't you have any respect for yourself?"

"I'm saying though, I didn't know he was married at first, and by the time I found out, we were already into things. I mean, I was mad, but I wasn't gonna give up everything he gave me. Plus, he said he's leaving you anyway. He said y'all don't have anything in common. He said y'all don't even have sex anymore. You're just fat and boring. The only reason why he ain't leave yet is 'cause he doesn't want TJ to grow up without you."

"What do you know about my son?" I said, getting angry.

"I know your son. He's been to my house a couple of times now. He doesn't know I go with his father though. He just thinks Tray is coming to see my brother, Paul."

"Paul? Richie's friend, Paul?"

"Yeah, that's my brother."

"You know his girl too?" I said, now interested.

"Simone. She's been to my house too. She doesn't know I go with Tray either. I know your whole family. I was at your family cookout on Labor Day. Don't you remember seeing me? I remember seeing you. I was the one standing next to Tray half the night, while you were with Tony's girlfriend."

"Tony?" I said, surprised.

"You thought I was lying. I know your whole family. I love your Aunt Trudy. She made me and my brother some pecan pie for my brother's birthday. Why do you think Tray spends so much time in Hartford? He is coming to see me. Why do you think he opened the shop out here?"

"Open what shop?"

"Damn, you're really out of the loop. Tray got, like, three shops, and I run one of them. He got that shop out by you too, but that's not where his real money comes from. He got one on the south end, where I live, and one on the north end. That's where he is all the time. He isn't even at the one out there in East Lyme. You wanna know what else? Tray bought the condo my mother and I live in. My mother loves him like her own sons. She said that he is the best thing that ever happened to me. She loves your son too."

I was speechless. There was nothing for me to say. Here was this woman, telling me stuff I never knew about my husband. It sounds more like it's her husband.

"Hello? You still there?" Maritza said.

"So how many months pregnant are you?" I said, not having anything else to say.

"I'm seven months pregnant yesterday. My baby's due on November 8," Maritza said proudly.

"Where are you from?" I said, wanting to know about her.

"I'm from Hartford, but my family comes from Puerto Rico."

"Wow, you're Puerto Rican," I said. *OK, that makes sense. He always did have a thing for Puerto Rican girls,* I thought to myself.

"Do you know how long we've been together . . . uh . . . Maritza, is it?" I asked, trying to sound like she was very unimportant to me.

"Yeah, like, fourteen or fifteen years," she said quickly.

"OK, so you know that I've invested a lot of time and effort into this relationship?"

"And . . . your point is?"

"Well, my point is, I would like to know what type of woman is OK with sharing another woman's man?" I said sarcastically.

"The kind that gets anything she needs and doesn't ever have to ask for anything," she said with an attitude. "Look, Sasha, I never meant to hurt you. I'm saying, when I met Tray, I didn't know about you or your son. Jade didn't tell me anything about you. That's one of the reasons we ain't cool anymore, and like I said, it all got too deep. By the time I found out about you, I was mad for the brother. He was my first black guy too. I didn't even like black guys before him. They were all so damn mean and hateful. But Tray, he treated me and my mother like we were queens. You just don't know. He bought my mother a car for her birthday last year and one for me the year before. He opened bank accounts for us and everything. Like I said, we've been dealing for almost five years. When Jade told me he was married, I wanted to kill him and her too. She said you were a bitch and that she ain't care nothing 'bout you. She said some shit had gone down, and she thought you were cool, and then you started acting really phony and shit with her. She said you were corny, and Tray needed somebody cool like me in his life. Anyway, I was mad as hell with her and him for a while, but then he bought me my Navigator—and shit, I ain't stupid. I forgave him quick. Tray does for me like no other man ever did for me. I'm not giving that up."

"Well, I suppose there's nothing else to say," I said, wanting to hang up now. This was all too much for me.

"Well, I got something to say," she said. "We need to meet and talk about things."

"Well, I don't know about that," I said, disgusted.

"What you don't know about is, I ain't gonna do anything to your ass. If I wanted to do something to you, I could've done it a long time ago. I know where you live."

"Well, I'm not the fighting type anyway."

"Oh, I know you're not like that. I know all about you," she said calmly. "Why don't you come down to the shop? It's off Franklin Avenue on Bushnell Street, in the south end of Hartford. One hundred thirty-four, second floor. Ring the bell. I'm 'bout to go down there now and check on things."

She sounded very eager to see me.

"You want me to call you on your cell phone?"

"What? You have my cell phone number too?" I asked, feeling quite intimidated.

"I got every number Tray dials. I don't play. I gotta make sure there ain't any more females out there he's messing with. If he could cheat on you with me, hell, he'll cheat on me with somebody else. I ain't stupid. Anyway, you want me to call you, or you're gonna call me or what?"

"No, that's OK. I'm sure I can find my way just fine. I know Hartford like the back of my hand." I hung up the phone, without saying bye. My heart was beating a mile a minute. I couldn't believe what just happened. Here I am, thinking we were just going through something right now, and he really was going through something on his own. He has a whole 'nother life. He got a baby on the way and everything. Damn, Simone was right. She told me to check out all that shit he's been saying and the fact that he's been sleeping on the couch and not wanting to have sex with me. I just thought . . .

I ran upstairs and got in the shower. I cried so hard my head was throbbing when I got out. I kept playing everything that's been happening these last few years in my mind. It's been right there in front of my face all along: him leaving early every day, 'cause he got to go all the way to Hartford, him not coming home till late in the night, he and Paul being so close all of a sudden, him always disappearing with Paul, him always having money, and him taking TJ with him all the time.

I just can't believe all this is happening to me. Now I have to go and meet some woman my husband has been screwing for the last four years or so, and she's pregnant seven months, and she drives a Navigator that he bought her. He only got me a Trailblazer. Well, I guess that's all I wanted. Here I am, feeling sorry for him, not wanting him to spend too much money on me, 'cause the shop wasn't making that much, and he's got two other shops. And he's out buying condos. Wow. Where have I been?

I don't know what to do. Should I call him and curse his ass out? Maybe I should call Simone. No, she's so ghetto; she'll wanna go fight. Maybe I'll call Tiffany. No, that bitch is over there. Maybe I should tell Tiff what's going on. I don't know what to do. I don't have anyone to turn to. I certainly can't turn to Melony. I need to talk to someone.

I know . . . I'll call my Nathan. Whenever there was something I wanted good, solid advice about, I always counted on Nathan to give me the answer. He was so spiritual and always looked to God for his answers. Sometimes, I wondered how someone that spiritual could smoke so much. The phone's ringing.

"Hey, Nathan. It's Sasha."

"Oh, what's up, girl? Long time I don't hear from you."

Did I mention Nathan thinks he's Jamaican?

"Yeah, I've been busy."

"Why do you sound like *dat*, Sasha? What's wrong?"

"How'd you know something was wrong with me?"

"You know I can always tell when something is bothering my Sasha."

"Yeah, well, this time, it's more than just a fight or TJ getting trouble in school."

"What can I help you with?"

"Nathan, I just found out Tray has been cheating on me for the past four years or so," I said, starting to cry again.

"Oh, man, sorry to hear that. Sasha, you know that man was no good from long time. He doesn't even treat you right anymore. You know we did talk 'bout this, right?"

"Yes, but I didn't wanna face that he could be cheating. I just wanted to think we were growing apart because we've been together for so long. Why did he have to go that far?"

"Well, you know, *a so it go*. What can I say? Some men just don't have any respect for their empress. You know."

"And the worst part, Nathan, is that the girl is pregnant."

"How'd you know all this?"

"The girl just called me and told me. She knows everything about me, TJ, Simone, and Aunt Trudy has even cooked for her and her brother. See, this is how it goes. Maritza, that's the girl's name, is a friend of Jade."

"Jade? How did she get in this? You see, me know that bad life would catch up to her. And see, it catch up to you too. She need *fi* leave that gay life alone. That is an abomination unto the Almighty."

"Nathan, you know Jade?

"Everybody know that woman. Her business is all over the streets, so of course, I would hear about her. Nothing pass my ears. I just don't talk everything I know 'cause it's not my place. You see me. Me is a very peaceful man, and sometimes, the things what me hear a no peaceful tings, so me just stay far from it. That's why mi na love come round *unu* people. You ina to much tings."

"Me, Nathan?" I said. I couldn't help but wonder.

"Not you, Sasha, but, you know, the gang, the crew. Them fulla too much bad vibes. Mi no really judge them still, but mi just wanna show you why me stay far. Mi wan deal ina the positive. And it cannot go on with them something round mi. You know wah mi a say?" "Yeah, I hear ya, loud and clear." Sometimes, I didn't understand what he was talking about. I just said yes so he wouldn't keep going on.

"So wah you want me *fi* do now?"

"I made an appointment to go and see her. Do you think that's a good idea?

"How you feel 'bout it?"

"I think I wanna see her. I wanna know who she is. She said he has two shops in Hartford. I can't believe I didn't know anything about this."

"OK, that's what is going on? That's a lot. Can't believe that one got by me. Well, nobody can tell you how you feel. If you feel like you want to see her, then go on and see her. Me tell you be careful. I don't want anything to happen to you. Mi love you."

"I love you too. Bye, Nathan."

I hung up the phone and thought for a moment about what I was about to do. You know, I can't believe Nathan. You could always tell when he had just finished talking to someone Jamaican, 'cause he sounded just like one, even though he was born in Hartford. Ever since he met that Rasta girl about ten years ago, he has been learning more and more about the culture. He just gets deeper and deeper into it every day. It's a pity she went back to Jamaica. They made a good couple. What was her name? Mallah? Malayah? Something like that; I wasn't really into her, but she made Nathan smile 95 percent of the time I saw him, and to me, that was a good sign.

Well, it was time for me to make a decision. Was I going or not? I sat on my couch, looking at the painting of Tray, TJ, and myself that I painted on the wall. I used a picture from when TJ was about six. It covered the whole length of one wall right in front of the baby grand piano. We looked so happy. I can't believe all this is slowly coming to an end. I can't believe he's made another baby with someone else. How could he? He vowed to love only me for the rest of his life. That's how it was supposed to be.

You know what, I'm going. Let me start by washing my face and putting on some toner, then let's see how I feel. OK, I think I'll wear my new hip-hugger jeans. They show off my big ass, and I'll have to wear a really tight T-shirt that shows a little bit of my stomach. I mean, it's not completely flat, but it does show off my pretty navel. Oh, and I'll wear my pointy toe boots. I should go get my nails done while I'm in Hartford before I go. Now what am I gonna do with my hair? Oh, and my eyebrows need to be done. I'll just stop at one of those Asian shops on the way.

When I finished getting dressed, I looked in the mirror; I looked like my cousin, Simone. She would have worn something like this. Shit, she dresses like this on a regular basis. I don't know how she could be in such tight pants and heels all the time. I couldn't do it. I gotta breathe, and I love my sneakers. I think I'll put my hair in a ponytail, seeing that it's so long, almost sixteen inches now, but I need a perm. When I was finished getting ready, I looked myself over one more time. Everything looked as perfect as it could possibly look.

I jumped in my car and headed for Hartford. I couldn't believe I was going through with this. All the wonderful times Tray and I shared together ran through my mind. I wanted to cry, but I didn't wanna mess up my eyeliner. My eyes were already puffy from crying all morning. I'm not gonna let this chick know she got to me in the manner in which she did. I'm so glad I talked to Nathan; he always puts things into perspective for me.

You know, I think I did know all along that Tray had something going on. I just didn't want to face it. I didn't want it to be true. Simone told me time and time again that this man wasn't right and that there was more than one reason he slept on the couch on most nights. He had another woman all this time.

Who would have known that he could live two lives and keep it such a secret from everyone in the family the way he did? Everyone is so focused on Paul that they don't even see this Maritza right before their eyes.

I know Aunt Trudy is gonna be mad as hell when she finds out she cooked for Tray's lover. There's one thing I can say about my Aunt Trudy: she loves me even if I'm not doing what she wants me to be doing. She is all about her family, and it is going to blow her mind when she finds out that all that time, Tray was cheating on her niece.

I remember the first time I brought Tray to meet my aunt. She asked me, "Who is that nappy-headed boy in my living room?"

She thought I could do better. I told her all about his poetry and how he wanted to open his own business. She was very impressed with his entrepreneurial ideas but said that that poetry-writing crap wasn't gonna get him anywhere. She was right. He stopped writing after about four years ago or so and just focused on his business. He hasn't written anything since. He said he didn't have time for things like that anymore and that he was a grown-up now. I thought it was silly of him to think that only children write poetry. Or maybe he had other things on his mind. I thought it was business, but I see now the truth comes out.

I remember when Tony met him; he said, "Yeah, he looks like one of those earthy, candle-light'n', finger-snappin'-type dudes."

I was glad he said that 'cause that's the type of guy I was looking for. I didn't want the business suit man that Aunt Trudy wanted me to be with, and I sure didn't want one of the drug dealers Tony tried to hook me up with. They were all off their rocker.

One tried to take me on a vacation to Europe, talking 'bout how we can go and stay out there for a couple of months. I told my cousin he was probably running from somebody, and why would I wanna go so far from everybody for several months with somebody I didn't even know? Weirdo.

All of Tony's friends thought that as long as they had money, they could get women to do whatever they wanted. Not me. Money does not make me. It may help me along, but if I was with a broke man, I would be happy as long as he spent time with me and really loved me. That's all that really counts.

I wanted to call Tiffany so bad and tell her what Jade had done, but I just didn't know how to break it to her. I knew that she would be pissed off, and I knew that I would shatter her world right along with mine. I loved my cousin, and I just don't think that's necessary right now. Not until I find out the whole story. I know that ever since Jade tried to come on to me again and I refused, she hasn't treated me the same. I know she has a problem with rejection, but I just never imagined she would take it to that level.

She came to my house a couple of months after the last incident. When I looked out the window, I couldn't believe who was at my door.

What was she doing here, and where was my cousin? I opened the door, and she was standing there with a big smile on her face.

"Hey, Sasha. How've you been? We haven't seen you for a while," Jade said, smiling at me. She was so beautiful.

"Oh, I've been busy . . . really busy," I said, stuttering.

"Well, can I come in?"

"Yeah, sure." I invited her in, but I wasn't really sure why. I didn't want to see this woman ever again. I was so embarrassed about how she made me feel that night, and I didn't want her to know that I still thought about her. I mean, I started masturbating because of her. I was fine before that night. Now all of a sudden, I was turning into this horny toad that is always thinking about sex. Now here she was, in my house, and we're all alone.

"Mm, Sasha, I've never been in your house before," Jade said, looking all over the place. "I like the doves on the lawn—and wow, go, girl. You have a baby grand. Who painted that picture on the wall?"

Who's the painter in the family? That was a dumb question. I guess she was just trying to make conversation.

"Sasha, baby, this is really nice. It's very different. I love that chandelier," she said, walking into the dining room. "And that fireplace is off the hook."

It wrapped around into the living room wall. The room had a balcony leading into the bedrooms and cathedral ceilings with skylights.

"Tiff never said your place looked like this. This is fierce," Jade said, sounding very impressed. I mean, what did she think? I was gonna live in some rundown shack?

"I love to decorate, so it was fun," I said, starting to brag a little.

"Can I see the bedrooms?" Jade said with a twinkle in her eye.

I brought her upstairs, and we went into TJ's room. He wanted to feel like he was in outer space, so I painted his room a deep-blue color, with stars on the ceiling. Then I painted a rocket ship on one wall and some of the planets on the other. Everything in his room was in deep blue and black. He loved it. He said it helped him think about being an astronaut, since that is what he wanted to be.

"Oh my gosh, Sasha! This is amazing. Can I see your room?" she said, sounding so excited.

"Well . . . ah . . . OK," I said, hesitating. "Go down to the other end of the hall."

As she walked down the hall, I couldn't help but watch her. I am not sure why she makes me feel this way. When she opened my bedroom door, she just stood there for a minute. She looked astonished.

"Girl, mirrors?" she said, holding her chest.

I had mirrors mounted on half of the walls in my bedroom, a black wooden canopy wrapped around my king-size bed, with red linen drapes coming down from the top and twisted around the poles. I also had a chandelier put in over an old-fashioned washbasin I had installed in the corner of my room. I wanted it to have a modern but woodsy feel to it. I also didn't want to have to go into the bathroom to wash up after all the sex. Jade stood in the middle of my room and just looked around. It was like a fantasy room. I had branches going up into the ceiling from out of one corner in the room, and there were plants everywhere. I didn't like a lot of clutter, so I only had my bedroom set and the sink in my room. The TV was embedded in one of the dresser tops, and the lights came out of the ceiling. We had different switches for each area of the room.

"So, Jade, what was it that you came over here for?" I said, leading her back downstairs as she rolled her eyes.

"Oh, I was in the neighborhood and remembered you lived somewhere around here, so I decided I would stop by and check on you."

"Well, I'm fine."

"Yes, I know. You sure are," she said, trying to look into my eyes.

I wasn't buying it though. I know damn well why she was here. She wanted to finish what she had started. It must have been on her mind; why else would she just show up for the first time out of nowhere? Tiff has never brought her to my house, but she sure did find her way.

"Uh, Sasha, I was thinking about what had happened that last time we were together, and I really wanted to know how you felt about all of it. I mean, we haven't seen or heard from you since, or at least I haven't. What happened to you? It was almost like you fell off the face of the earth or something. I didn't know if it was something that I had done or not done or what."

"Well, Jade," I said, taking a deep breath, "the fact of the matter is that I'm not gay and don't intend to be, and as a matter of fact, I don't even remember half of what went on. I was so out of it I couldn't remember anything the next day. It was only days later that little bits and pieces started coming back to me, and I didn't like what I was remembering. I mean, Tiff is my cousin, and I can't believe she let things get that far."

"Sasha, she wasn't even in the room. What are you talking about? It was just you and me," Jade said in a protective voice.

"I am very sorry that it happened, and I never want it to happen again!" I said angrily. "I don't know what I was thinking. I mean, don't get me wrong, Jade, you're a nice girl and all, but I am not a lesbian, and I don't enjoy being touched by a woman. Frankly, I don't know how you can do that nasty shit. I love men, and my man is the best lover there is. There will never be another, and there definitely would never be another woman."

Jade's face was red with fury.

"You know what, Sasha? I think you're lying to yourself! You were not all that drunk or high. You liked what happened. People don't get as wet as you were for no reason. You just don't wanna face the fact that you liked what happened and that you like me. What you don't realize is that I really got a thing for you, and I would leave your Tiff to be with you in a heartbeat. I've always liked women that looked like a woman, not a woman that looks like a man. What would be the point of being with a woman? I could just be with a man. You don't know what you're missing. I could make all your fantasies come true. And from the looks of your bedroom, you got a lot of them."

"Jade, I may have a lot of fantasies, but I also have a very sexy and desirable husband to fulfill them, in case you forgot. Now if that was all you came over for, I'll be seeing you," I said, leading her to the front door. "I have a lot of things to do. Thanks for stopping by, but next time, maybe you should call first. Make sure I'm not busy."

Jade left without saying another word. I know she was mad 'cause she didn't get what she came to get, even though I did lust after her. I wasn't about to give up all that I had going with my husband and hurt my cousin just for some damn desire. Blood is thicker than that. She pulled off in a rage. I hoped she wouldn't go home and share the conversation with my cousin, because I had no intention of telling her.

Now that I think back on it, I should have told Tiff, because now if I try to tell her what's going on, she won't believe that Jade could do that to me. I don't think she really knows who she's dealing with. This is one of the reasons why I need to talk to this Maritza today. I need to pluck her brain about Jade while she's angry with her.

When I reached Hartford, I got off on Sigourney Street so that I could go to the Asian nail shop off Farmington Avenue. When I went in, there were only two people there. I had to see Lillie; she was the best in the shop.

"Lillie, I wanna get a full set of tips, with a fancy airbrush design to match my outfit, and I also need my eyebrows done."

Lillie is the only one I would let touch my nails or my eyebrows. I have had too many bad experiences. As I walked over to her booth, she smiled and took out some cotton balls. We never spoke to each other. She was always very quiet. I loved it because it gave me time to just be. When she got finished with my nails, I gave her a five-dollar tip because they looked so good. She grinned and told me to come back and see her again.

When I was younger, my cousin, Simone, and I would always go together and have our nails, toes, and eyebrows done. The works is what they call it. She was the one that told me about that shop. They've been around for about eighteen years now, in the same spot, and Lillie still looks like she's eighteen.

I pulled out of the driveway, scared to death about what was about to go down. Suppose I got to her shop and Tray was there. I would lose my mind. Suppose she had a posse of girls waiting there to beat me up. I didn't know what I was getting myself into, but I was going anyway. I guess I'm more curious than scared. Driving down Franklin Avenue, all I could think about was how I used to hang out with my friends not far from here. Everything was so simple then. My life was so much easier, and you know what, Tray was such a big part of it. Yeah, I would spend time with him, but I had a whole lot going on with a whole bunch of friends. I don't even know where any of those people are right now. We did poetry and laughed. We danced and sang out in the streets. We didn't care who was watching or listening. I miss those days. They brought out the artist in me. I remember when I introduced my cousin, Melony, to some of my friends; she felt so out of place she didn't know what to do with herself.

I turned down Bushnell Street and started looking for the address. It wasn't hard to find, with the big sign on the front lawn saying, "You know you wanna look." I wonder where that name came from? I parked in the back and went around to the front to go up the front steps. I checked myself one last time before going in.

I opened the door to her shop, and what a surprise. It was so upscale, very classy. It was painted red and brown, and everything was shiny and clean. Her stations had big lightbulbs over the round hanging mirrors, which were framed, and recessed lighting. The floors were a sort of stone tile. It really looked nice, like somewhere I would go. I looked at the services she offered, which were carved on a big slate stone that was hanging from some large black hooks, over her front desk.

I was going to talk to the girl at the front desk, but Maritza's station was the first one. The moment I saw her, I instantly remembered her as the pregnant girl from the Labor Day cookout the other day. In fact, I remember seeing her at a few other family functions; we just never spoke to each other.

"Man, she is really pregnant," I said in a whisper. She looked like a skinny woman that had swallowed a watermelon. Her hair was black, curly, and long, way down past her breasts. She had on a little T-shirt, with half of her stomach hanging out, and a little jacket over it, hip-hugger jeans, and some cute little sneakers. Unfortunately for me, she was very cute. Her nails were really long, and she had rings on all her fingers, including both thumbs. She had, like, two or three diamond tennis bracelets on each wrist.

Walking closer to her, I wondered if Tray bought everything. I mean, I know she told me that he took care of her, but her shop looked almost as good as my house. I walked closer to her, but she had a client, so she didn't see me until she looked up.

"Hi, Sasha. I'll be with you in just one minute. Let me put my client under the dryer," she said, putting in the last roller. "You can have a seat right there," she said, pointing to the seating area.

I couldn't help staring at her as she put her client under the dryer; she was beautiful. Damn, it's no wonder Tray doesn't want me anymore. This girl is seven months pregnant, and she doesn't have one stretch mark on her stomach.

"Let's go in the back and have a seat," she said, leading me to the back of her shop. The other girls in the shop looked at me but didn't say a word. As I followed Maritza into the back of the shop, I could hear them whispering.

"So we finally get to meet," she said, sitting down slowly in a black leather reclining chair. The back room of her shop was kinda split into two sections. The right side of the room was set up like a living room. She had two reclining couches facing each other, a glass coffee table in the middle, with matching end tables, and a big screen TV. The other side was set up as a kitchen, and she pulled no punches. She had all stainless steel appliances, brown granite countertops, and an island.

As I looked around the room, I realized that a lot of the photos were of her and Tray. There was a picture of them together at the beach; he doesn't even like going to the beach, and there was one with them all dressed up. They had a real life together. I can't believe all this is going on; it was so painful to watch all this. I fought to hold back the tears. Maritza took a seat on the couch, and I sat down across from her.

"So, Sasha, I think there are some things we need to be discussing right about now, don't you?"

"Yes, that's why I am here."

"Well, I wanna know where your marriage is going. I need to know what's gonna happen when my baby is born. See, I'm tired of having a part-time man."

"Don't you think you should have thought about that before you got yourself pregnant?" I said calmly.

"Well, that's true, that's true. But I didn't get myself pregnant, and I can't change what has happened now. The only thing I can do is think about how it's gonna be for Tray Marie and me. My daughter doesn't need to grow up in all this confusion. That's why I need to know what you intend to do about all this. Tray told me he was gonna leave you, like, two years ago, and I don't see that happening. I don't know what kind of hold you got on him, but I know it can't be all that if he's been with me for the last five years."

I looked at her, slightly confused, before speaking; I thought about how cold she was. What about the life Tray and I shared before she came along?

"Maritza," I said, "I think it has something to do with the fact that I was his first love and that we have a son together, not to mention the fact that we've gone from rags to riches together. See, you've only been around for the riches, but I was there when he didn't have anything," I said confidently. "There's no way that you could ever be me or have the hold on him that I do. I've been with Tramaine my whole life. I made him the man he is today, and aside from him finding you, I think I've done a damn good job."

"He said you were cocky," Maritza said, grinning slightly.

"What do mean by that?" I said, wanting to jump off the couch and stomp on her belly till it was flat. "You mean to tell me you two have actually talked about me?"

"Yeah, all the time. I always ask him questions about you. See, Sasha, I'm not in this to hurt you or your son. I never wanted anything like this to happen, but the more I spent time with Tray, the deeper I got into him. I always wondered about this day and what I would say to you. I knew that I would be able to talk to you, woman to woman, because of how Tray talked about you. He respects how mature you are, and he loves you a lot. He's just not in love with you anymore. I know I may sound really cold, but I need to make sure you know how I'm getting all this. He doesn't dog you out to me or anything like that. He really only talks about the sweet side of you, and I wonder to myself sometimes, why is he cheating with me if you're so sweet? But when he touches me or says just the right thing, like I know you know he can do, I forget all about you and everything else. I lost a lot of my dignity dealing with this man. I always said I would never go with another woman's husband, and like I said, I didn't know in the beginning that he had a wife. He didn't tell me, and Jade didn't tell me either."

"Speaking of Jade," I said, interrupting her. "How do you two know each other anyway?"

"Jade and I, we used to hang in the strip club together. We were both bartenders in a strip club. That's where I met Tray. I used to hang out with Jade and scheme on all the hotties in the club."

"You worked in a female strip club?" I said, wondering if she might be a lesbian too.

"Yeah, but I don't do girls, if that's what you were thinking. It's Jade that goes both ways. Shoot, she goes with one right now. He lives down the street from here. She talks to this Italian guy named Frankie. They always are in the club together. I saw them, like what, last week or something. Tray and I went to this club—yeah, big belly and all—and her ass was up in there with that cat. She only talks to Tiff for her money and a good booty-licking game. She doesn't love Tiff or Frankie. She just wants their money. Jade doesn't love anybody 'cept herself. The way I got it, she only hooked me up with Tray 'cause she was mad at you for not playing her little lesbo game. She said you were a closet bisexual, and she was gonna take you out of the closet. When you went off on her, she was pissed. I'm saying, I didn't know about any of this until a couple of years ago. She never told me that before, and the only reason she told me then is 'cause I wasn't into her like that anymore. I was all about Tray, and she was jealous. I mean, we never had any sexual dealings or anything like that. But that was my girl. Shit, we shared everything, including men, except Tray. When I found out what she did, I stopped dealing with her altogether for a while. She could've gotten me killed or something, hooking me up with somebody's husband. I had a girlfriend that got shot behind some shit like this. She didn't know that damn man was married, and the wife found out about them, walked right up to her, and shot her dead in the face. She ain't dead or anything, but still. Half of her funking face is gone. That shit is crazy. I would've never thought about doing anything like this, and she knows it, 'cause we used to talk about it all the time. She would be like, 'If they give me what I wanted, I would do whatever they want,' and I used to say, 'Not me. I want my own man. I don't want anybody's leftovers, and I ain't sharing. What's mine's supposed to be mine.' You feelin' me?"

I didn't say a word. I just looked at her stomach jumping as she spoke. This woman was so ghetto and yet so nice. She seemed like she was a victim in this too. She really didn't seem like she meant any of this. I know how persuasive Tray can be. He got me, didn't he? I didn't even really like him, and he found out what I liked most in a man and became just that. I didn't know what to say to her. I had no intention of giving her my man. I'm sorry she's pregnant and sorry she has to share, but at this point, I was sharing too, and I already had a child. I really didn't know what she wanted from me. It sounded like she wanted me to give up on my relationship.

"Well, Maritza," I said finally, "I'm sorry about the position you and Tray Marie got yourselves into, but I have no intention of giving up my man. This is the only man I've ever been with, and I don't want anyone else. Yeah, we have a lot of things to work out, but I feel like we can get through them as long as we stay together. Besides, when I leave him, where does that leave TJ? He'll be without his daddy. I can't do that to my son, on account of one little indiscretion. We have to find a way to work this whole thing out."

"You know what, Sasha, I really admire you. Tray always has wonderful things to say about you and how you're so smart and so pretty. He's right too. But it only makes me feel even worse about what I'm doing to your family. I just don't know what to do. I don't wanna be a kept woman. I don't wanna be mean or evil and have my daughter grow up and go through the same things I'm doing to you, but I'm in too deep. Tray changed my life.

How am I supposed to just give all that up? I got everything I ever wanted from him, except him to myself. I feel like nobody can have it all, but I'm pretty damn close. If he can make both of us happy, well then, I guess things will just have to stay the way they are, for now."

I couldn't believe what I was hearing. This young woman was telling me to my face that she had a piece of my husband and that it was too good for her to let go. After saying all what she had to say, she got up, walked over to me, bent down, and hugged me. I didn't even have time to stop her.

"I know if we met on the street somewhere, we would've been friends. You could teach me a lot," she said, with tears in her eyes. "I am truly so sorry about all this, and I hope that one day, we can be friends, since our kids are going to be brother and sister. It would be nice for them to grow up together. TJ's not an only child anymore, and since I don't plan on having any more, I don't want TrayMarie to grow up that way either." She held me so tight and whispered in my ear, "Everything is gonna be all right if we stick together," like we were girls or something.

I couldn't bring myself to hug her back. I just sat there, feeling confused. When she let me go, I got up. I didn't know what to say to her, so I didn't say anything. I just wanted to get the hell out of there. I grabbed my bag and headed for the front. I walked out the front door without even saying bye, and I didn't look back.

That was the strangest thing I had ever encountered in all my years on this planet. The girl was actually nice. I wanted to hate her, but I couldn't. I didn't know where to go next. I didn't wanna go back home, and I sure didn't wanna see Simone or Auntie Trudy. Still sitting in the parking lot of Maritza's shop, I called Nathan. As soon as he answered the phone, I busted out in tears.

"Sasha, are you all right?"

"No, Nathan, I'm not OK. I don't know what to do."

"Just come over here," he said. "You don't need to be driving right now."

It was a good thing he only lived off Park Street. I didn't have far to drive. When I got to Nathan's house, he was boiling some water to make me a cup of tea.

"Here. You need this right now," he said, handing me the cup of tea. "It will calm your nerves."

I sat at the kitchen table, sipping and sniffling. Nathan left the room and came back with a joint.

"Light this and take your mind off things for a while," he said, handing me the joint.

"I don't wanna take my mind off things, Nathan. I need to figure out what to do about all this."

I started telling him the whole story from the beginning: that she was so sweet to me and that she had nothing but good things to say about me. She even told me how smart and pretty I was. She really left me confused. I thought I was going in there to get jumped or end up fighting with this woman or something; instead, I felt sorry for her. I wanted to hug her and tell her everything was gonna be all right. I felt like she was one of my friends telling me about a bad situation she had gotten herself into.

"Well, you see, Sasha, sometimes, when we only look at things from one perspective, we only see one thing, but when we can open up our minds and see the whole picture, then we can see the world in a whole new light."

"Yeah, I guess so," I said, feeling ashamed for me and her. She didn't have a husband, and the fact that Tray tricked her into being with him made me realize how manipulative he can be when he wants something. This was a side of him I didn't really know. Just thinking about how he kept everything from her, the fact that he didn't even tell her he was married, it makes me wonder how many more girls he has out there that I know nothing about. The first thing I thought about is going to get a checkup.

"You know what, Nathan? I think I need to make a doctor's appointment. I haven't been feeling well lately. I wonder if that man gave me something."

"So go and get yourself checked out then."

"I'm gonna call and make an appointment on Monday."

Sipping on my tea, I still couldn't believe what just happened. It all felt like some crazy nightmare I couldn't wake up from. I just can't believe Tray has another woman—and a pregnant one, no less. How could he do this to me? My head was spinning. I need to get myself together.

"You know what, Nathan, I think I wanna stay with you for a while. I'm gonna take a leave of absence from work, so I can figure this shit out, put things into perspective."

"It's no problem with me, Sasha. You know my door is always open."

"Thanks, Nathan. I am so fortunate to have you in my life. I don't know what I would do without you."

"Sasha, I just want you to take care of yourself. If you're not OK, TJ won't be OK. You know what I mean?"

"Yeah, I know what you mean."

I think I'm gonna ask Lee if he can help me out with TJ for a while. He can stay with him until I figure this all out. I called over to Lee's house to talk to TJ. Lee answered the phone.

"Hello."

"Hey, Lee. How's TJ?" I said, trying hard not to cry.

"Hey, Sasha. He's all right. He's out back playing. You wanna talk to him?"

"Oh, no, that's OK," I said. "Um, Lee, I need you to do me a favor. I need to stay in Hartford for a couple of weeks, and I need someone to take TJ to school for me. I was thinking if you could take him, he could just stay over there with you for a while, just until we go back home."

It got harder and harder to hold back the tears.

"What's going on? Is everything all right?" Lee said, concerned.

"No!" I said, crying out. "Everything is not all right. Tray has been messing with someone else for the last five years, and she's pregnant with his baby."

"Sasha, are you sure about this?" Lee said in disbelief.

"Yes, I'm sure. I met her and everything."

"Wow, that's a lot. Did you talk to Tray about this?"

"Talk to him about what? There's nothing to talk about. I saw all that I needed to see. She even has pictures with him. He can't lie his way out of this one."

"Damn, so what are you going to do?"

"I am not sure yet, but I know I can't look at him right now."

"Well, you know I will keep him for you, Sasha. What do you want me to tell him about why he is staying here? Do you want me to tell him you had to go out of town?"

"No, Lee, don't tell him that. I'll call him and talk to him myself. I want to make sure he understands everything that is going on."

"All right, Sash, I won't say a word. Are you gonna call back and talk to him?"

"Yeah, I can't talk to him right now. I'm too messed up. Anyway, thanks so much for helping me out, Lee. I really appreciate this."

"Sasha, you know I'd do anything for you. You're my baby girl. I'll tell TJ that you called and that you'll call him back later."

"Thanks, Lee," I said, sniffling. "I'll call him around eight or so before he goes to bed."

"All right, baby. You should get some sleep."

"I know. I really do need to. I'm gonna finish the tea Nathan made me and take a nap. I love you, Lee."

"I love you too, Sasha."

When I hung up the phone, I took one more sip of my tea and headed for the spare bedroom. Nathan came in and checked on me right before I was about to go to sleep.

"Are you all right, Sasha?"

"No, but I will be, I suppose. I'm gonna take a nap."

"All right then, I'm gonna go out for a while. I'll be back later."

Nathan left the room, and I turned over and went to sleep.

Chapter 4

I woke up with a killer headache. I got up out of bed and headed for the bathroom. Nathan was in the kitchen, cooking.

"Morning," I said, walking past him, going into the bathroom.

"Morning, Sash. Are you hungry? I made some veggie burgers."

"No, thanks. I am not in the mood to eat."

"Damn, Sasha, for the last couple of days, all you've been doing is smoking and sleeping. You have to eat something."

"I know, Nathan. I will."

"Don't make this man kill you off. You have to be strong. Come and eat something."

"What's today?" I said, bewildered.

"Unbelievable, Sasha. Today is Wednesday."

"Do you know I still haven't spoken to Tray?" I said, sitting at the table. "I just don't know what to say to him. I've been playing everything over and over again in my mind, and I just can't see where I went wrong. I thought we were so in love. He was my knight in shining armor. Now he just looks like an old cheating bastard."

"Sasha, you are focusing on the wrong thing. Don't focus on Tray. Focus on yourself and your son. What are you going to do? You need to get yourself together. Are you going to talk to Tray about everything?"

"Nathan, I just can't," I said, starting to tear up.

"All right, all right, let's not talk about this right now. I want you to eat."

He handed me a plate with a veggie burger and potato fries on it. I didn't want to eat anything, but I knew he wasn't gonna let up until I did. Every bite I took hurt—not physically but somehow mentally. All I could envision was my broken home and how I had to start all over again. I called TJ last Sunday and told him everything that happened. He sounded really hurt, but I didn't want him to hear it from anyone else.

Even though I am still not sure what I'm going to do, the one thing I do know is that it is over between us. He can never touch me again. Just the thought of him touching me makes me sick to my stomach. I gave him the best years of my life, and this is how he repays me? No, he will never have the chance to do that to me again. Never! I don't know if I should start looking for a place to live or what. I just know, right now, I have no intention in ever going back to him. There's just no way.

I ate half of the sandwich and got up. Nathan didn't say a word; he just looked at me. I know he had a lot he wanted to say to me, but I was grateful for his silence. I went back into my room, sat on the side of the bed, and lit up the joint I left in the ashtray last night. I just need something to numb the pain.

I've been talking to TJ every night before he goes to bed. Yesterday, when I spoke to him, he had a million questions. He wanted to know when we were going back home and if he was going to get to see the new baby. Somewhere in his mind, I think he believes we will all be together, like one big happy family. I had to explain to him that that wasn't our home anymore. I couldn't live with Tray ever again after this. Every time he would kiss me or touch me, I would be thinking about how he kissed her. I just couldn't live like that. I know TJ has always wanted a sister or brother, and I know that someday, I will have to let them meet, but right now, I couldn't think about any of that. Right now, I need to figure out what I am going to do with myself.

I picked up my cell phone to see I had a ton of missed calls. I knew it was my job, because I called them on Monday and told them there was a death in the family. I explained that I needed to go out of town, to help take care of everything. I know I shouldn't be talking about deaths in my family, but I just need some time to figure things out. I mean, I didn't really lie. I feel like I was dying inside. I still can't believe I didn't see any of this coming. How could I be so blind? It was all right there in front of my eyes, and I was just too damn blind to see.

When I looked at my call log, there were ten from Tray, eight from Maritza, like, ten from Simone, and five from Tiffany. Damn, they've been blowing up my phone. I couldn't bear to respond to anyone right now. I just need time.

I feel so confused. A part of me wants to hate her with a passion, but oddly enough, I like her. I can't understand it. Maybe if she behaved like an old tyrant, I wouldn't feel this way, but I really like her. I also feel sorry for her. I would never want to be in the position she is in. How painful it must have been for her to find out her boyfriend was married. She couldn't have been more than twenty years old when they met, and she did say that he gives her everything she wants.

I wonder what's going to happen between them when Tray finds out she confronted me. I know all hell is going to break loose. He may even leave her. Either way, I am not going back. I don't know why I even care about what happens between them. I should be thinking about me and my son, like Nathan said. I put down the phone and lay back down.

"Sasha," Nathan called from the living room. "I have to make a quick run to New York and come back. Make sure you check the mail for me, OK?"

"OK, I'll see you later."

He was probably going to get more weed.

"Are you gonna be all right till I come back?"

"Yes, I'll be fine," I said from the bedroom.

Nathan went to New York with one of his friends, so I had his place all to myself. I didn't feel like doing anything much. I know I shouldn't stay in bed all day, but I just don't feel like doing anything. I feel so angry inside.

"I just don't know how I could let this happen," I said out loud. "How could I have been so blind? Why is this happening to me?" I screamed. "What did I do to deserve this? God, you said you wouldn't give me more than I could bear, then what is this? What am I supposed to do with this? I have nothing! My whole life is going down the drain, just like that. What the hell do I do now?"

I am so freaking confused. I really need to talk to Simone. I miss her so much. Oh, shit, what time is it? It was one o'clock in the afternoon. I went downstairs to check Nathan's mailbox. He lived in a three-family house, and I didn't have to go outside to check it, so I didn't mind.

When I opened up the box, there was a letter addressed to me. I was shocked. It was from Tray. I guess he knew where I was all along. I ripped it open.

Dear Sasha,

> *I'm writing to let you know that I miss you and TJ, and I want you to come home. I know you're over at Nathan's, 'cause whenever we fight, you either go to Tiffany or Nathan. Since Tiffany's been calling here for you, you gotta be with Nathan.*

I hated that he knew me.

> *What I've been doing to you is inexcusable, and I need a chance to sit down and talk to you about it. I know TJ is probably over at Lee's house, 'cause you wouldn't want him to miss any school, but I was too embarrassed to call him. Maritza told me that you went to see her. She said she couldn't believe I could do something like this to such a nice woman. She's right. I didn't know what I had, and now that you're gone, I'm losing my mind. It's only been a couple of days, but for me, it feels like a lifetime. Please come home so we can talk, or at least answer my calls.*

> *Your husband forever,*
> *Tramaine Stephen Longston*

Wow, he wrote me a letter. He's never done that before. He must really miss me. I can't believe he had the nerve to write her name in this letter. He really got balls. Why should I call him? Why should I make this easy for him? I've been faithful to him for the last fifteen years of my life, and this is how he repays me—by not only sleeping with someone else, but also getting her pregnant. Shit, he has a whole 'nother life. Plus, he opened two shops I know nothing about. He has too many secrets. I wanted to call him, but I really wanted to find out what the doctor had to say first. Make sure I was clean. My appointment wasn't until tomorrow, so he would definitely have to wait for another day at least. I picked up the rest of the mail and went into the house.

This moment deserved a joint, a glass of wine, and the back porch. I played one of Nathan's Jamaican CDs and went to the back porch. Nathan had it set up really nice with plants and a hammock. Being out here always made me feel nice; plus, the sun was shining bright, and I just needed a moment to just be. As I took a couple more puffs and downed the rest of my drink, I began thinking about Tray again and this damn letter.

"Yeah, right. You don't know what love is. Why would you cheat on me if you loved me?" I said out loud to myself. "Why did you have to go and destroy everything we worked so hard for? I was with your ass when you didn't have shit! Why are you such a self-centered womanizing asshole?" I said, looking at the letter. "Why?" I screamed. "Why?" I started to cry.

I am trying very hard to deal with this by myself. I don't have my mom, and there isn't anyone I feel I could talk to right now. I wished my mother was still alive. She would know what to do.

"She was the greatest," I said out loud. She would know what to do. "Oh my, I think I'm drunk," I said, going to sleep.

Chapter 5

I woke up, turned over on my back, and looked up into the ceiling. It's been three weeks now since I've been home. I was supposed to go back to work last week, but I decided to take a leave of absence. I'm not sure if I wanna go back to that job. The more I think about it, the more I realize it really doesn't do it for me. I want to feel alive in my spirit. I mean, teaching does have its gratifying moments, but I want to do something bigger than that. I mean, I am an artist. It's time for me to get back to that woman I left behind.

I remember, when I was younger, how good it felt to travel back and forth to New York for poetry readings and art exhibits. If I didn't have my son, I would move to New York in a heartbeat. There are so many more opportunities to pursue my art, but I know I need to keep my son here near the family. He's gonna miss them too much, especially Tiffany. If I did that, I would only be doing the same thing that Maggie did. She ran away to New York by herself, and we haven't heard from her since. Running away from my family is not the thing to do right now. I just need to get a job and find a place for me and TJ to live. I sure can't leave TJ over at Lee's house forever, and I can't live here. I love being with Nathan, but when I'm around him, I am not the most responsible person. I mean, I haven't been sober for more than an hour in the last three weeks.

I don't remember much of anything that has happened after meeting with Maritza that day. I have the worst hangover ever. My body hurts—I mean, physically hurts. My eyes are all puffy, and my face is swollen. Did I fall or something? I don't even remember.

The other bad thing about staying here is that I haven't been to church for the past three weeks. My mother would be so ashamed of me. I wish I was strong like her. I always seemed to run to the wrong direction to soothe my pain. My mom was one of the strongest women I have ever met. She raised me all by herself until the day she died. She never asked a soul for a dime. She worked and took care of me. I miss her so much right now. I just can't handle this on my own.

I began to cry. I hate this feeling. How can I make it go away without smoking and drinking myself into a coma? I got up, went into the kitchen, and put on the kettle. While the kettle was boiling, I went and knocked on Nathan's door.

"Nathan," I said, knocking.

There was no answer. I cracked opened the door to find that his room was empty. He didn't even wake me up and tell me he was leaving. Anyway, I suppose it's for the best. I need to shower and get myself together. I am going to make some phone calls and plan out my next move. I haven't answered any phone calls.

Looking at my phone, I notice there are a ton of messages and missed calls. I had to disconnect for a little bit. I had Nathan tell the family what was going on. I couldn't bring myself to talk about it with anyone right now, but I knew everyone would be worried if they didn't know where I was. Nathan said they had ten million questions, but he told them that I would explain everything when I was ready.

No matter how much I drink and smoke, I just can't get this knot out of my stomach. I feel like someone kicked me in my gut. I never knew I would ever feel this way. I know it's not my fault, and I need to stop blaming myself for all this. Tray would have done this regardless of what was going on with us. He is just a cheating-ass man. I feel so sorry for him and Maritza. He will never be happy with anyone. He's not happy with himself. Now he's broken up his family and lost his son. I don't even want him around my son. Why should I? So he can teach him his foul ways?

Sitting down at the kitchen table with my cup of tea, I began to go through my messages. Wow, I have seventeen missed calls from Maritza. Are you kidding me? What does she want from my life? I decided to listen to them.

"Hi, Sasha. It's me, Maritza, calling. Um, give me a call when you get this message. A lot is going on, and I need your help."

She needs my help? Who's gonna help me?

"She has got to be joking," I say out loud, as I deleted her message. As I checked the rest of the messages, the next sounded more desperate than the last.

"Hi, Sasha. It's me, Maritza, again. I really need to talk to you about Tray. I'm really scared right now. He is threatening to hurt me because I broke up his family, and I just don't know what to do."

She needs my help? Really? What does she expect me to do? I couldn't believe how helpless she sounded. When I met her, she was so strong and sure of herself. She sounds like a helpless child now. I am sure she is going through a lot with Tray. Didn't she think that would happen after she told me everything? How is that my problem though? I didn't tell her to tell me. Now she wants me to rescue her from her "baby daddy." She got some nerve.

I was fine in my own little world, taking care of my son and doing my own thing, until she destroyed everything. Well, I mean, Tray destroyed everything by thinking it was OK to cheat on his wife. Did he think I would never find out? I mean, it was bound to happen eventually. Where did he think I lived? In a bottle? I have no respect for him. I have more respect for Maritza for telling me. At least she was woman enough to confront me, even though she only did it because she wanted me to step aside. Well, guess what, I am not going back to Tray, so she can have him.

I don't know why she is calling me to get her out of her own jam. What did she do when they had arguments in the past? And I'm sure they did. She didn't come running to me then. Why does she, all of a sudden, think I'm gonna help her out now? Why does she think she could even call me with this? That bitch better take care of this shit by herself.

I went and lay back down for a moment. I had to think. As I lay there, I began going through the rest of the messages. Simone called me, telling me she is done with me because I didn't call her and let her know what was going on. Is she serious? I am going through the hardest time in my entire life, and all she can think about is herself. Who cares if I didn't call and tell her everything that happened? I don't have to. This is my damn life. Was she gonna figure things out for me? Was she gonna find me a job? I don't need that shit right now. I am going through enough on my own without her adding her shit to the mix. I deleted all the messages from her. I don't have time for that right now.

I listened to the rest of the messages. Tiffany called; she wanted me to give her a call when I am ready. See, that's what I'm talking about. That's why I treat Tiffany the way I do, because she so understands me. She knows I'll come around in my own time. I always do.

Sitting here, thinking, I started remembering when TJ was a little boy. Tray and I had gotten into this big fight. I packed all my things and went to Tiff's house. When I got there, I knocked on the door. Tiff opened it and went right back to bed. She didn't ask me any question for anything. The next morning, she asked if I was all right, and that was it. When I was ready, I explained everything to her, but she never once asked. You know, maybe I will call her back.

I really need to call Maritza and ask her to stop calling my phone. I don't want to hear from her. I don't know why she thinks we're friends or something. She needs my help with Tray? Can you believe the balls on this chick?

As I picked up my phone, I hesitantly dialed her number.

"Sasha," Maritza said, answering on the first ring.

"Yes, Maritza. Why do you keep calling me?"

"Sasha, we really need to talk. Tray is threatening to take the baby when she's born, and he said he's putting me and my mother on the street. I don't know what to do!" she cried frantically.

"Well, what do you want to talk to me about?" I said, trying to sound like I didn't care.

"I need you to talk to him. Make him understand that I wasn't trying to hurt y'all. I just wanted you to know what was going on. It was your right to know, and now I am paying for it."

"Maritza, I didn't tell you to tell me, and I am not calling Tray on your behalf. Who do you think I am? You come into our lives, destroy it, and now you want me to help you fix up your life with my husband? You must be out of your damn mind."

"Sasha, please, I really need your help. I have never seen him this mad before."

"That's not my problem. You should have thought about that when you started messing with a married man in the first place."

"Sasha, I told you, I didn't know about you from the beginning."

"Yes, that's true, but as soon as you found out about me, I didn't see you come running to tell me what was going on then. Now that you're pregnant, you want us to be girlfriends? Are you insane?"

"Sasha, I don't have anyone else. I can't tell my mother everything that is going on right now. She would be so mad with me and Tray. She treats him like her own son."

"OK," I said, still unsure of what she wanted from me.

I am certainly not going to call Tray for her and tell him anything. I haven't even spoken to Tray for my damn self. Why would I call him for her?

"Hello, Sasha? You still there?"

"Yeah, I'm still here," I said with an attitude. "Look, Maritza, I agreed to come and meet you because I was curious, but that doesn't mean I am OK with all this. You and Tray ruined my son's life and mine and now you want me to fix things between you and Tray? Have you lost your mind?"

"No, I haven't lost my mind, but I'm desperate. My baby is due next month, and I don't wanna do this by myself."

"Well, you should have thought about all that before you went and got yourself pregnant. You knew he was married when you got pregnant. You could have avoided that, but you didn't. You chose to do big-girl things. Now handle it like a big girl. I am not here to help you out. I can't believe you would even ask me."

"Sasha, do you think I thought things would turn out like this?"

"I don't know what you were thinking."

"Sasha, please, I am begging you. Tray is going to put me and my mother out on the street. Is that what you want?"

"Is that what I want? I couldn't care less."

"You don't really mean that. Tray said you were one of the sweetest women he knew."

"Really? Then why did he cheat on me with you?"

"Sasha, it wasn't like that."

"Maritza, I don't know what it was like. All I know is, three weeks ago, I was in my house, living my life, and you changed all that. Now you want me to help you from being homeless. Well, guess what, my ass is homeless."

"Sasha, you are not homeless. You can go back home anytime you want. Tray would never put you out. He loves you too much. I see that now. I thought that I could make him stay with me if I got pregnant, but he really loves you. That's why he would never leave you."

"Well, it didn't stop him from starting a whole 'nother family with you, so you're on your own. Anyway, I have to go," I said, and I hung up. Can you believe this chick, the nerve of her, wanting me to call Tray to talk about, who, her? I know I will have to speak to him eventually, but I figured I would let him sweat it out for a while longer.

I honestly didn't wanna go back to East Lyme. I really didn't wanna move out there, but Tray thought it would be better for TJ. He didn't want him to be raised in Hartford with the hood rats. Now that I think about it, Tray probably moved us way out there so he could do want he wanted to do in Hartford. He knew what he was doing all along.

Oh, man, I really need to do something fast. I got up and got Nathan's newspaper from the kitchen. I need to find a job. I don't care what it is right now; I just know I need to get on my own two feet. I have always been able to get jobs easily. I mean, I can do almost anything. Maybe I should try to work in the office or something for now. At the very least, I'll be able to get a place of my own. I've never been on my own before. I went from Aunt Trudy to Tray.

I know that's my phone ringing again. I picked it up. It was Tray calling me again. I let it go to voice mail. I didn't want to talk to him right now, even though I wondered about how he was feeling. His letter made him sound like things would be different if I went home. I wonder if I would really see a change in him after all this. Would he treat me different now?

I believe when people mess up and get a second chance, they will sometimes learn from their mistakes. On the other hand, you have people out there that make the same mistakes over and over again, and they never learn from it. They don't see the harm that they've caused.

I am really curious to see what type of relationship we'll have now. Would he be the husband I always wanted? I mean, he hasn't always been in the past, but I let it go on because I thought we were going through something, and all along, his mind was on someone else.

This was all so much to think about. I looked at all the missed calls on my phone. Tiff called me almost every night. She was so worried about me. She knew something happened with Tray, because Nathan told her, but he didn't go into detail. This made Tiff furious. She felt like she had always been there for me in the past, and now that I am going through something, I exclude her from it. She is one of my best friends.

I just couldn't bring myself to tell her everything because that will mean I have to tell her what part Jade played in all this—how she deliberately set Tray up with Maritza because she was mad with me. She is crazy. Why would she think I would leave my husband and mess up my cousin's life for her?

I only took two of her phone calls, and I made them as brief as possible. The first night she called, she wanted to know if I was ready to tell her what was going on and why my ass wasn't home. I told her I needed some space and that I felt stifled in the house all the time. I told her that I wanted to start painting again and that I needed to change my scenery in order to do that. She wanted to know what made me feel like that. I told her it was just a feeling I had in myself.

The next night she called, she wanted to know if I would stop by for lunch with her and Jade. I told her that I couldn't because I was working on my project and that I really didn't wanna leave. I couldn't bring myself to tell her the truth, and obviously, either Jade didn't let her in on what was going on, or Jade didn't know.

Tiff was really upset with me, but she accepted what I had to say and told me she was gonna give me one more week, and then that was it. She would be coming to find out for herself what was going on. I loved the fact that she respected my wishes. She was always good for understanding things.

I really should ask Maritza about Jade. I was so curious that I decided to call and check on her. The last time we spoke, she said she was in a lot of pain and wouldn't be able to go down to the shop for a while. I think she was just depressed about how Tray was treating her and that she needed some time to figure things out too. Dialing her number, I wondered if she thought this was all so weird that we were starting to talk more.

"Hello," she answered, sounding really tired.

"Hey, Maritza. How are you?" I asked, trying to sound concerned.

"Well, I'm alive."

"What do you mean by that? What's wrong?"

"Everything? I need to see you, Sasha. Do you think we could go have lunch somewhere or something?"

"Sure, what time do you wanna meet?"

"Right now. I need to get out of this house," she said anxiously.

"All right. Where do you wanna go?"

"We could go to Mickey D's or something."

"OK. How about the one on the corner of Washington and Park Street?"

"That's fine with me," she said.

"See you in a minute," I said, putting my socks on.

"OK, Sasha, and thank you."

She sounded so bad, like she was having a nervous breakdown or something. I didn't think about looking my finest. It wasn't important anymore. She was more important to me now. I couldn't believe Tray would just abandon that poor woman in the last months of her pregnancy. He's such an ass. I was really starting to hate him more and more with each day we were apart. Being alone can do a lot for a person. When you're not all caught up in things, you start to see the whole picture.

I got to Mickey D's and sat in the parking lot since I didn't see her car anywhere. She pulled up about five minutes after I did. We both walked in together.

"What do you want to eat?" I asked.

"I really don't want anything. Maybe just some fries," she said.

"OK, I'll get them for you. Go find a seat."

I found myself treating her like a kid. After all, she was still a kid in my eyes. I ordered a cup of water and a salad and fries and a cup of juice for her. When I got to the table, she was already in tears.

"Sasha, I can't believe how nice you've been to me. You didn't have to be. You could have been a coldhearted bitch and told me that whatever I got myself into was my problem. But instead, it seems you're here more for me than Tray. Why is that? Why are you being so nice to me?" Maritza said, confused.

"Because," I said, positioning myself for the conversation, "number one, you're not a bad person, and I don't know how old you are exactly, but you're kinda young to have all this shit going on in your life."

"I know that's right. I'm only twenty-two, and I don't have a baby daddy. I'm not even married, and here I am, about to have a baby in a couple of months. I just can't believe all this is happening to me. I don't know what I was thinking, getting involved with Tray. When I found out he was married, I should have just backed off until I could get rid of him. But there was so much at stake. And now, he doesn't wanna take care of me anymore. I never thought about how it would be if he didn't take care of me. He told me he would be there for me forever."

Maritza had streams of tears flowing by this time. I wanted to wipe her tears.

"Maritza, do you remember when we were in the shop and you told me that if we stuck together, everything would be OK?"

"Yeah, I remember."

"Well, it will be OK. I'm not going anywhere. I'll be here for you, even if Tray's not."

"Oh my god, you don't know how scared I was to talk you. I really just want us to be OK. Tray is such an asshole for cheating on you. You're everything that I wanted to be. But now look at me. I didn't even graduate from high school, and now I'm pregnant. I don't have a trade or anything. I don't even have my hairdressing license. You remember that older lady you saw in the shop? The shop is in her name. I couldn't even do that right, and Tray said he was giving me the money, but he wasn't putting his name on it."

"Maritza, you have your whole life ahead of you. You could go back to school and get your high school diploma and then go to hairdressing school, if that's what you want to do. You can do anything you want. This is America, girl. All you have to do is want it. I knew I wanted to be an artist, even when no one else thought I would or could do it. And look at me now. I can basically work anywhere I want because of the connections I've made over the years."

I really did have connections in high places. I just wasn't ready to use them yet. They may involve some old sexual tabs being paid.

"I am my own person, Maritza, and you can do the same thing. You can become self-sufficient. When you do that, you don't have to answer to anyone. You can do as you please. My family hates that I paint for a living instead of becoming a doctor or something. But, Maritza, you can't live for people. You have to live for yourself and do what makes you happy, 'cause in the end, you have to live with you. People will come and go, but as long as you're alive, you have you."

"You really think I could do it, Sasha? You really think I could take care of this baby on my own? There's so much to do. How could I possibly do it by myself?"

"You're not by yourself, Maritza. At least you have your mother. I didn't have that, growing up. My mom died when I was fourteen. I basically raised myself, I mean, with help from Aunt Trudy and my cousins. But mostly, I raised myself. I had to figure out what would be good for me, not what someone else wanted for me. That's harder than what you have to do. You have your mother to help and support you through all this."

"Sasha, I didn't even tell my mother about this yet. She doesn't know Tray is married, and she doesn't know that I know you. She thinks he had a son with a girl from a long time ago and that Tray lives with him. What am I gonna do when she finds out the truth? She's gonna disown me. I'm a disgrace to her. She would never do what I've done. She thinks too highly of herself to stoop to this level, and when she finds out that I knew about you and still took things from him . . . shit . . . when she finds out that she took things from him, she's gonna hate him and me too."

"Maritza, your mother's not gonna hate you. She may be upset at the choices that you've made, but I don't believe she'll hate you. You've done nothing but look out for her, right?"

"Well, yeah. And I did do all this to get us out of the ghetto. Shit used to live in the projects before Tray came along. My mother was so overjoyed when I told her we were moving out of that roach-infested hellhole. That's why she loves Tray so much, 'cause he changed her life, and she didn't have to think 'bout the fact my father left her for another woman anymore, 'cause she was doing all right for herself. That's why I know she's gonna hate me. My father did the same thing to her that I did to you. That lady he was messing with knew about us, but we didn't know about her. And my father used to bring us around her and tell us it was somebody he worked with. She used to make us dinner and everything. I know she's gonna be so hurt. I'm so stupid."

"Maritza, you're not stupid. You just made a mistake."

"Yeah, a big mistake—a mistake that I can't take back."

"Maybe you're not supposed to take it back. Maybe this baby is what you need to get yourself together. Just think, you can't be irresponsible anymore. Now you have to think about what's best for your baby. And in my opinion, you've already started doing that. You called me, didn't you? You wanted to know where I stood with your baby's father 'cause you were thinking about the well-being of your baby, right?"

"Yeah, that's true. I wasn't just thinking about that though. I wanted to know what you were about, and I really wanted you out of the picture. But after I met you found out you were nice and everything, I felt, like, a little guilty for even messing with Tray in the first place."

"Well, don't worry about a thing, 'cause we know each other now, and I'm not gonna let you go through this alone."

Maritza wiped her eyes one last time. Her face was all red and puffy. To think the young woman I first talked to with the chip on her shoulder and an attitude problem a wide long turned out to be this confused, naive little girl who now needed my help. I wasn't gonna let her down. My stepdaughter deserved more than that.

I honestly did understand what it was like to feel alone. Remember I grew up with Trudy Walker and her crew. When we left, she gave me a big hug in the parking lot. I started to feel like I was the champion in all this. I mean, if he never cheated, I wouldn't have ever thought about doing something different with my life. And seeing that Maritza ended up pregnant, and after my doctor's appointment, I'm in perfect health—other than a minor broken heart, which I'm sure I'll get over and come out on top.

Tray, on the other hand, came out alone. He doesn't have me, or Maritza, for that matter. I really didn't want him anymore, and I can't believe that I didn't even miss him this whole time I was gone. I told TJ that we wouldn't be going back, and he wanted to know what was going to happen to all his stuff and if he would still see his dad. I told him that I was thinking about getting my own place for a while and that I wasn't divorcing his father—just taking a break from him. Maybe we need to be apart from each other in order to see where our heads are. I planned on telling Tray today.

I wanted to go and check on Maritza. She was admitted to the hospital, and Tray didn't even bother to go and check on her. I felt so bad for her. I had to go and see if she was all right. I just don't have it in me to be a coldhearted bitch. I've been talking to Nathan a lot about the situation, and he said that whatever I did to help this young woman, God would reward me tenfold. He said it showed the true substance of my being and that I was a beautiful woman.

I truly believe this girl needs me right now. There she is, having her first baby, and her mother doesn't even know anything about her baby's father being married. She's going through a lot, and it doesn't matter if she caused it on herself. I'm sure there have been plenty of times that we've caused things on ourselves and would have loved for someone to bail us out. Everyone is entitled to another chance. I think it's even harder for her now, considering how distant she felt from her own mother. That poor woman doesn't even know that her daughter is pregnant by a married man.

I know a lot of people would say, "Well, she made her bed. Now she has to lie in it," but I just don't think she has to lie in it alone. Tray lay with her in the beginning, and now he's left her alone. I think he's just trying to sort things out in his head.

I, however, couldn't abandon her. This was gonna be a rough time in her life, and I just don't think she's strong enough to endure all this pressure. If she had her mother by her side, I would back off, and I know this sounds crazy, but I would like to help deliver this baby. I don't know what has gotten into me.

I've been reading the Bible about forgiveness and that we shouldn't judge lest we be judged, and you know what? I kinda think that's right. I've done things in my life that I'm not proud of, and I don't think I would want anyone to judge my actions. As a matter of fact, I know I wouldn't want anyone to judge me. I'm not a saint either. Look at what happened with me and Jade. I believe I owe it to God to right that wrong in some way. Maybe I'll be forgiving. I did go against one of the Ten Commandments: thou shall not commit adultery. It didn't state what gender.

When I got to the hospital, Maritza looked so helpless. She just lay there, crying. I thought something was wrong with the baby, but she was fine. Maritza couldn't keep down any food, and they said her blood pressure was really high. They told her she would stay until it came down, and she went back to holding down solids again. The doctor told her she was under too much stress and that it wasn't good for the baby.

All Maritza kept talking about was how bad she wanted her mother to be there and that when she would find out what she had done, they'd never be close again. I didn't believe that for a second. If her mother was any kind of woman, she would forgive her. I just kept reminding her of that. After all, that's her only girl child. She would somehow understand; I just knew it. I could feel it in my heart.

It was lunchtime now, and I spent the whole morning with Maritza. We watched TV and talked about what she would do to keep her blood pressure down when she got out of the hospital. I couldn't believe she had been here for two days and that the only person that gave her flowers was me. This was partially her fault. She didn't tell her mother or brother that she was in the hospital. I guess she has her times when she used to disappear with Tray, so no one looked for her.

"So do you have a lot of clothes for the baby?"

"No, not really. I need to get a lot more winter stuff. You know it's gonna be cold before you know. I don't want her to freeze out there."

"Well, who's gonna give you a baby shower?"

"I don't even know. I heard some of the girls talking in the shop one day about something, but whenever they see me, they stop talking, so I know they're planning something. I also heard my mother talking to my aunt about renting some place, but I don't know. After all this goes down, I don't know what's gonna happen there."

"Maritza, don't you think your mother is going to be angry when she finds out you're in the hospital and you didn't tell anyone? I really would like to know where she thinks you are right now. If you were with Tray, wouldn't you call her and tell her where you are so she doesn't worry about you?"

"No, she never worries about me. She said that as long as I am with Tray, she doesn't care. She knows he'll take care of me. Little does she know, Tray ain't even thinking about me right now."

"Does she normally call you on your cell phone or something?"

"She'll leave a message or something once in a while, but she doesn't like to crowd me. I told her off once because she wanted to know my every move, and ever since then, she just leaves me alone. Now, I wish I didn't do that, 'cause I need her now more than ever."

"Why don't you just call her? Tell her that you're in the hospital, and while you're here, maybe you could talk to her about everything that's going on. I'll stay with you, if you like. Maybe she won't be so mad when she finds out that I'm all right with all this. I mean, what can I do? It's already happened, right? There's no point in hating you. That wouldn't solve anything."

"You know what, Sasha? I have to say it again. You are a beautiful a person. Here you are, spending the day with your husband's lover. I don't think I would've been as understanding as you've been. I probably would've tried to kill you or something."

"Maritza, that wouldn't make any sense. Kill the baby, and then spend the rest of my life in jail. Meanwhile, Tray is free to find someone else and start a new life. Not to mention the fact that my son would have to grow up without his mother. I went through that. I would never want my son to go through that. Not in a million years. That just doesn't make any sense to me. I always look at the whole picture before I do something. I don't just feel the moment and run with it. The only time I feel the moment and just go with it is when I'm painting. That's when the good stuff comes out. You know, Maritza, I've been thinking about opening an art studio out here somewhere, maybe downtown or something. I'd like to do something different, seeing that I'm not going back to East Lyme. I need to find something to do for work too. I can't live off my cousin forever."

"Good afternoon," the young lady said to us as she brought in Maritza's lunch.

"Good afternoon," I said to her with a smile.

"Good afternoon. Is all this for me?" Maritza said to the young lady, opening her tray. "I can't eat all this."

"You're gonna have to try."

"Yeah," I said to Maritza. "If you want them to take that IV out of your arm, you're gonna have to try to eat some real food."

"Well, you ladies have a nice day. You know, if you want to have lunch here, there's a cafeteria downstairs," the young lady said, as she was leaving the room.

"Oh, that's OK. I'm leaving soon."

"Do you have to leave now?" Maritza said sadly.

"Yeah, I got some things I need to take care of, and remember what I said to you. You need to call your mother and let her know what's going on with you. I wish I had my mother to tell stuff to."

"Yeah, I guess you're right. She does need to know that I'm in the hospital and that her grandbaby is OK. I don't know about the part about you and Tray though. I don't think I'm ready to tell her that part."

"Well, all I know, Maritza, is that the longer you keep it from her, the more painful it's gonna be for her when she finds out about it. She is your mother, you know. And if there's one thing I know, it's that mothers always want to feel close to their children, especially in a time like this. She is probably wondering why you haven't called her. And what if they decide to keep you in here for another week? You mean to tell me you're not going to speak to your mother for a week? If I was her, I would call the police and report you missing. Anything could happen to you, and she would want to know that you're OK."

"Well, Ms. Sasha, I could say the same for you. Are you going to call your husband and let him know you're all right? I think it's time you talk to him and let him know how you feel about everything. I mean, regardless of whether you go back to him or not, he's out of my life. I'm not gonna be with something today, and they disappear tomorrow. I don't need that in my baby's life. He ain't even concerned that I'm in the hospital or anything. I guess he wouldn't even care if the baby died either. He probably won't even buy her anything. All I know is that he's gonna have to give me child support. That's all I want from him. He doesn't ever have to see me again if he doesn't want to."

"You know what, Maritza, you shouldn't say that. I think your baby has the right to grow up with her father. At least let her see him and let him take her places. You wouldn't want her to miss out on that part of her life. She'll hate you for it later."

"Yeah, you're right again. I'm just so fuckin' pissed off with his ass. Right now, I don't want to see him anywhere near me. I know I'mma change my mind later, but right now, fuck Tray."

"Yeah, I kinda feel the same way. He's gonna have to beg for me to come back. I was wondering though, where is this other shop he has in the north end?"

"Oh, it's on Tower Avenue, at the corner of Main Street, across from that car dealer. He thinks he's so damn slick. I may just have to pay him a visit one of these days, let him know I know what's going on."

"You know what, I'm really leaving now. I said that already, and I'm still here. I'll talk to you later." I gave her a kiss on her forehead and left. I couldn't believe I had developed a relationship with my husband's lover. Hey, I suppose you should keep your enemies close.

I decided to pay Tray a visit right now. I had time to waste; plus, I wanted to see what this shop was all about. I can bet he got a whole bunch of women working around him.

Jumping on the highway, I checked the clock in the car. It was around one thirty now. Shoot, I'm getting hungry. I wonder what I can eat. Not anything fattening, that's for sure. It's time for me to get my body right. I sat in the hospital, looking at Maritza. Even with the belly, she was thin. How'd she do that? I really need to get it together. I want Tray to look at me and lust after me like he used to. I need to get me a personal trainer or something, work my fat ass.

I pulled up into the parking lot near the rib-and-chicken place. I can get something to eat from here and then go next door and see what's going on with my so-called husband.

Before I could even get out of my car, someone came up to my window. "You got some change?"

"No! I don't have any change."

"I'm hungry. Can I get a dollar so I could buy some chicken?" the beggar said.

"No! I don't have any money to give you. If you want some chicken, I'll buy you a piece, but I'm not giving you any money." These druggies are always trying to get money for their crack. They use food as an excuse. When I said that, he walked away. He wasn't hungry then. I ain't stupid.

I walked into the rib house and ordered a slab of ribs and a diet soda. "No fries, please," I told the man behind the counter.

"Damn, baby, you look good. What's your name?" a man standing next to me said.

I looked up at him and smiled. "Sasha."

He was fine—I mean, superfine. He was tall and slim, with hazel eyes and curly hair. He was very well dressed too, casual but nice. His clothes looked so neat on him. They fit his body. Nothing baggy or hanging over.

"Hi, Sasha. How are you doing today? I'm Nick."

"Hi, Nick," I said, feeling giddy. I think I was even blushing.

"So where are you from?" he said to me, with his suave, deep voice.

"I'm from Hartford, but I live in East Lyme."

"East Lyme? You're kinda far from home, ain't you?"

"Yeah, I'm thinking about relocating back here. I've had some bad experiences in East Lyme lately."

"Yeah, maybe we can get together later and discuss this over dinner," he said, smiling at me. His teeth were so white and straight. I love a man with nice teeth. It says a lot about them. "Let me give you my number. Would that be all right?"

"Sure," I said, with a slight grin, to show half of my dimple.

He pulled a pen out of his little briefcase and took my hand. His hands were so soft and pretty. He even looked like he had a manicure. I got all tingly inside.

"I'm gonna write it on a place you won't lose." As he wrote his number on the palm of my hand, he said, "Call me at about six o'clock or so. That's the time I get home from work. Don't wash that hand until you call me now," he said to me with those beautiful eyes.

"OK," I said and laughed.

His order was ready before mine, so when he got it, he left. As he grabbed for the bag with his left hand, I looked for a ring. I didn't see a ring or a mark from a ring. To me, that was a green light.

As he was leaving, he looked back at me again. "Don't forget to call me now."

"I won't."

When my order came up, the man behind the counter handed it to me and said with some kind of Indian accent, "Today is your lucky day. That man got the big bucks. He's a lawyer here in Hartford. He comes in here all the time. You go, girl."

I laughed and said, "Thanks for the information." As I walked out, I had a smile on my face. *A lawyer. Mmm. Sounds interesting*, I thought to myself.

I saw Tray's truck outside the hair shop next door. It wasn't there when I pulled up. I wonder if he noticed that it was my car. He probably didn't pay it any mind. I sat in the car and ate some of my ribs. I didn't want to talk to him on an empty stomach. He might make me sick, and then I wouldn't want to eat my food.

I watched the shop. We Got It was the name outside the shop. We Got It, where does he come up with these ghetto names? He could have at least come up with something family oriented. But, oh, I forgot. He's not family oriented.

Looking through the window, I could see there were a lot of women in this shop. One side was all women, and the other side was all men. I guess he wanted to make sure he covered all his bases. It looked pretty nice in there.

I took a couple more sips of my diet soda and cleaned up my mess. I checked to make sure I didn't have anything in my teeth and touched up my eyeliner. *I always look good*, I thought to myself. Thought I'd give myself a little pep talk before I went inside. I had on a tight jean miniskirt and a tight T-shirt, with some cute little jogging sneakers, my ankle bracelet, my diamond tennis bracelet, and the diamond-studded watch Tray bought me for Christmas three years ago. I wondered why he gave me such an expensive watch. It cost about four thousand. My hair was in a ponytail, and I had on big hoop earrings and a herringbone necklace. Simple but fly. Oh, and did I mention I took off my wedding ring? I got out of the car and headed for the door.

The minute I walked in, the guys started on me. "Damn, Ma. You sure you need your hair done? You look perfect."

"Is Tray here?" I said, ignoring the one man's comment.

"Yeah, he's in the back. Let me call him for you." He picked up his cell phone and used that walkie-talkie thing. "Yo, Tray, there's a fine-ass black woman out here to see you."

"All right. Tell her to have a seat. I'll be out in a minute."

"He said he'll be out in a minute. I'm Jeff, by the way. Your name is?" he said, trying to get in business.

"I'm your boss," I said with an attitude.

"Yeah, you got it like that?" Jeff said.

"Yeah, I got it like that," I said, looking him square in the eyes.

Tray came out of the back room and took a step back when he saw me. "Sasha, what up? What are you doing here?"

"What am I doing here?" I said, looking at him like he was stupid. "That's all you have to say to your wife?"

"Your wife?" Jeff said, looking in amazement. "Damn, Tray, you ain't tell us 'bout this dime piece. Come to think about it, if my wife looked like that, I would tell no niggas 'bout her either."

"Let's go in the back and talk, Sasha."

"Oh, now you wanna be private. All your business is all over town. Why'd you wanna be private now?"

"Come on, Sash. Let's talk in the back."

"Ooh. That female's hot," another one of the guys said.

"She sounds like she's gonna whip his ass," one of the ladies said.

"Oh, Tray done got himself in some more shit," another one of the ladies said. Then they all started laughing with one another.

Tray brought me into the back room and started in on me. "Why'd you gotta come in here and embarrass me in front of my employees?"

"Your employees? Last time I checked, we were still married. Don't you mean 'our employees'?"

"You know what I'm saying, Sasha."

"No, Tray, I don't know what you're saying. You never told me about this shop or the one on the south end. What have you gotta say for yourself?" I started getting loud.

"Sasha, baby, calm down."

"Calm down my ass!" I said, making sure everyone in the front could hear me. "You're probably dating one of them bitches working in the front too—or one of the men. Who the fuck knows what you'll do or won't do."

"Sasha, you're going too far. Don't get me mad up in here."

"What are you gonna do, Tray? Hit me? Kick me out? Yeah, that's it, you fuckin' punk. Kick your wife out of the shop you never told her you had. All I know is that when I divorce your sorry black ass, Imma get half of all your shit—the secret shit and the shit I know about. You're so fuckin' sorry."

"Oh, you gonna divorce me, Sasha? Why'd you got to take it that far?"

"Take it that far? Bitch, you got two shops I didn't even know you had, a girl on the side, and a baby on the way. Don't you think you took it far when your ass did all that?"

"Sasha, I wanted to tell you, but the more time that went by, the harder it got to tell you. I didn't want you to leave me. You're the best thing that ever happened to me."

"Yeah, you should've thought about that when you were buying Maritza her condo and her car. How you gonna date a girl ten years younger than you, get her pregnant, and then leave her to fend for herself? You are a sorry excuse for a man and a father. You let your son down, and now you wanna let your daughter down."

"Damn, you sure do know a lot about Maritza."

"Well, how else am I gonna know what's going on with you? I had to do something. When she called me, it was the best thing that ever happened to me. I knew you'd been acting strange, but I didn't know you were going on with all this. You are such a liar."

"So what are you saying, Sasha? You don't love me anymore?"

"How could you possibly think about whether or not I love you right now? You have a one-track mind."

"Sasha, if you still love me, we can work all this out. Don't you know that? I still love you."

"Yeah, right. How'd you put it to your little girlfriend? You love me, but you're not in love with me? Is that about right, Tray?"

"That bitch is just trying to break us up. Don't you see that? She's just trying to make sure that we break up before her baby is born."

"*Her* baby, Tray? Don't you mean *your* baby?"

"Sasha, I don't even know if that kid is mine. She was still messing around with her old boyfriend."

"Yeah, and you still hit it raw, huh, Tray?"

"Sasha, it wasn't even like that."

"Yeah, it wasn't like that, but she got a condo and Navigator, right? It wasn't like what? You're so full of shit it ain't even funny anymore. I really think you need help, Tray."

"Help? Baby, I don't need help. All I need is you. If I have you, everything else will be fine."

"Well, you had me, and everything ain't fine. It may be fine for your cheating ass, but it ain't fine for me or TJ. You had your son thinking you were this great man, and you let him down. The funny part about it is that he forgives you, but he doesn't understand why you're staying away from him. You know where he is, but you won't go see him or even call him. But I know why. 'Cause your sorry ass is too ashamed of what you did to our family. We would've been fine if you didn't go out there and do all your little foolishness. But you know, that's OK. 'Cause now I'm starting to realize that there's a whole life out there I've been missing, being stuck under you."

"So what are you saying? You're gonna start seeing other people?"

"Hell, yeah. Why not? Shit, you've been doing it for years. It's about time I got in the game. And you know what else, I'mma start tonight. I got a date with a lawyer. A lawyer, Tray. And he makes your ass look poor and dumb."

"Poor and dumb, huh? Sasha, you ain't going out on a date with anybody. You're my wife, and what I say, you do."

"Oh, Tray, back in the days, you might have been able to pull that shit, but this is the new millennium, and I'm a new-millennium chick. And you know what else? I may not be skinny like Maritza, but I'm fine as hell, and there are a lot of guys that are just waiting to see what I'm all about. And by the way, I want your shit out of my house by this weekend, 'cause I'm coming home, and I don't expect to find you there!"

I walked out of the shop with a force before he could say another word.

"You go, girl," one of the stylists said.

When I got in my car, I felt like a new woman. I had really taken charge for a change. He wasn't gonna be the boss of me ever again. Not in this lifetime.

Pulling out of the parking lot, I screamed, "I'm free! No more chains holding me!"

I opened up my hand to see that Nick's number was still there. Now I had a chance for a new beginning. It was time for me to start meeting new people. I was coming out of bondage.

Chapter 6

I spent the rest of the afternoon shopping at the mall. I ran up at least three of Tray's credit cards. I'd say I spent about seven thousand easily in three hours flat. Shit, I had to look good for my date tonight. I got a new outfit, shoes, and handbag. And, of course, I need accessories. I treated myself to a five-thousand-dollar diamond set—earrings, necklace, ring, bracelet, and anklet. Full princess-cut double rows. It was fabulous. I wanted to look rich but elegant.

I also needed to rent a car for the night, so since I had to tell Simone what was going on eventually, I figured I could kill two birds with one stone. I called her and asked her if Richie could drop her down at the car dealer so she could drive my car back to Nathan's house. When she got to the dealer, which was in, like, twenty minutes flat. Nosy ass, she had twenty-one questions for me.

"So, Ms. Sasha, where have you been? Why haven't you returned any of my calls? What is going on with you and Tray? I know you ain't been at the house, 'cause I've been calling over there too. Where have you been? I called Tiff, and she said she didn't know what was going on. I saw Nathan, and he said he hadn't seen you either, but I knew if he had, he wouldn't tell me. I know how the two of you are. You've been missing a lot that's been going on in the family."

"OK, Simone, can you take a breath?" She was so excited. "Let's just get the car, and then I'll tell you everything."

"All right. I'mma go in and get it, and then you can follow me back to the house."

When I pulled out of the parking lot, I was pushing a bmw x5—black and fully loaded, to match my outfit. I even had little diamond studs on my high-heeled sandals. I'm wearing a sleeveless black dress, one side higher than the other, with my hair in an updo off my face, with maybe some curls in the front. I'm also gonna get a French manicure and pedicure.

I looked in my rearview mirror and saw my cousin driving at the back of me looking at me like I was out of my mind. My cell phone rang when I turned the corner to get on the highway. It was Simone.

"Sasha, what is going on? Why did you rent that truck? Where are you going? As a matter a fact, where are we going now?"

"Simone, would you shut up for a minute?"

"Hello? Was that Sasha that just told me to shut up? What is going on with you?"

"Simone, just be quiet and follow me. I'll talk to you once we stop."

I pulled into the nail salon on Farmington Avenue. When she got out of the car, I looked at her and said, "Does this bring back memories?"

"Yeah, it does. Now what's going on?"

"Girl, I got a date tonight," I said as we walked into the salon and signed in.

"A date with who? Tray?" Simone said, having a seat on the couch.

"No, with this lawyer named Nick," I said, sitting next to her.

"What?"

"With a lawyer named Nick."

"What's been going on? Why are you going out on my boy like that? I thought y'all were so in love and y'all were gonna be together forever?"

"All I can tell you, Simone, is that there's a lot that's happening between Tray and me right now. And the last two weeks have been showing me some things. I'm 'bout to take control of my life. One thing I know for sure is, I'm going on this date tonight, and I'mma love every minute of it. I'm not holding back anymore. In fact, I gotta give him a call at, like, six or so. What time is it now?" I said, looking up at the salon clock. "OK, it's five. I still have some time left. I'mma call at, like, six fifteen," I said to Simone as two pedicurists came to get us.

Sitting down in the pedicure chair, Simone just looked at me. She didn't have anything at all to say. That was the first time that shit ever happened.

Sitting there in that chair with my feet getting massaged, I thought about how fine Nick was and how his voice was so deep and manly, with his soft-ass hands. He was so different from Tray. Nick was a real man. Tray was still trying to act like a young boy, with his baggy-ass clothes and them damn jerseys, like he couldn't ever wear anything else. But

Nick, he dressed more like a rich white boy. And the ass on that man was unbelievable. Damn. He must be doing a whole lot of squats.

"So, Sasha," Simone said, still looking at my face, "you're going on a date?"

"Yeah, I already told you that. You don't believe me?"

"I'm just checking, 'cause all this shit is news to me."

"OK, Simone, what do you wanna know?"

"Sasha, I wanna know everything—everything you can tell me and definitely everything you think you can't."

"Everything like what?"

"Why are you dating somebody else? What exactly happened between you and Tray? And what's up with the BMW rental? Since when does the style of car matter to you?" Simone said, confused.

"Girl, a lot of things have changed," I said, giving her a little grin.

"I see that," she said, looking me over. "When did you get fake nails in the first place, and where are your bushy eyebrows? What is up?"

"I'm turning over a new leaf on life. I wanna be the finest, richest chick you would wanna see. Shit, my husband can afford it. Why not?"

"Since when can Tray afford all that?"

"Since he opened up two new shops I know nothing about."

"What?"

"Girl, yes," I said. "And since he got a baby momma that ain't me living in a condo, driving a Navigator."

"What? Nah, you're lying. Not Tray?" Simone said, amazed and a little pissed. "Girl, I told you that man was up to something," Simone said, sounding really angry now. "That son of a bitch. Oh, he's gonna pay for that shit."

"Yeah, I know you told me, Moni, but I didn't wanna listen. I didn't wanna believe my husband was like that, but oh well, I guess he is. Such is life."

"Now what did you say 'bout a baby momma?" she said curiously.

"Yeah, he got this little young girl pregnant, and now he doesn't wanna take care of the baby. He says it ain't his."

"Yeah, you know that's the typical excuse," she said. "I didn't do it. She was messing with other men too."

"That's just what he said, Simone. Well, you know what? His ass is gonna have to take a blood test to prove to me that that baby ain't his, and Imma still divorce his sorry ass and take half of every fuckin' thing he got."

"Sasha, I never heard you talk like this before. You must be serious."

"Yeah, well, I guess I never felt like this before."

"You know I'm here for you, girl. Whatever you need, just let me know. Or do you need anything? 'Cause, girl, I'm diggin' that diamond ring," Simone said, with sparkles in her eyes.

"Oh, this? I just picked them up at the mall. I tried to spend all his damn money. Shit, I'm worth it. He ain't gonna do anything but give it to the next female anyway," I said, with an attitude.

I never noticed how ghetto I sound when I'm talking to Simone. She really pulls it out of me, and now that I'm turning over a new leaf, I'mma show Tray some of the ghetto in me too. I'm tired of him running over me. He won't get the chance to do this ever again.

"Sasha, what does this guy look like anyway?"

"Who? Nick?" I said, sounding like he was already my man. "He's about six foot two maybe, and he weighs, or I'd say, two twenty. He's really thick and full of muscles. He got curly hair and hazel eyes, with dimples and long eyelashes. And, girl, he got the sweetest ass," I said, laughing in lust.

"Ooh, sounds like you snagged a hottie," Simone said, sounding a bit jealous. "Shit, he got a brother?"

"Shit, I don't know yet, but I'll let you know. I know his hands are really big and really soft."

"You know what that means," Simone said, and we both laughed. The two Asian ladies doing our toes laughed too.

When we got over the manicure table, it was almost six o'clock. I was getting anxious to call him. I decided to put his number in my phone so that I wouldn't lose it when Lillie got ready to do my nails. Simone didn't get the manicurist next to me; she was two seats down.

"So what design do you want this time?" Lillie said.

"I want a French manicure like on my toes. I have a big date tonight."

"Oh, yeah, very special, huh?"

"Yes, very," I said, smiling.

"OK, I'll make sure I'd do an extra special job for you."

By the time Lillie gave me a fill, it was six twenty-five.

"Lillie, I need to use the bathroom before you polish my nails." I got up and went into the bathroom. Passing by Simone, I gave her my pocketbook and took my cell phone to give her a hint at what I was about to do.

I looked for his name in my phone and pressed the green phone button. I sat on the toilet seat, nervous as hell. I felt like I would have to go in a minute. The phone rang three times, and he answered it. "Hello."

"Hi, Nick. It's me, Sasha."

"Ooh, Sasha. Right on time. I just stepped in. So what's up? How've you been since I saw you last?"

"I'm fine. Can we still get together tonight? What time did you plan on getting us together?" I said, trying to sound like I might have other things to do.

"Oh, I'd say around eight thirty, nine. We can get a bite to eat and maybe go out dancing somewhere, if that's OK with you."

"Oh, that sounds good. Eight thirty will be fine with me," I said, sounding as calm as possible.

"All right then. I'll see you then."

"OK." I hung up the phone and just sat there for a moment. I was shaking, and I could feel my heart beating so fast it was gonna jump out of my chest. I went back to Lillie and got my nails airbrushed. Simone looked down at me and grinned. I grinned back and looked down at my nails. This was going to be a night to remember.

I got finished with my nails and eyebrows at about seven fifteen. Simone was done before me since she didn't get a fancy design on her nails and didn't get her eyebrows done. They already looked perfect. She wanted to know what happened when I called him and begged me to come to her house to get ready for the date. "Just come over so I could see how you look before you leave," she said persuasively.

"OK, OK, maybe you can do something with my hair. I don't have much time left."

We took the back roads to her house, which was only about ten minutes away. Her place was always so clean. She didn't like anything out of place, unlike me. I kept things tidy, but not like her. Everything had to look perfect.

When I got there, I took a shower and put on some of her body spray and lotion. When I pulled my dress out of the bag, Simone was shocked to see what I was wearing. "Go, girl. That's a bad dress. How much did you pay for that?"

"I got this for two fifty."

"Two hundred and fifty dollars?" Simone said, with her eyes wide open.

"That's right, I need to look fabulous. I don't want this lawyer to think I need his money. I want him to think I got my own."

"Girl, you got it going on. It's a good thing you're small on the top though."

"That's one of them exact-fit dresses. It stretches after the waistline," I said, assuring her I could get my big behind in it."

When I put it on, Simone looked at me and said, "That ass of yours is talking in that dress, girlfriend. It looks like you got four pieces."

"Should I put stockings on with it?"

"No, Sasha. What do you need stockings for? Just wear a thong," she said. "I got some new ones I just bought, if your big ass can fit in one."

"What size?" I said, thinking about the fact that she was a couple of sizes smaller than me and didn't have all the ass I was blessed with.

"It's a seven, 'cause they didn't have any six, and I really wanted to catch the sale."

"Oh, I can fit them. That's my size."

"Now you know you shouldn't be putting all that ass in a seven."

"Just shut up, Simone, and gimme the drawers. Ooh, these are cute," I said, smiling. "How much were they?"

"I got six pairs for sixty dollars," Simone said, sounding like she got a bargain.

"Ten dollars a pair, Simone? That ain't a sale," I said, looking at the drawers one more time before putting them on.

"Yes, it is, girl. My drawers usually cost twenty dollars a pair."

"What! You are really living the life, Moni." I slid them on, and when I did, I could see why she paid so much for them. They fit like a glove, and it didn't feel like I had anything on at all.

"Now do you see why I bought them?" she said, looking at my facial expression. "They look nice on you. I guess your ass ain't that big after all."

"Girl, you are so right. These are nice. I suppose you get what you pay for, 'cause I've never worn anything that felt like this before," I said, pulling the bottom of the dress down over the thongs. "Can you see my bare ass through the dress?" I said.

Simone went behind me to check my behind. "That looks much better. I can't see your bare butt, and now I don't see your whole ass split in four."

"OK, Moni, now just do my hair and stop talking all that mess."

"You need to do some kinda updo with that dress," she said, looking me over.

"That's just what I was thinking," I said, sitting down at her vanity. "Now do my hair and stop talking. You're gonna make me late."

"Girl, you know it's good to be a little late."

"No, Simone, that's a black thing. It's not good to be late. It's not polite to make a man wait—or anyone else for that matter, and it sure doesn't make any sense to pretend you're not prepared when you've had the whole day to prepare."

By now, it was going on eight o'clock. It took her about twenty minutes to do my hair.

"You like it?" she said, looking at me through the mirror.

"Yeah, it's fine. I like the little curls on the sides and in the middle coming down to one side. That's sharp. Now for the final touch." I got up and got my pocketbook.

Simone didn't know I had the whole diamond set. All she saw was the ring. I pulled out the jewelry bag, with all the little boxes in it. When I pulled out the ankle bracelet, she almost lost her mind. "What else have you got in that bag?" She grabbed it from me and pulled out everything else. "No, you didn't, Sasha. You got diamond teardrops, the choker, and the tennis bracelet. Tray's gonna kill you when he finds out."

"Yeah, but he won't know till next month, so I'm not worrying about it right now." I put on all the pieces and then my shoes. "Oh, bitch, those shoes are fierce. No, you don't have a little diamond on the front of that sandal. You are too much."

"It looks like too much, Simone?"

"No, you look like you got serious money, bitch. What the hell are you gonna bust for the next date?"

"Let me get past this date first, all right?" I went downstairs and took one final look in Simone's mirror at the bottom of her stairs. I looked perfect. My lipstick and hair were flawless. I grabbed my little handbag and my cell phone and went out the door.

Simone stood by the door, watching me. "Don't hurt anybody, girl!" she screamed from the door.

I used the remote and opened the car door. I felt like a million bucks. I've never looked this good. Sitting in the car, I looked up his number again and dialed it. I didn't wanna call him in the house with Simone's big ears on standby.

He answered on the first ring and startled me. "Hi, Sasha," he said, sounding delighted.

"How'd you know it was me?"

"I put you in my call list on my home phone and my cell phone."

"Oh, excuse me?" I said, pleased to hear he has taken an interest.

"So where shall we meet?" he said, sounding so damn sexy.

"Well, I was thinking, should we drive separate cars, or should I just come to your house?" I said, seeing if he would object to me knowing where he lived.

"Well, what do you want to do?" he said, leaving it all up to me.

"Well, it would probably be best if I left my car at your place and drove with you."

"OK then, let me tell you how to get here. I live in Simsbury."

"Oh, OK, I'm in Bloomfield."

"OK, then it shouldn't take you that long to get here," he said. He gave me all the directions and then said, "I can't wait to see you." It gave me goose bumps. He lives at 385 Cold Springs Drive. Wow, that's where the mansions are. I wonder if he lives in one too. I can't wait to get there. He gave me really good directions.

I decided to call Simone and tell her where he lived. She was screaming on the phone. "Girl, no, he doesn't! No, he doesn't! Wait a minute, why isn't he married?"

"Oh, Simone, don't start."

"What do you mean 'don't start,'" she said adamantly. "I would really like to know why he's not taken."

"Well, I don't wanna know. All I want is to have a good time with someone that is really attracted to me. Even if it's for one night."

I drove right past the address. 385, this can't be it. This can't be right. Oh my lord. The man is rich. Thank you, Lord Jesus. Thank you for answering my prayers—my original prayers, the ones I used to say when I was twelve. I would say, "Lord, when I grow up, please don't let me have to work to make a living cleaning somebody's butt like my mama or mopping floors like my Uncle Peety. Please let me meet a rich man that lives in a big house on a hill." Wow. Better late than never, Lord. Better late than never.

I pulled into the long driveway that went up on a hill. It was nine o'clock by now. Dear Lord up in heaven, his house was amazing. I wonder if I have the right address. This is 385. I decided to call him and make sure.

"Hello."

"Hi, it's me. I think I'm outside."

"Come on up to the side and park next to that black Hummer."

A Hummer. "OK."

"I'll be coming out the side door."

I was in awe. This couldn't be happening for real. I wonder how much this house cost and if he owned it. I also wonder if other people lived here with him.

He came to the side door in a black suit with a pink dress shirt. He had on one thick herringbone necklace and a Fab Watch, which had to have cost around two or three thousand. He looked good enough to eat. This is what I'm talking about. I was so curious to see what the inside looks like.

Nick came right out to my car, opened my door. "Hey, Sasha," he said as he helped me get out of the car. "You look amazing."

"Thank you. You don't look too bad yourself. Are we ready to go?" he said, leading me over to his white Lexus 470. Damn, it was gorgeous. It had leather interior, and everything in it was computerized. I can't believe this man has money. Who would have thought? He seems so simple. I suppose he had a simple elegance about him.

"Well, should I tell you my plans for the evening?" he said after putting me in the car and then getting in himself.

"Sure," I said, trying to sound nonchalant about it.

"Well, I thought we'd start out at the Wilburton for dinner."

Oh my god, the Wilburton, I thought to myself. That's like a "two hundred dollars a plate" dinner.

"And then I thought about maybe going to the Radisson Club for some dancing."

Damn, that place is by invitation only. It is sweet up in there. I know 'cause I saw it in a magazine before. "Oh, that sounds nice," I said, trying to sound like I'd been there before. I knew where the bathrooms were and everything because the magazine did a tour of the place when they first opened. I can pull this off. We pulled out of his driveway, and all I could think about is that I may live here one day, if I play my cards right.

"So, Sasha, tell me about yourself."

"Well, there's not much to tell. I'm a painter."

"A painter? How interesting. You must do well."

"Not as well as I'd like, but I get by. I sell a lot of my paintings in New York. People don't seem too interested in my work or my prices out here."

"Yeah, well, some people are very closed-minded, and they don't know good art when they see it. Just from looking at you, I know you must have some amazing pieces. You must let me check out some of your work one of these days."

"Oh, sure," I said, wondering to myself, how long could I carry this one lie? "So what do you do for a living?" I said, pretending not to know what he did.

"I'm an attorney, and I also play the piano."

"The piano?"

"Yeah, there's an artist that lives inside me too."

"OK, you'll have to play for me sometime." I didn't want him to think I was thrilled about him being a lawyer.

"So do you have any other interests?" he asked me.

"Yes, I'm very interested in raising my twelve-year-old son."

"Oh, you have a son?"

"Yes, from a previous marriage."

"Oh, OK. Yeah, I myself was married before. No kids though."

"It must be fun."

"Yeah, sometimes, but it's hard to raise a boy. Their needs are sometimes so very different. So what's his name?" he said, sounding interested.

"TJ."

"Yeah, isn't that funny? I have a good friend of mine named TJ at the law firm. That makes three things we have in common so far."

"We do, don't we?"

"Yes, we're both artists that have been married before and have someone close to us named TJ," he said, laughing.

I laughed too. He was such a nice guy. It kinda made me feel bad about lying to him about my profession, but there was no way I could tell him I was an art teacher.

As he continued to drive, it seemed like for hours, we laughed and made jokes and even listened to music. I found out so much about this man and the fact that we had so many things in common it was amazing to me. Could he be my soul mate?

We got to the restaurant at around nine forty-five. It was all the way in Suffield. Nick pulled up to the front door, and he got out of the car. He came over to my side and opened the door for me and took my hand. Then he gave the keys to the valet.

Wow, what a place to be eating. I hope the menu wasn't too fancy. I think I'll just be safe and order a salad and maybe some chicken breast.

I will also order some white wine. I think that's what goes with chicken. I won't take charge of the night, but I will act like I know what's going on.

When we were escorted to our table, which he had reserved in advance, Nick pulled out my chair. I felt like a princess. I really felt like a million bucks and then some. This man's game is tight. We sat there for all of two minutes, and then a waiter came to ask us what we would like to drink and if we wanted to start with an appetizer. I let Nick take control. "Sasha, what do you think you might want to eat?"

"I was thinking somewhere along the lines of chicken breast."

"OK, then I think we should start with a white wine." He told the waiter what type of wine we would have. I can't even say the name. Something I never heard of before. All I know is that the waiter said it was a very good choice. "So, Sasha, are you enjoying yourself so far?"

"Oh, yes, this is very nice. You have good taste."

"I just wanted to make sure you had the best. I know that's what you're used to."

You're damn right, I thought to myself. "Oh, that's so nice of you," I said to Nick, with a little grin. I excused myself and got up and headed for the bathroom. He watched me as I went out of the room and straight down the hall to the left. It was nowhere near where we came in. I knew I had him thinking now.

When I walked into the bathroom, it looked exactly how it did in the magazine. There was even a lady in there to give you cloth napkins to dry your hand when you were done. This was incredible. People were just waiting on you everywhere, even in the damn bathroom. I gave her a tip and pretended it was no big deal to me.

When I got back to the table, the wine had arrived. The waiter brought it over and left it on a little table next to the table in a bucket of ice. There was already about a swallow in my glass. When I went to sit down, Nick got up, and then we sat back down together. He really had manners.

"So, Sasha, have you ever been here before?"

"Yes, a couple of times when they first opened."

"That was about four years ago."

"Yes, something like that."

"I noticed that you were very familiar with the place."

"It is a very nice place. Thank you for bringing me here."

"Oh, you're welcome. It was my pleasure. I just want to get to know you better. I think you may be just what I need in my life."

"Why do you say that, Nick?"

"Because all work and no play makes Nick a dull boy. I work so many long hours, and sometimes it's only because I have nothing to look forward to after leaving work so I'd just rather stay there. I don't go out often. As my friend, TJ, puts it, you're not going to meet a woman locked up in my office—unless she's outside, cleaning your windows." We both laughed. "I'm not comfortable with the nightclub scene. I just don't think you should go to a nightclub to pick up women. Half of them are drunk, and they don't even remember meeting you the next day."

"Oh," I said, interrupting, "but you do, however, believe in picking up women in rib houses."

He laughed. "I know a diamond in the rough when I see one little lady, and I wasn't about to pass it up. Someone else may have seen that diamond and shined it up. That's gonna be my job."

"The shining part?" I said.

"Yes, ma'am," he said, grinning at me.

"Well, I do believe, sir, you've already started shining." We laughed again.

We talked all through dinner about my son and his work and how his house is so big and lonely. He said that after the divorce, he moved into that house, and he's never really gotten used to being there alone.

"So, Nick, what happened with you and your wife?"

"Oh, man, she was such a wonderful person in the beginning, and then all of a sudden, she turned into this paranoid stalker. She would come by the office and just sit outside my door and watch what type of clients I had. She would follow me and the fellows when we go play basketball and just sit in the car and watch us. It was crazy," he said, cutting his chicken. We both ordered the same meal: chicken breast sautéed in garlic and asparagus. "I had to get away from her," he continued. "She lost all her own interests and became obsessed with me. I never want to go through that again. I believe everyone should have their own interests. Don't you, Sash?"

"Oh, yes, I certainly do. I think you might have the opposite problem with me. I sometimes lock myself in a room and paint for hours."

"That's not a problem to me. I could be working on cases while you were doing that," Nick said, calling the waiter to bring another bottle of wine to the table. "I don't need to be with someone 24-7, but when I do come up for air, it's nice to know there's someone there. You know what I mean?" Nick looked so sexy talking to me.

"Yeah, I do know what you mean."

"So, Sasha, what happened to TJ's father?"

"Oh my goodness, he was a very active man in the community, if you know what I mean. I started getting phone calls from all sorts of women asking me if I knew where my man was and all sorts of nonsense. I suppose I just didn't spend enough time with him. He was too needy. I guess he found another woman to fill the gap."

"Well, it seems we have something in common. We are really turning out to be a pair, aren't we?" Nick said, smiling at me.

"Yes, Nick, I suppose we are."

When dinner was over, we headed for the nightclub. I didn't even know what time it was. I didn't have to go anywhere else at that point. I had a wonderful time just sitting and talking with him over a meal. He was so sweet and so damn fine. "I think I may have had a bit too much to drink," I said to Nick, giggling.

"Are you OK? Do you still want to go dancing? We could go back to the house if you want. I promise I'll be a perfect gentleman."

"Yeah, maybe that's best. I feel kinda woozy."

"You're not a drinker, are you?"

"Not really. I do drink once in a while, but maybe not two bottles."

On the drive back to his house, we talked some more. "So how often do you go out to New York, Sasha? I'd like to come with you one day."

"Oh, about every two, maybe three, weeks. Sometimes sooner, depending on what's going on. I try to make all the big openings. That's how I sell most of my pieces. People always like to have the first pick at things, and I notice they're more apt to buy when they know that they're the first to see the painting."

"You've got that right. I acquired a lot of my pieces at art openings. The first night is the most important," he said, showing so much interest in my damn lying ass.

"Yes, it really is. After the first night, people that come wonder why no one else wanted the paintings that were left. Isn't that crazy? Once in a while, you'll find someone that has the idea, that everyone else may have passed up a good one, but that's rare." I fell asleep after about five minutes of silence. Nick didn't even bother to wake me until we got to his house. We pulled up in the front of the house instead of the side.

"Sasha, we're here," he said, gently touching my shoulder. I woke up to see his handsome face looking over at me. "I didn't want to wake you.

You looked so beautiful sleeping." He helped me out of the car and closed the door. Every time he touched me, he gave me chills down my spine. I never wanted a man more in my life. I didn't want to seem too easy though.

When we entered the front, I woke right up. His house was amazing. He had the biggest fish tank you could imagine—the length of a whole wall, and it had all sorts of different colored fish in it. Some were very big and kinda scary, if you ask me. He led me in to the living room, where there was a fireplace and leather sofas surrounding a shag big white rug; it was all centered in front of the fireplace. "Would you like me to light the fireplace?" he said, taking off his jacket.

"Sure, I am a little chilly," I said, still feeling drunk.

"How about something to drink? Juice, water, or anything?" he asked while lighting the fireplace.

"Some more wine would be nice."

"Are you sure about that?" he said, walking out of the room, with a grin on his face.

"I'm fine now. I just needed to sleep it off," I said, looking at the pictures above the mantelpiece. "I suppose I just had a longer day than I thought. I'm so sorry for falling asleep on you!" I yelled out.

"Oh, no, that's fine," he said from the kitchen down the hall, I assumed. "I'm just glad you felt comfortable enough with me to fall asleep."

I hadn't looked at it that way. I did trust him. He made me feel like we had been together forever. His house was so warm and cozy. This definitely didn't feel like a first date.

"Here you go," he said, handing me the glass of wine.

"Oh, thanks." Before Nick could sit down, I sat down and turned my bottom to adjust myself in the seat. The wine spilled all over the front of my dress. It was a good thing it was black, but now I was all wet.

"Uh, I think maybe you want something else to put on. I'm sure if we hang out your dress, it'll dry."

"Sure, that would be nice."

"I think maybe that was a sign you shouldn't drink anything else," he said, leaving the room.

"Yeah, maybe," I said, taking a sip, thinking, *Maybe I spilled it on purpose.*

He came back with an oversized white T-shirt and a pair of slippers. "This may fit you. I got it for when my sister and her daughter come to visit me from Maryland. You might wanna get out of those shoes too."

"That's perfect. Thank you," I said. "Where's your bathroom?"

"There's one just down the hall to the right. Here let me show you." He walked down the hall, and I followed. In the hallway, his walls were painted dark brown on the bottom and light brown on the top. He had beautiful paintings of sceneries and a couple of portraits on the walls. He turned on the light in the bathroom and allowed me to enter. "I'll be in the kitchen, just down the hall. Make a left when you come out."

"OK," I said, like a child. His bathroom was so pretty. It was all blue. Dark blue at the bottom and light blue at the top. He had a big painting of a waterfall and plants by the window. I had never seen a man live like this before. He even had a stand-up shower made of glass, with a bench that could fit two people, with doves imprinted on the doors. It was plain but so damn elegant. This house was phat, and I didn't even see the rest of it yet. I wonder how the bedroom looked. I wanted to call Simone and tell her all about everything that was going on, but I left my cell phone in the car.

After I changed, I walked down the hall to the kitchen. He stood there, pouring the wine, with his shirt open and pulled out from his pants. He had taken off the tie and was looking rather scrumptious. I want to jump him.

"I see you found your way. Here," he said to me, handing me the glass. We walked back down to the living room and sat on the couch. It was very cold. I shivered slightly, and Nick said, "Do you want a blanket?"

"Sure."

He went to a closet on the side of the fireplace and came out with a furry green blanket. We sat on the couch together. He put one foot up on the couch slightly so that he would be facing me, all wrapped up in his blanket. He looked me in my eyes and smiled. "Would you mind if I kissed you?" he said so politely.

I have never had a man ask before. I didn't know how to respond. "Sure, you can," I said, leaning closer to him.

He put down his glass and leaned in to me. The first kiss was soft and sweet, and then I had to put down my glass 'cause I thought I might drop it. Then he leaned further into me and held me back under the blanket. The blanket slipped down to my waist, and I put my arms around his neck. We sat there for, I don't know how long, lip locked in passion while he rubbed and caressed my back. "Ooh, I better stop," he said, sitting back, facing forward to grab his wineglass. "I'm getting a little warm. Is it hot in here to you?" he said, putting the wineglass back on the table and adjusting his pants.

"No, Nick, it feels just perfect," I said, leaning into him and kissing him again. Before I knew it, I was on top of him between his legs, with one of his feet still on the floor. He rubbed my back as he kissed my face and neck. His tongue was so sweet in my mouth.

"Oh, damn, Sasha. It's been a long time since a woman has kissed me like this."

We both started to get hot. I took the blanket off me completely and pushed it to the side. Nick took his shirt off to expose the rippling muscles in his arms. He was so fine. I looked him in those hazel eyes of his. It feels so good to be in his arms, and we started kissing again. We talked some more as I lay there on his chest. And before I knew it, I woke up to see daylight gleaming into his living room from the double doors leading out to a back patio and swimming pool. Nick was asleep, with his arms around me. We both had drifted off, wrapped up in the blanket. The fireplace was out, and the house was so quiet. The only thing I heard were the birds chirping outside. I couldn't believe I was still here. I tried to get up without waking him, but he opened his eyes as I rose up off his chest.

"Good morning," he said, looking into my eyes and brushing his hand across my cheek.

"Good morning," I said, getting up. "I have to go to the bathroom," I said to him.

"You know where it is," he said, sounding so sweet. "Let me know if there's anything you need," he said, stretching as he sat up.

There were windows all over the house. I felt wonderfully alive in here. I closed the door and looked at myself in the mirror. "Sasha, this could all be yours," I said to myself. Nick . . . Damn, I just spent the night with this man, and I don't even know his last name. "Hey, Nick," I said, coming out of the bathroom.

"I'm in here," he said. The voice was coming from the back where the kitchen was. I walked into the kitchen, but I didn't see him. "In here, Sasha." There he was, in another bathroom that was right off the kitchen, brushing his teeth. "I have an extra toothbrush, and you can take a shower if you'd like. I won't peek. There's a towel in there already."

"Thanks," I said. "Nick," I screamed from the shower, "what's your last name?"

"Abraham!" he screamed from the kitchen. "Why? What's yours?"

"Longston."

"Oh, nice to meet you, Ms. Longston," he said humorously.

"Nice to meet you too, Mr. Abraham," I said, putting toothpaste on my toothbrush while I was still in the shower.

"I'm gonna make some coffee. Would you like some?" Nick said, peeking into the bathroom.

"Sure, that'll be fine." He made coffee and whipped up two omelets. "Oh, so you're a chef too," I said, sitting down on the barstool off the kitchen counter.

"No, not really. I'm only good at breakfast and grilling."

"I'll have to remember that," I said, looking around the kitchen. "Your house is really nice," I said.

"Thanks. It was my grandparents', about twenty years ago. It got sold to someone else when they retired and went to Florida. When I was looking for a place to live after my divorce, I saw it was back on the market. Of course, I grabbed it. After all, there were so many memories here for me. The only problem is that since the whole place had been done over, everything feels very different from what I expected. I'm still trying to make it a home, if you know what I mean."

"You sound like you were very close to your family," I said, sounding a bit jealous.

"Yes, we are a very close family. I have one sister and one brother who both live very far from here. My sister, as I told you yesterday, lives in Maryland, and my brother lives in Mexico."

"Mexico?"

"Yeah. Strange, right? When you meet, you'll see why."

When I meet him, I thought to myself. This sounds promising.

"Then my father lives in Michigan with his new wife, since my mother passed away about ten years ago. She died of cancer."

"Wow, Nick, we have something else in common."

"Yeah, what?"

"My mom passed away too. Only it happened when I was thirteen. I lived with my aunt until I was nineteen and then got married to TJ's father. I basically wanted to get away from my aunt. She was, and still is, somewhat of a nightmare. She's the type of person that wants you to do what they want you to do. She hates the fact that I'm an artist. She wanted me to be a doctor or lawyer or something. Not to say there's anything wrong with that, but she was too controlling. Maybe I would have done something else if she hadn't been so persistent. I'm the opposite when it comes to my family. I don't know half of them, and the ones I do know, I don't care for too much—except for only four of my family members: my cousins, Nathan, Simone, Tiffany, and Lee—who, ironically enough, are the children of the aunt I don't care for. Lee is the one my son stays with most of the time. He loves it over there because there are a lot of boys in his neighborhood. He's been hanging out with them since he was little, so it's almost like he lives there. I make sure I spend time with him though, because I don't want him to think I don't love or care about him." Nick just watched me eat and talk. He looked like he might wanna rip this T-shirt off me, throw me down on his kitchen floor, and have his way with me. "What are you thinking about?" I asked him.

"Oh, just thoughts. I don't think I'd be a gentleman if I shared them with you."

"Dare I ask?"

"You may, if you're prepared for the consequence."

"What kinds of thoughts," I said, licking the fork.

"Don't do that," he said, looking at my tongue going around up and down the fork. "You can make a grown man cry, doing things like that."

I laughed. "You are so funny, but I'm serious though. What kinds of thoughts are running through your mind right now?"

"You really wanna know?"

"Yes," I said, persisting. "I really want to know."

"I was just wondering what you must taste like."

I dropped the slice of bread I was about to put in my mouth. "What was that?"

"Oh, you're wicked."

"No, I'm serious. What was that you just said to me?"

"I said . . . I was wondering . . . what . . . you taste like."

"Well, why don't you come over here and find out?" I wanted him so bad. Damn, I couldn't believe it. I finally got a man that goes downtown. There's gotta be something wrong with him. He's too perfect.

Nick came up on the side of me and spun me around to face him. Then he knelt down in front of me. Since I hadn't brought another pair of underwear with me, I had nothing under the T-shirt I was wearing. He opened my legs and started biting on my thighs. And oh my god, I thought I was gonna lose my mind from just that alone. He touched me in all the right spots. He licked me back and forth across my thighs and teased me so bad I let out a moan. He took his hand, put it on my chest, and guided my back down unto the barstool that was next to the one I was sitting on. He then put my legs behind his shoulders and wrapped them around his neck. With one easy thrust, he plunged his whole face into my vagina. I couldn't believe it. He rubbed his lips back and forth over my clit and entered me with his tongue. I wanted to scream. In fact, I think I did. I grabbed his head and pulled it into me more. "Ah" was all that came out of my mouth.

"Oh, Sasha, you taste so good. Damn, baby. Come here." Nick took my hand and led me upstairs to his bedroom. I didn't even have time to look around before he threw me on his king-size bed. He took his T-shirt off and grabbed my thighs, and again, his whole face disappeared between them. He must have stayed down there for a half hour. I was so wet. I think I passed out and woke up. It was so good. I must have come ten times before he said, "I want you so bad. Can I have you, Sasha? Say yes."

"Oh, yes, Nick, you can have me. You can have all of me."

He took off the T-shirt I was wearing and then his pants and little Speedo boxers. Oh my, he had a gorgeous body. He stood there in front of me for a minute, with his caramel self, just looking down at me lying on his bed. I wanted him as bad as he wanted me. He gently knelt down on top of me and began sucking on my breast. "Mmm, so sweet. Damn, it's so sweet," he said. I could feel the tip of his erect long thick penis brushing across my thigh. I wanted him inside me now. I couldn't wait any longer. I pulled him down on top of me, and he entered me with one smooth thrust. Ah, I was in heaven. He sent chills up my spine and down to my toes. He kissed me all over, and I felt like I was the only woman in the whole world. We made love for the next two hours, and I thought he would never come. I felt like I was a virgin before he came along.

We fell asleep in each other's arms, and when I woke up, I could hear singing coming from downstairs. I lay there for a minute, looking around his bedroom. It was so big, and everything was neat and in its place. He had black art on the walls, and his bed was a brown wooden canopy similar to mine, without the curtains. All his furniture was huge, and he had one very large plant touching the ceiling in the corner, draped over one of the windows. He also had a bathroom in here. I wondered if he had a cleaning person come in because the place was so big. I got up and walked to the bathroom. I looked in his cabinet to what I could see. He had shaving lotion and toothpaste and dental floss. Oh, and aspirin. That was it. This house was so damn clean. Wow. I washed my hands and dried them on his monogrammed towel. It had the initials NGA. I wondered what the *G* stands for. I spread his bed and went downstairs to see what he was doing.

"Good afternoon, Ms. Longston," he said, with a smile on his face, while making sandwiches in the kitchen.

"Good afternoon, Mr. Abraham," I said, daring to sit back in the same barstool seat. "Can I ask you a question?" I said.

"Go ahead, shoot, ask away," he said, eager to hear what the question was.

"Well, I was upstairs in your bathroom, and I couldn't help but notice your towels. What does the *G* stand for?"

"You promise you won't laugh?"

"Well, I'll try."

"It stands for Gladstone. It was my father and grandfather's middle name."

"Well, that's kinda neat. Your middle name has substance."

"Yeah, if I ever have a little boy, that has to be his middle name too."

"I can understand that. Can you tell me something else?"

"OK. The first question was pretty painless," he said, stopping and looking at me.

"Do you always have sex with a woman on the first date and without protection?"

"Well, first of all, I haven't had a date in some time now, and second, I don't know what came over me. It just felt like the right thing to do. This may sound strange, Sasha, but I feel like I've known you forever. It's very easy and effortless being with you."

"I feel the same way about you, Nick."

"Let's go sit out on the back patio."

"OK, but I should be leaving soon. This is the longest date I've ever had. I don't want my cousin, Simone, to start worrying about me."

"Oh, she knows you're here?"

"No, she knows we were going out, but that's all she knows. She may be looking for me by now."

"Well, I have some things to take care of at about four. Do you think you can stick around until then?"

"Yeah, but I should get my cell phone out of my car and see if she called."

When I went out the side door from the kitchen into the car and checked my phone, I had gotten nine calls from Simone alone, not to mention four from TJ, four from Tray, and two from Nathan and one from Maritza. Jeez, you would think I fell off the face of the earth. I sat there for a moment, checking my messages. Simone wanted to know how my date went, and by the last message, she was worried something had happened to me. She said she was going to call the police if she didn't hear from me in the next twenty-four hours, since that's how long you had to wait to report someone missing. TJ wanted to let me know that he was going over to Tiff's house for the weekend. Nathan wanted to let me know he had come back in town. Tray wanted me to call him, and Maritza was crying and told me to call her as soon as I got the message.

I really didn't feel like being bothered by anyone right about now. I just want to be back in Nick's arm where it was warm and felt safe from harm. I must have been outside for about ten or fifteen minutes before Nick came out to check on me.

"Everything all right?" he said, as I sat in the car with the door open.

"Yeah, everything is fine. My cousin called to be nosy, and my son is going to my cousin Tiff's house for the weekend."

"Does this mean I can kidnap you for the entire weekend?"

"Nick, I don't think that's a good idea. I don't want you to get sick of me, and besides, you said you had something to do at four."

"That's no big deal. I can cancel. I'd love it if you'd stay with me. You make me feel so good inside."

"All right, I'll tell you what. Let me make a few phone calls, and then I'll tell you whether or not I can stay. Is that OK?"

"That's fine. Then I'll know whether to cancel my appointment or not. After all, I was just going to hang out with the fellows, and they probably just want to drill me about my date with you. I'd much rather be with you instead of talking about you."

I laughed inside. I couldn't believe this man really wanted to spend this much time with me. What are the odds of finding a rich man that is single and is this sweet. I better not let him go. "I'll be right in a moment, OK?" I said to him, trying to hint to give me some space. I called Simone first.

"Hello, bitch, where the hell have you been?" was the first thing she said to me. "I've been trying to reach your raggedy ass all day. You know I was only giving you, like, four more hours before I call the cops and lie and tell them you've been gone since six. Shit, you scared the hell out of me. I thought that damn man did something to you."

"Oh, girl, he did," I said. "He did a whole lot."

"You know I want all the details," she said, being her usual nosy self.

"Well, I can't give them to you now. I've got to go back in the house."

"You're still there?"

"Yeah, he wants me to spend the weekend with him."

"The weekend? At his house?"

"Yes, girl, it is so phat. You just wouldn't believe it. He's been treating me like a queen."

"What? I can't get over the fact that he wanted you to stay with him for the whole weekend. Did his phone ring yet?"

"As a matter of fact, no, it didn't ring at all."

"Girl, he probably turned it off. You gotta check for things like that. If he turned it off, it probably means he got other bitches calling his house and he doesn't want to have to deal with it right now. You gotta think, Sasha. Don't just be over there and get caught up in some more bullshit. You should know better by now. No matter how sweet they are, they always got something going on with them. Our job is to find out what it is and figure out whether or not we can deal with it in the long term."

"Yeah, OK, Dr. Simone. What, you're my therapist now?"

"I'm serious, girl. Keep your eyes open."

"Bye, Simone." I hung up the phone and went back in the house. I didn't want to call TJ over at Tiff's house 'cause I wasn't in the mood for twenty-one questions. I hoped TJ didn't go over there and ask her what's going on.

Nick and I spent the next two days making love over and over again. We even went swimming in his pool and played pool in his basement. He had an amazing personality. On Sunday night, when I was leaving, he put me in my car and said, "Sasha, this has been the best weekend I've had in a long, long time. Thanks for making it happen. I hope you know we're gonna be seeing a lot more of each other now. You're my girl, so you make sure you tell any of those guys that try to get beside you that you're taken. Have a great night. Take care, and I'll call you in the morning."

"Bye, Nick. You have a great night too." I pulled out of the driveway, looking back at the house on the hill in my rearview mirror. What a weekend. On my way back to Nathan's house, I couldn't help thinking to myself how this was the best weekend I had ever had with the opposite sex. It was fantastic. I've never had a man that attentive to me. That man had thought of everything. I didn't have a care in the world. Tray would never be that way. He just didn't have it in him.

I wonder if this is the real Nick or if this is just an act. I don't want to get all wrapped up in this man and find out that he's a Jekyll-and-Hyde type of guy. I would really like to know what it was about him that led his ex-wife to believe that he was cheating on her. Women don't just think these things on their own. I can't believe this. I sound like Simone. I have to say for once, she's right. It will really be interesting to know what makes this woman give up all that and what part he's played in it, 'cause there's no way you're gonna tell me that Nick doesn't have a role to play in their breakup.

Men always make it seem like it's all on the woman, but the truth of the matter is that it takes two to tango, and when you really love someone, you find a way to work things out. I know I did for years. I loved Tray so bad that no matter what was going on, I found a way to overcome it. I mean, until he got another woman pregnant. That's my life we're talking about. I'm not willing to risk that again. That's just too valuable to me, and I don't love him more than I love myself.

Pulling up into Nathan's driveway, I wondered what questions he would have for me. I know I disappeared and that he called, and I didn't even bother to let him in on all that was going on. I usually share everything with him, but a part of me knows that he's not gonna approve of what I'm doing, so why bother? I know he's gonna tell me that I need some time to sort things out and that Nick is a rebound. I know all that, but I need to feel cared for, for a damn change. I am sick and tired of being the one doing all the caring. Who knew that all this time, that damn man was playing me for a sucker. I don't even know all there is to know either. I am so sure there's much more.

I walked into the house, and Nathan and one of his friends were in the back room, smoking and playing the guitar. They just kinda grinned at me and kept on playing. I went to the kitchen and got a glass of juice. I wanted to talk to Nathan, but I didn't want to interrupt his session. I didn't have to though 'cause when I closed the fridge door and turned around, there was Nathan, standing in front of me with his spliff in his mouth.

"So, Ms. Hot Pants, where have you been all weekend? And don't tell me 'nowhere' 'cause I spoke to Simone already. You know she can't keep her mouth shut, and from what she told me, you didn't call her back either. You have the whole of us looking all over the place for you. I thought something really happened to you, until Moni told me that you're on a play date at a man's house. What kind of something is that, Sasha? You don't even know the man, and you went to his house. Now, suppose that man did something to you. Nobody knows where this man lives."

"Simone knew where he lived," I said, trying to get a word in. "I told her the address of where he lived."

"Yeah, but she didn't know that's where you went all this time. She just found out, said you were there for the whole weekend. Boy, that dick must have been really good to make you forget about your family for the whole time, especially your son. You didn't even call over to Tiffany's and see if he's all right."

"I know that he's all right."

"Yeah, if you called, you would've known that he had gone home with Tray. Tiffany called here, looking for you, to tell you that Tray came and got him. I know you didn't want that to happen."

"What! Gone with Tray? Why did she let him take him?"

"From my understanding, Sasha, TJ wanted to go with him. TJ said it seems like you're too busy to take care of him right now, and he wanted to live with his father. He said maybe you needed to be by yourself for a while."

"My son said that? I don't believe that. I don't believe that TJ would say that about me."

"Sasha, you know your son is very outspoken. Aah, you raise him to speak his mind and to always be honest. Well, the honesty comes back to bite you now."

"I can't believe this. I can't believe he would choose his cheating-ass daddy over me. You know what? I'm not gonna fight it. If that's what TJ wants, then he can have it. I really do need a break from everything. This whole life I've been living has been a lie. I can't take it anymore."

"Sasha, dis doesn't sound like you at all. You never give up on your son like this. Look how much time you and Tray go tru things. You never once made him have his way."

"Well, you know what, Nathan? Tray's been getting his way anyway, whether I want him to have it or not. There is just too much going on in Tray's world for me to handle right now. I'm trying to do me. I've never been on my own before, and maybe it's time I get a taste of what it's like, and you know what, I don't even want that job in East Lyme anymore. That was the job of a married woman with a child. I want to be free, single, and disengaged. That's the way I'm gonna start thinking. There's so much in my life I've missed out on because of Tray. I'm not gonna allow him to make me miss out on another thing."

"I guess this new man really whipped it on you. You have a whole new talk."

"It's not about the new man. It's about me not selling myself short anymore. I have a whole life ahead of me, and if I sit back and follow Tray,

I'll be living this lie for another fifteen years and still be unhappy and confused. I don't want to be in this state of unconsciousness anymore. I am awake and alive, and now is the time for me to start embracing it. No longer will I be the damn fool in this mess. He's gonna have to be the fool for a while. Nathan, did you know that that girl is about to have his baby and that he's saying the baby is not even his. What kind of shit is that?"

"Well, Sasha, my question to you would be, how do you know that it is his baby? How do you know she wasn't messing around with someone else too? I mean, if she could mess with a married man, it would be likely that she could mess with somebody else at the same time."

"You know, I have thought about that, but this chick is in love with him like how I was. I think even though she thinks she's so smart, she got caught up in the same trap as me. I don't think she would have someone else because she would be scared of Tray taking everything away from her. He's the reason why she lives in a condo instead of the project, and he's the reason why she's driving a Navigator instead of taking the bus, and don't forget, she got control of one of the shops. He's the reason for all that, so I don't think she would really give all that up to be with another man that probably wouldn't do all that for her."

"Tray doing all that *fi* her? Damn, that man is serious."

"I don't know how I could let myself be fooled for so long. Here I was, thinking I was going to spend the rest of my life with this man, and all the while, he planned on spending his life with me and ten other females. You know what, Nathan, I don't even wanna think about it anymore. Like I said, I want to start over again. I want a chance to see how life would be without Tray guiding me through it. He's been the one making all my decisions since I was just twenty, and to think he hasn't really been into me this whole time. He probably had been looking for someone else to pass his time with from the beginning. I just can't believe I fell for it for so long. I need to call Tiffany and find out what is going on."

While I was dialing Tiff's number, Nathan walked out the room. I know he was disappointed with me, but all I could think of at that time was what I was going to say to Tiff. It was time she knew what was going on. I really didn't want to mess up her relationship, but the fact of the matter is, she had no relationship—if Jade was sleeping with some guy, and Tiff thought she was the only one. Jade was just as bad as Tray. Shit, maybe they should be together. He'd probably be happy with her. They think a lot.

Chapter 7

I put all my stuff in the car and headed for East Lyme. I was kinda scared to see Tray's face. I didn't know what to say to him. All I knew is that I was fuming. How dare he take my son from Tiff's house, and why didn't he stick up for me when TJ was saying all that stuff about me? As bad as things have gotten, I never wanted TJ to bad-mouth his father. I always wanted him to love and respect him no matter what. See what happens when you're honest. TJ wanted to hear the truth, and now that I've told him, it backfired on me. Never again. It's better to lie to them damn kids. I don't care what anybody says.

I was pulling up into my driveway when my cell phone rang. It was Nick checking to see if I had gotten home all right. I didn't want to talk to him outside the house. You never know, Tray might come out being all loud, and I didn't want Nick to hear all that. I pulled back out the driveway while answering. "Hello."

"Hey, you. Everything all right?"

"Yeah," I said, driving around the corner. "I'm fine. I'm just about to pull up into my driveway. I'm exhausted."

"I bet you are," Nick said, sounding pleased with himself. "I had a wonderful weekend."

"I did too," I said, exhaling.

"Well, I better let you get in the house and get yourself ready for bed."

"Yeah, I better do that. I think I have to take a trip out to New York tomorrow," I said, still going around corners. "I'll have to see how things go."

"Well, if I don't hear from you before you go, have a safe trip."

"Thanks, Nick. Have a good night, OK?"

"You do the same. Bye, baby."

Nick sounded so sweet. Made me just wanna get on the highway and go back to his house. I pulled back up in the driveway. What a man. Why couldn't Tray be more like Nick? Why did I get stuck with the ghetto, self-centered, egotistical, nappy-headed jerk?

I got my stuff out of the car and went into the house. I didn't bother to change my clothes because I wanted to make sure Tray knew I had gone somewhere. I turned the key and went inside to hear Tray on the phone with one of his friends talking about some girl.

"Yeah, man, she is blazing. You ain't seen an ass like that anywhere. Not even that Puerto Rican chick in the movies got an ass like this one." I slammed the door, and he looked up from the couch.

"Yeah, man, well, I'll call you back. I got some shit to take care of."

"Where's TJ?" I said, looking around.

"Where do you think he is? He's in his room."

"Yeah, he's in his room, and you're down here, talking about some chick with a big ass. Really nice, Tray."

"Oh, please, girl. He can't hear me. He got his headphones on, listening to some CD Tiff bought him."

"OK, Tray, if you say so."

"So where have you been, all dressed up?"

"I've been out. What is it to you? You're not controlling this anymore. You got your own shit going on."

"Yeah, all right, Sasha, that's what you think. Let me catch your ass with somebody else. See what I do."

"What are you gonna do, Tray? Ah, you are so fuckin' unfair. You've been cheatin' on me for the last five years. Now you wanna act like you care about somebody. You ain't shit."

"Sasha, don't talk to me like that. I'm not having it."

"You're not having what? I'll talk to you any damn way I feel. You ain't anybody. Got a nerve. I thought I told you to be out of my house by the time I got back here. Why is your sorry ass still here?"

"Sasha, how are you gonna put me out of my own shit? I pay more of the bills on this shit than you do. If anybody was leaving, it would be you. And your ass ain't going damn anywhere till I say so."

"Oh, you think so. I'mma show your ass something. Wait till tomorrow. You're gonna see something."

"What are you gonna do, Sasha? Divorce me?"

"Oh I'mma do more than divorce you. I'mma take half of everything your ass got and some. And don't think your baby mama ain't gonna be an issue. 'Cause I'mma drag your tired ass through the mud."

Tray got up off the couch and walked toward me. "Sasha," he said, backing me up to the bottom of the stairs, "I better not hear another thing about that woman, or your ass is gonna be sorry."

"I'm already sorry," I said, looking him dead in his eyes. "Why are you so close to me, Tray? What are you gonna do? Hit me?"

"Oh, yeah, I bet you'd love that. So you can go run and tell your cousins that I'm beatin' you over here. No, Sasha, I'm not gonna put my hands on you," he said and walked up the stairs. "Just know that you ain't going anywhere till I say so. And I ain't saying so. You're my wife!" He screamed from the top of the stairs. "You hear me? My wife!" he said and slammed the bedroom door.

This man is fuckin' crazy. Did he really think I was gonna stay with him after he got someone else pregnant? That nigga done lost his mind. I went into the closet and got a blanket and pillow we kept downstairs, in case it got cold. I wasn't sleepin' upstairs with that maniac. I laid it out on the couch and then went upstairs to check on TJ. He was in bed, fast asleep with his headphones on. I took them off, put them on his night table, and gave him a kiss. He opened his eyes.

"I knew you'd come back home. I love you, Ma."

"I love you too, baby. Now get some sleep. We'll talk more in the morning. Wake me up before you leave. I'll be on the couch downstairs."

"Ma, you wanna sleep in here with me?"

"No, baby, that's OK. Now get some sleep. You have school in the morning."

I went back downstairs and made a cup of tea. Imagine, that arrogant asshole thinking he was going to still have me after all this shit. I just can't get over it. I took my tea and went to the living room. I didn't even wanna be here anymore. If it weren't for TJ, I'd be long gone. I couldn't get to sleep, and it was about twelve thirty now. I really did have to go to work in the morning. I still can't make up my mind if I just want to give them my two weeks or what. I just really want a change from all this shit. I don't know what I want, but I know I don't want this. I know this is not what God had intended for me.

I got up off the couch and went out to the car with my cell phone. I really just need some air. I dialed Tiff's number and then hung up, then

I dialed Simone's number and hung up. I didn't know who to call, but I needed to talk to someone. While I was thinking about who to call, I had already scrolled down to Nick's number and pressed it.

"Hello."

"Hi, Nick. It's me, Sasha."

"What's up, Sasha? Everything OK?"

"Nick, I have a lot to tell you, but I just wanted you to know that I'm making some changes in my life, and I'm gonna need your help. Do you think you can help me?"

"Sure, Sasha, I'll try. Whatever you need, just let me know."

"Well, for starters, I need a good divorce attorney. Do you know one?"

"Divorce? I thought you were already—"

"Don't say anything, Nick. Just help me."

"OK, baby, I won't ask any questions right now. When the time is right though, I expect you to come clean about everything that's going on."

"I will, if you're still around."

"Oh, I'm not going anywhere. I've been hooked since I first laid eyes on you. I don't know what it is, but I know we're supposed to share something special."

"Oh, Nick, you just don't know how that makes me feel."

"Well, I know how you make me feel, Sasha, and I wouldn't trade it for the world. Now get some sleep, and I'll call you tomorrow or, should I say, later on today."

"All right. Good night, again."

"Good night, baby. Get some sleep, OK?"

"I'll try."

I hung up the phone, looked up, and there was Tray, coming out to the car. I got out of the car and started to walk past him, but he grabbed me by the shoulders.

"What are you doing out here? Who in the hell was that you were talking to on the phone? Your little boyfriend?"

"Tray, don't question me. You don't have the right to, and you don't have the right to touch me either." I shook loose from his hold and walked into the house.

"Sasha," he said, closing the door behind us, "I hope you don't think I'mma make it easy for you. You've been my wife for the last fifteen years, and I don't plan on changing that just because some little bitch says she's pregnant with my baby."

"Oh, she wasn't your bitch when you put her in charge of one of your shops or when you were buying her a condo and a car? She wasn't a bitch then? No, Tray, she wasn't a bitch when you were fuckin' her and sneaking your sorry ass around town with her? She wasn't a bitch then?" I said and went upstairs to my room. I locked the door and got in my bed. Now maybe I can get some sleep.

"Sasha, open the door. Sasha."

"Go away, Tray. I don't want your sorry ass anymore. There's a pillow and blanket on the couch in the living room. Have a good night."

Chapter 8

I woke up to the sound of my son knocking on my bedroom door.

"Ma, get up. It's seven o'clock. I have to leave soon, or I'mma be late."

"I'm up, baby. Good morning."

I jumped in the shower and threw on some sweats. This morning was gonna be a better one for me. I was gonna make sure of it. When I went downstairs, TJ was sitting outside on the front porch with the door open. I didn't see any sign of Tray. That was a good thing. A hot cup of coffee was sitting on the kitchen counter, along with my car keys and a folded piece of paper under them. My son always thought ahead. The piece of paper was a note from Tray that said, "Sasha, we need to talk about some things. I know it's gonna take a while before you can forgive me, but I am willing to wait. I love you. Talk to you tonight. I'll be home early. Tray."

"Yeah, you'll be home early now since you're busted." I don't have anything to say to his sorry ass. I'm going to have a productive day, and it won't include Tray and his nonsense. I'm gonna start by taking my son to school. I grabbed my coffee and keys and left the note on the table. "OK, TJ, let's get it moving." It was now seven twenty. I had about twenty minutes to get him to school.

TJ hated being late for anything. He said that people look at you funny when you walk in late, and then you're the joke for the rest of the day. In the car, we talked about how he had been doing in classes and why I needed to try to make it without his dad. I told him that we had been together for so long I needed to prove to myself I could do things on my own.

He didn't say much. In fact, he didn't say anything at all when I talked about his daddy and me separating. He didn't want us to part, and I could understand why, but nothing lasts forever. I didn't believe it before, but I know it now. No one stays together forever. This was just something that I would have to learn to get used to. I thought my marriage would last forever, and look at me now.

After I dropped TJ at school, I decided to stop by Tiff's shop and let the cat out of the bag. I didn't care if Jade was there or not. I was telling it all today. When I walked into the shop, I was surprised to see that Tiff was alone.

"Hey, stranger," she said, looking up at me and then back down at some papers on her desk.

"Hey, Tiff. Sorry for not letting you know what's been going on, but there's just so much."

"Yeah, I gathered from our last conversation that there was a lot of something that you weren't telling me."

"Well," I said, sitting down at her desk, "first of all, do you know everything there is to know about Jade?"

"Why? Why do you ask that, Sasha?"

"Well, there's a lot going on that I don't think you know about."

"Like?" Tiff said, putting the papers in a neat pile.

"Like the fact that she has a boyfriend."

"A what?"

"Or like the fact that she hooked my husband up with one of her friends and—"

"Wait a minute, Sasha. You're going way too fast for me. She has a boyfriend? How do you know this?"

"Her friend, Maritza, told me."

"I know Maritza."

"Did you know she was having a baby?"

"Yeah, by some deadbeat, right?"

"Yeah, the deadbeat's Tray."

"What? Tray? How did he get in all this?"

"Well, Jade didn't like the fact that when she came to my house, I would give her none, so she backstabbed me and introduced Tray to her girlfriend, who, by the way, didn't know he was married."

"Wait, Jade came to your house? When did all this happen?"

"Tiff, this was about five years ago."

"Five years ago. Why are you just telling me now?"

"'Cause I didn't think it was important before. I didn't want to break you guys up, and I thought as long as I didn't do anything, there was nothing to tell."

"Oh, so you're telling me for the last five years, you've been looking at my face and lying to me?"

"No, I haven't been lying to you. I just didn't tell you."

"Oh, and you think that makes it OK?"

"No, I just didn't know what to do. You seem so happy, and I didn't want to be the one to destroy that."

"All right, let's look at the whole picture here. You say what now? Jade introduced Tray to Maritza and what?"

"Yes, Tiff. Now Maritza's having his baby. They've been together for almost five years now, Tiff. Right under my nose."

"What? And you're telling me that Jade is the one that hooked all this up?"

"Yeah, 'cause Maritza told me."

"Hold up, Sasha. You talked to her?"

"Talk to her? I went to see her. Her and her big belly. She called me one day and asked me to come down to the shop."

"What shop?"

"Oh, I didn't tell you that. Tray got two other shops in Hartford he told me nothing about."

"What the hell is going on around here?"

"That's what I said, Tiff. Shit, Maritza is running one of his shops. He bought her a condo and a Navigator, girl."

"And he got you driving around in that old car."

"That's what I'm saying, Tiff."

"Damn, Sash, all of this shit is news to me."

"Tiff, I didn't know what to do."

"Oh, now it all makes sense. That's why you camped out at Nathan's house. You know, you need to stop running away from every fuckin' thing. Every time something happens, you run your ass to Nathan's house and leave that boy for everybody to take care of. Keep that shit up, you're gonna make him hate you. He said some pretty foul shit about you this weekend. I think he's tired of all the drama."

"Tiff, as long as I stay with Tray, it's always gonna be some drama."

"I'm not talking about the drama, Sash. It's how you handle the drama. You can't keep running away from it. Nothing is gonna change if you do that. Nothing but the faith your son has in you."

"Well, I know one thing. I hate Tray. I will never love him again as long as I live."

"Now, Sasha, you damn well know what your mother always said. You can dislike a person's ways or even the person for who they are, 'but never hate.' We all have our ways about us, and we wouldn't want people to hate us for the thoughts we think or the mistakes we've made. It's just human nature to fall short. That's the one thing my auntie, your mother, said that has always stayed with me. Why do you think I'm still with Jade? I always somehow manage to understand where she's coming from. And even though I don't like the way she handles herself at times or her reasoning behind some of the things that she's done, I'll never hate her."

"Well, I do. I hate every bone in her body, and there's nothing anyone can say to make me change the way I feel. My mother could come back from the grave and stand in front of me here and now, and I'd tell her the same thing."

"What about karma? Did you forget about all that too?"

"Tiffany, I don't have time to think about all that bullshit right now. I just wanna get the fuck out of that house and get on with my life."

"Get out of that house? Where are you gonna live, Sasha?"

"I don't know yet, but it won't be there with him. I want a fresh start. So what are you gonna do about Jade? Are you just gonna let her get away with all the shit she's done to your family?"

"Sasha, I know you're mad with Jade, but I have to think this thing through. I wish you told me when all this shit went down. I invested a lot in Jade over the past five years. Shit, we're two years away from being a common-law-married couple."

"What the fuck are you talking about, Tiffany? Jade's a woman, if you haven't forgotten. You really need to stop pretending like you're a real couple and get with the program. I can't believe you honestly feel that you and Jade are a couple. Y'all are a couple of freaks, if you ask me. You need to find yourself a nice guy, settle down, and have some damn kids."

"Now you sound like Aunt Trudy, Sasha. What is going on with you? This whole thing is really bringing out the bitch in you. Now you know I've always let you say whatever you wanted about me being a lesbian, and even though you didn't approve of my lifestyle, you've never actually come out and dissed me before. You're really going too far now, Sasha."

"Tiffany, you went too far when you brought that woman into this family. I don't know what you thought you were doing bringing that ex-stripper into our lives. She was bound to do something with someone sooner or later. Don't you think you deserve better than that?"

"Sasha, I don't wanna talk about this shit anymore. You're really starting to piss me off. Don't tell me how to run my life."

"Oh, but you can tell me how to run mine?"

"I was only talking about my little cousin. I don't give a fuck what you and Tray do, just as long as it doesn't affect my little cuz. If you didn't want to be responsible for someone else, you should've never had a child."

"How dare you talk about what I should and should not have done. You won't even rise to the challenge of being a parent much less. I guess it's easy for you to look in from the outside and see all my mistakes, but try living it for real, and you'll see. It's fucking hard to raise a child. You think all you have to do is just provide them with food and clothes. You don't know the half of what I have to go through. A lot of times, I'm doing it all by myself. What about all those nights everyone was going out partying, and I was home, stuck with TJ?"

"Oh, that's how you felt, Sasha? Stuck? That's what you think of him?"

"Just forget it, Tiffany. I wish I never came over here. I gotta go. I'mma be late for work."

"Oh, you still work, do you?"

"Bitch," I said, storming out of Tiff's back door. Who did she think she was, counseling me on how to be a good mother to my son? She couldn't even be a woman. She couldn't even face the fact that she was living a lie, acting all manly all the time. And Jade. Who the fuck was she? The housewife? What a joke. I should tell Aunt Trudy all the shit that's been going on with her lying-ass lesbo daughter. That butch has got a lot of shit with her. I'mma fix her ass.

I called my job and told them that I wouldn't be in today and that I needed to set up a meeting with the administrator and the counselor. On my way to Aunt Trudy's house, I called Maritza.

"Hello."

"Hey, it's me."

"Me who?"

"It's Sasha, Maritza."

"Oh, you're still alive. I called you so many times it ain't funny. What's up?"

"I need a favor from you."

"You need a favor from me?" Maritza said curiously.

"Yeah, I need you to find out how I can get in touch with Ramón."

"Oh, that's easy. He is down at the corner store from the shop, playing cards with them cats in the back."

"Well, it's time we put an end to all this shit Jade has been doing."

"What's up, Sasha? What brought all this on?"

"I'm tired, Maritza. Will you help me or what?"

"Yeah, I'mma help you. Anything to get that bitch back. I've been thinking of a way forever."

"Here's what I want you to do. I want you to get Ramón to go out to my cousin's house and ring the doorbell at about eight o'clock tonight. Tell him it's a surprise party for one of Jade's friends and he's invited. Tiff and Jade will be home together by then, and I want Tiff to finally have to deal with something right on the spot instead of thinking everything out." *Them bitches are gonna see what it feels like to be on the spot,* I thought to myself.

"OK, Sasha, I could do that."

"All right, call me later and let me know what happened." This bitch tries to tell me how to raise my son. Who the fuck does she think she is? I need to get Simone in on all this. When I dial her number, I feel devilish inside.

"Hello," she said, answering like she was still sleeping.

"Moni, how about me and you do lunch?"

"Sasha, do you know what time it is?"

"Yeah, I do."

"The question is, do you?"

"Yeah, I know what time it is. I don't have classes until later on."

"Why ain't you at work?"

"I called out."

"Again? Sasha, they're gonna fire your ass."

"I don't give a damn."

"Oh, OK. I see that Nick got your head stuck in a cloud."

"Bitch, are we doing lunch or what?"

"Yeah, around twelve thirty. I got class at two."

"Well, why can't we do it earlier?"

"'Cause I got a dick in my pussy right now, bitch. Bye."

I laughed. She is so damn nasty. I called Aunt Trudy when I was close to the house to make sure she was home.

"Hello."

"Hi, Auntie."

"Hi, Sasha. What's going on?"

"Auntie, I need to talk to you about a couple of things. Can I come over?"

"Sure, baby, come on. I was just getting off that exercise bike. I did it for a whole twenty minutes."

"OK, I'll be there in about ten minutes or so."

"Oh, you're that close. Oh well, all right."

I drove around for about fifteen minutes before I pulled up in the driveway. I rang the door and had to wait for, like, two minutes before she came to the door.

"Sorry, baby. I was trying to take a quick shower before you got here. Come on in. You want some coffee?"

"Sure. Who's here with you, Aunt Trudy?"

"Nobody. Is somebody supposed to be here?"

"I just thought maybe."

"No, there's nobody here but me."

"Auntie, how do you stay in this big old house by yourself?"

"I love it. Everybody has grown up and gone 'bout their business, leaving nobody here but old Whiskers and me. That dog keeps me company enough. I enjoy my quiet time. Now come on in here and sit down." We went to the kitchen and had a seat at the table. "Now what's bothering you, Sasha?"

"Auntie, there's a lot of stuff going on right now and has been going on that you know nothing about."

"Like what, baby?"

"Like the fact that Tray and I are getting a divorce."

"What? Oh, baby, what happened?"

"Well, Auntie, it's a long story. Well, first of all, you know Jade, right?"

"Yeah, that's Tiffany's roommate, right?"

"Well, she's more than just a roommate. Auntie, Tiffany is gay, and she's been that way for a long time."

"What? You mean that girl, Jade, is her lesbian lover? I knew they were too close. See what happens when you live with a woman."

"Auntie, they've always been lovers, ever since they met."

"OK, so what has she got to do with this?"

"Well, Jade tried to come on to me about five years ago, and I told her I wasn't like that, so she was mad at me and hooked Tray up with one of her straight girlfriends. Now, Auntie, the girl is pregnant."

"She's what? What did you say?"

"And the worst part about it, Auntie, is you know the girl."

"I do?"

"Yeah, it's Maritza."

"That nice girl that came over here with her brother? I cooked some food for them one time. She's sleeping with Tray?"

"Yeah, and has been for almost five years now."

"What are you saying to me? I can't believe Tray would do that to you. You mean so much to him."

"Well, I guess I didn't mean all that much to him, 'cause he bought that girl a condo and that truck they probably drove in over here."

"Oh, baby. How are you managing with all this?"

"I don't know," I said, now crying. "I don't know what to do. I wish Mama was here. She'd know what to do."

"Well, your mama's not here, but I am. What are you gonna do?"

"I don't know. All I know is that I don't want to live out there with Tray anymore."

"Oh, that's all right, baby. You come and stay right here with me. I've got plenty of room for you and TJ."

"Well, see, Auntie, that's the other thing. TJ wants to stay with Tray," I said, breaking down.

Aunt Trudy reached over and hugged me. "Oh, there, there, baby. Everything is gonna be all right. I'm here for you. Now you go out to that house and you get those things of yours and come right back. Everything is gonna be fine."

"Yes, Auntie," I said, sounding like a child.

"Now you hurry back. I'll make something for us to eat while you're gone. We'll figure this thing out together."

"OK." I went through the door and wiped my eyes. I couldn't believe it. The woman I hated most of all was coming to my rescue. Ain't this something?

While driving back to East Lyme, I started thinking about Nick. I wonder what he's doing right now. Let's see, it's almost ten thirty.

"Hello."

"Oh, you sound so sexy early in the morning."

"No, you're the sexy one. What's up, baby?"

"Oh, nothing. I was just calling to let you know that I'm not going to New York and to tell you that I'm moving today."

"You're moving? I hope not far."

"Well, actually, I'll be closer."

"Oh, I like the sound of that. Where are you going?"

"I'm gonna stay with my aunt for a while. She has a house in Hartford at Gramby Street. You know where that is, don't you?"

"I sure do. I'm not far from there now."

"Well, I'm on my way to East Lyme to get my things."

"Do you need some help?" he asked, sounding anxious to me again. "I have a couple of hours to kill."

"Well, I think it's best if I do this by myself."

"Oh, I hear you."

"Nick, can I ask you a question?"

"Shoot."

"Why do you think we'd make such a good couple?"

"I told you, you and I have a lot in common."

"What if you found out that we didn't have so much in common?"

"Like what?"

"Well, for instance, Nick, I'm not some famous artist selling my paintings in New York. I'm just an art teacher at the local college in East Lyme."

"OK, well, I guess I could live with that. Is there anything else?"

"Yes, I am moving out of my and my husband's house, whom I've been with for the last fifteen years."

"Mmm, interesting. But you're moving out now. Why?"

"Because we haven't been together for a long time, but I just never really made things final."

"So you think now is the time?"

"Yes, I do. I believe there's more for me out there in life, and staying in this marriage is only bringing me down."

"See, we do have a lot in common. That's one of the reasons why I couldn't stay with my ex-wife. We were going in opposite directions. She wanted to do the housewife thing, and I wanted to travel. The two just didn't click. So are you gonna be all right, Sasha?"

"Yes, I'm taking the whole thing one day at a time. I just wanted you to know that you're not a rebound. I really care for you, and I enjoyed being with you."

"I enjoyed your company as well. I know we have a future doing something together. I don't know what yet 'cause that's up to you, Sash. The balls are in your court. Your wish is my command."

"Oh, Nick, stop playing. I'm serious."

"I believe that anything you feel deep inside shouldn't be ignored. Some of the greatest couples I know are together because they felt a spark the first time they met and went with it. And I don't just mean lust. I think I'm old enough to know the difference between just lusting over a woman and genuinely wanting to know a woman. I wanna know how you think and feel about things. I wanna know what makes you happy and sad. I wanna know you, Sasha. I don't feel like this about a lot of women. Believe me when I say, I know when it's right. And this feels right. I was talking to my friend, TJ, about you. I told him that I met a woman that could possibly change my life for the better and that you were one of the deepest women I've met in a long time. I also told him how beautiful you were. You know what he said?"

"What, Nick? What did your dear friend, TJ, tell you?"

"He told me I sounded like I was in love and that I didn't even sound this way with Yvette. And I married her for Christ's sake. I don't know if you feel what I feel, but what I feel makes me smile every time I think about us together. And I hope this doesn't scare you when I say I could see me spending the rest of my life with you. I know it's all too soon, but everything is gonna be all right. I wanna see you later. Let's have lunch."

"OK, that's fine with me, Nick. What time?"

"How about twelve?"

"All right, I'll see you then."

"Bye, baby, and remember, everything is gonna be all right."

In that instant, I forgot I had made plans with Simone. I'll just call her and cancel; she won't mind. "Simone."

"What, Sasha? What do you want now?"

"I'm not gonna make it for lunch. Nick called me, and he wants to have lunch with me. I couldn't turn him down. This is a new relationship."

"Yeah, all right, Sasha. I'mma let you do me like this, this time, but don't think I'mma let you put me on the back burner for this man all the time. I'm just not having it."

"Oh, Simone, come on. You've put me on the back burner for Richie so many times I lost count."

"That was then. This is now."

"You know that ain't right, don't you, Simone? How you gone say it's OK for you and not me? Anyway, I have something else to tell you."

"What, Sasha? What have you got to say?"

"I wanted to tell you that I was gonna be staying with Aunt Trudy for a while."

"What? Get out. How did you manage that?"

"I went to talk to her about everything that's been going on, and she told me to come and stay with her until I could figure out what I was going to do."

"What about TJ?"

"He wanna stay with Tray. He said he didn't want to leave his house and school and move somewhere else."

"Oh, excuse me. I didn't know he had a choice. Didn't you tell him he better go where you go and shut up?"

"No. What I told him is that if he wanted to be with his father, he could and that it was fine with me."

"Is it fine with you, Sasha?"

"No, but hey, maybe it's best for the both of us. I need to get my shit together."

"Damn, you're just gonna let go of your son like that?"

"No. Don't say it like that, Simone. I'm not just letting go of my son. I'm just taking a break."

"Sasha, you've been taking breaks from TJ for as long as I've known you. You don't ever keep him with you for too long. Anytime something goes down, you're always dropping him off somewhere."

"Why does everybody keep saying that? I don't do that to my son."

"Sasha, I'm just calling it like I see it. The truth hurts. Take it or leave it."

"You know what, Simone, I gotta go. Bye."

I can't believe these people. Why are they all ganging up on me? You would think I would get some damn support from these people who are supposed to be my family. But no, all I'm getting is negativity. I pulled up in the driveway and left the engine running. I ran into the house and grabbed my suitcase. Got around ten outfits and put six pairs of shoes in another bag and got back in the car. I didn't wanna see this house anymore. I didn't want to see East Lyme anymore either.

I called Aunt Trudy to tell her I was on my way back.

"OK, baby," she said. "I made us some of them turkey burgers. You want some fries with that?"

"No, thank you, Auntie. As a matter of fact, I had a couple of errands to run, so I will just drop off my stuff in the spare room."

"Well, it's almost twelve, so I guess I'll go on ahead to the grocery store like I was planning on doing. I'mma leave a spare key on the back porch in the garden under the little man with the lantern. Don't leave it out there though. You can use that key for yourself. You can sleep in Melony's old room. I just washed all the sheets in there."

"Thanks, Auntie. I'll see you later when you come back, OK, Sasha?"

"OK." Hanging up the phone, I felt so excited about moving. I was glad she wasn't gonna be there when I got there. I needed some time to unwind before I went out for lunch with Nick. Oh, let me call him and tell him I'm gonna be a little bit late.

"Hello."

"Nick."

"Hey, what's up?"

"I'm gonna be a little bit late. I'm on my way back to my aunt's house now to drop my stuff off."

"Well, you know what, Sasha, how about this? When you're done, why don't you just come to the house? I'm having a meeting there in a little while, and I figured we could have lunch after. By the way, I'm free for the rest of the evening."

"Oh, you are, are you?"

"Yes, I am, and I was wondering, of course, if you're not busy, if you'd like to go to the movies or something later."

"Oh, I don't know, maybe. I'll have to see what's going on. I should check in with my aunt. I don't want her to think I just needed somewhere local to store my clothes."

"Yeah, Sasha, I suppose that wouldn't be right. Well, I'll see you in a little while, and we'll take it from there, OK?"

"That's fine with me, Nick."

When I got to my aunt's house, she was already back from the store. She was in the kitchen, cooking again. Damn, she loves to cook.

"Sasha? Is that you?"

"Yes, Auntie, I'm just gonna put my stuff in Mel's room. I'll be right there."

Walking into Mel's room brought back so many memories. I remember when she first had Alezandria, before Alex came along. She and the baby would be up all hours of the night. Aunt Trudy would be fussing over her in the morning when I came over to pick her up for school. "I'm not gonna be missing my sleep for you and your baby. Now you wanna leave her with me and go on with your day. This is crazy," she would complain. She hated the fact that Mel had a baby so young. She said she always wanted more for her. "Why can't you be like Tiffany?" she would say. Little did she know Tiff wasn't out there messing with boys; she was after the girls.

"Sasha!" Auntie screamed from downstairs. "Are you hungry, or do you still have errands to run?"

"I'm not staying, Auntie. I really got to get stuff going. I'll grab something outside." I didn't dare tell her anything about Nick. She would kill me with advice. "I'll see you later, OK?"

"All right, baby, don't stay out too late now. I like my door locked at a certain time. You know I gotta put that chain on the door."

"If I'mma stay out, I'll call you. Simone wanted me to come and spend the night with her."

"All right, baby, let me know."

I gotta bring back this rental car. I wonder how much it's gonna be. I really need to stop over Simone's house. Let me call her. "Hello."

"What, loser?"

"Why are you calling me a loser, Simone?"

"'Cause you are. How you gone stand me up after all we've been through for some nigga?"

"Listen. I got a favor to ask of you. What time did you say you got to be at class?"

"At two. Why?"

"'Cause you know I still got this car."

"You didn't bring that car back yet? It's gonna be, like, two or three hundred for that shit."

"Yeah, yeah. I don't care about that. I just need to bring it back."

"Why don't you call them and see how much it would be to keep it for the week?"

"Simone, it's, like, seventy-five dollars a day as it is."

"Well, you said you didn't care about Tray's credit card. By the way, does that man know that's not your car?"

"Oh, shit, I forgot to tell him that."

"Yeah, I bet you did. You're diggin' a deep hole. You think that man's gonna wanna be with a liar? You keep on lying to that man time and time again."

"Yeah, you're right. You know what, I got a good idea. I'll talk to you."

"So you don't need me then?"

"Nah, I'mma handle it on my own."

I called Nick.

"Hello," he answered after about the fourth ring.

"Nick."

"Oh, hi, Sasha. I can't really talk to you right now. I'm in the middle of a meeting."

"Are you still coming?"

"OK then, I'm just wrapping up. I'll call you back as soon as I'm done."

"OK then."

It was now twelve thirty, and I couldn't believe he asked me to get together with him at twelve and that he was in a meeting. The nerve. I decided to call the car rental company. I know the numbers are in the glove compartment.

"Baller car rental. This is Brandy. How may I help you?"

"Ah, yes, this is Sasha Longston. I'm renting the BMW X5."

"Yes, what can I do for you?"

"I'd like to know how much it would be to keep this car for the rest of the week."

"Would you be keeping it until Sunday?" she said.

"I would like the rate for both days."

"OK, can you hold on for one moment, ma'am?"

"Sure."

"OK, that will be six hundred until Sunday. Would you like me to change your scheduled return to Sunday?"

"Yes, would you do that? Oh, and take it off the credit card number I gave you to rent it. You can do that today."

"OK, that'll be fine."

"Thank you, Brandy."

"Thank you for calling Baller car rental, Ms. Longston. Have a good day."

I called Simone back and told her how much it would be to keep it until Sunday.

"Ooh, Sasha, Tray's gonna whoop your ass."

"Yeah, whatever. He owes me, Simone."

"So where is your hot ass going now? To see Nick, I'm sure."

"Yeah, he told me to come to his house for lunch. He said he has the rest of the day off after this meeting, and he wanted to go to the movies or something."

"Yeah, I bet he does. He just wanna fuck. I don't believe shit men say."

"Simone, you're just jealous. When was the last time you and Richie went to the movies?"

"I don't do movies. Whatever I wanna watch, I can get it bootleg, girl. You know that. Besides, Richie and I don't hang out together like that."

"Simone, I don't get y'all. He sleeps over there whenever he wants to. Y'all don't really do anything together, and you're always checking for him. What's up with that, Ms. Advice Giver?"

"I know what my man is up to. That's what's up with that. He is making a lot of moves. You know that too. He and Tony aren't even in this state half the time. You know how that shit goes."

"I wouldn't be able to take it. Aren't you scared something's gonna happen to him out there messing with that shit?"

"Richie is a big boy. He can handle himself. Plus, I'm not getting myself all mixed up in that shit. When it all goes down, I ain't going down with it. You feelin' me?"

"Yeah, I guess I do. I just don't know why you won't go get a nice guy that is dealing the straight life."

"'Cause you know I got a thing for bad boys. I can't help it. That's just me. And besides, I get whatever I want regardless of whether I see him or not. You see the ring. Shit, I can hardly lift my finger some days," she said, laughing.

"You are something else. All I'm saying is, there comes a time when you have to grow up."

"Look who's talking, Sasha. You're reliving your childhood, living with my mother. You got to be crazy. I would never do that. No matter how bad things get, I won't be going back there. Anyway, where is your crazy ass right now?"

"I'm 'bout to get on Cottage Grove Road. Why?"

"Stop by here before you go see your man."

"Yeah, I do need something else to put on. I want one of them tight back-out shirts you got to go with my sweat suit."

"Oh, you're actually wearing a sweat suit?"

"Yeah, why? Something wrong with that?"

"No, I just thought your rich man was too good for sweats."

"Well, that's what I got on. He ain't never seen me in sweats before. I got on my red suit, the one that stops right about my butt crack."

"Sasha, you know your ass is too big to be wearing them kinda pants."

"Shut up, Simone. I'll be there in, like, five minutes."

When I got to Simone's, she had, like, five shirts laid out on the bed. This bitch got clothes for frigid days.

"I should put my hair up, right?"

"No, Sasha, you got on sweats. Put it in a ponytail."

"OK, do it for me."

"Damn, you want me to fuck him for you too?"

"No, bitch, I can handle that. Simone, you know what? Every time I get around you, I get really ghetto. Cussing and stuff. I didn't use to be this way."

"Sasha, I don't know who you're foolin'. You've always been this way for as long as I've known you, and that's your whole life. You change your speech like I change my damn drawers."

"Simone, that's not true."

"Yes, it is. You're always flipping the script. When we get around white people, you become some white wannabe, and when we get around our people, all of a sudden, you're so cool. Don't put the blame on me, 'cause it's not just when you're with me."

"Whatever," I said, trying on one of the blouses. "How's this one look?"

"It got black and red in it, and since your sneakers are black, they go together."

"You don't think it's too much cleavage showing?"

"Oh, bitch, you need to show off your little-ass titties."

"OK." Just then, my cell phone rang. It was Nick. "Hello," I said, trying not to sound too excited.

"Hey, I'm sorry about earlier. It's just that they are very important clients, and we've been working with them for a long time. I didn't wanna make them impatient. You can understand that, right?"

"Sure, I'm fine with it. I understand. After all, you did tell me you had a meeting."

"What did you need me for?"

"Oh, don't worry about it, Nick. I took care of it."

"Oh, all right. You know, Sasha, TJ is still here. How about if you bring one of your cousins with you, and we'll all have lunch together?"

"Oh, I don't know about that, Nick."

"Oh, come on, Sash. It'll be fun."

"OK, let me call you back."

Simone was looking at my mouth, and she could hear every word he said. "Hell yeah, I wanna go."

"What about Richie?"

"Fuck Richie. He ain't here, and he ain't coming back till next week. Shit, I'mma just have some harmless fun. So who is this guy anyway?"

"He's a lawyer too. It's Nick's best friend."

"What does he look like?"

"I don't know, Simone. I've never met him before. Are you coming or what?"

"Yeah, I'll come."

"Let me call him back. Nick."

"Hey, did you get in touch with one of your cousins? Yeah, I'm gonna bring my Simone with me. We'll be there in a little while."

"Great. Um, could you do me a favor and pick up some Italian bread on the way? I made spaghetti."

"OK, sure. Be there in a little while." I hung up the phone, and Simone screamed.

"Oh, shit, I need to wash my ass. I got a date with a fuckin' lawyer."

"Simone, you better not go over there cussing and carrying on like some old sailor. Don't embarrass me."

"Oh, bitch, don't even try it. I know how to act in front of people. You act like we weren't all raised together."

"OK, I'm just letting you know they're somewhat intellectual."

"Intellectual my ass. Sasha, they're just horny black men. You gotta remember that. You make them out to be so much."

"Whatever, Simone. Just don't act up."

"What am I gonna put on, Sasha? Maybe just some jeans and a nice shirt, or maybe I should wear sweats too."

"You know what I just thought about, Simone? They just had a business meeting. I bet they're gonna be in suits."

"So what has that got to do with me?"

"Maybe we should just wear something else."

"No, Sasha, I'm going casual. As a matter a fact, I'mma put on my black sweat suit, with a really tight white wife beater tee and some white tennis sneakers."

"You know what, just get ready, Simone. It's already going on one fifteen."

We left in the beema and stopped at the store for bread. When we drove up Nick's driveway, Simone started laughing. "This is not where he lives, Sasha. No way. This shit is off the chain. Nah, yo. He ain't got it like this."

"See that's why I told you to act like you got some damn sense."

"All right, all right. I'mma play the role. Damn. Whose Jag is that?" Simone said.

"I don't know," I said, ringing the doorbell. No one answered, so I called him on my cell phone.

"Hello."

"Nick, I'm out front."

"Oh, I'm sorry. Come around back. We're out by the pool."

"Oh, shit, how do I look, Sasha?"

"You look fine, Simone. Now relax."

We walked around to the back of the house. There were beautiful flowers growing all along the sides of the walkway.

"Sweet," Simone said, whispering.

"Hey, ladies," Nick said, getting up from his seat. A very tall dark-skinned brother with curly jet-black hair and bushy eyebrows stood up next to him. Damn, he was bowlegged and fine.

"Hi, Nick. This is my cousin, Simone."

"Well, hello, Simone. I've heard so much about you."

I chuckled.

"And this is my friend, Terrance, but we like to call him TJ."

"Well, hello, ladies," TJ said, rubbing his hands together. "How are you today?"

"Sasha, you can bring the bread in the house," Nick said, leading me to the side door where the kitchen was.

"So nice day we're having, huh?" TJ said to Simone.

"Yeah, it's a really nice day. Nicer now."

TJ just grinned and pulled out a chair for Simone to sit down at the patio table. Nick and I went inside to put the bread in the oven, which he had preheated. His kitchen had the double ovens that were stacked on top of each other. When I bent down to put the bread at the bottom, Nick came up behind me and grabbed my waist. "I missed you," he said as I stood up and turned to face him.

"I missed you too," I said, hugging him.

He gave me the sweetest kiss. "Mmm, your lips taste so good. Damn. I better go outside before I have to cancel lunch and take you upstairs." I laughed as he went back out the side door. I watched the bread turn brown, which took all of two minutes.

Simone came in laughing. "Girl, this place is bad."

"I told you, Simone."

"Yo, TJ is fine as hell. I didn't think he would look that good. That's what money will do for a brother. You know money can make anybody look good. Girl, I'm saying though. He got some pretty white teeth, and them dimples are driving me wild. I could stick my finger in one of them. Oh my god."

"Simone, you better remember about Richie. This is just a social gathering. Not a date. You do have a man already."

"Shit, does TJ have a woman?"

"I don't know. I never asked."

"Probably. Looking like that, I know he got somebody he's seeing."

"Well, I guess time will tell, Simone."

The guys walked through the door, talking about basketball or something. They both looked like a million bucks. They had taken off the jackets and ties and opened a couple of buttons of their shirts to show their T-shirts. Their jackets and ties were on a lawn chair out back.

"I feel so overdressed," TJ said, looking at Simone's ass half hanging out of the back of her sweatpants.

"Oh, you look fine," Simone said, turning around and looking him in his eyes.

"If you say so."

"Why don't you ladies sit down in the dining room, and we'll serve you," Nick said, interrupting them. "Oh, would you like to eat on the back patio?"

"The patio would be fine with me," I said.

"Yeah, me too," Simone said.

"OK then, the patio it is. Now go on and let us cater to you."

I watched TJ watch Simone walk away. Simone and I went out to the back and sat down on the lawn chairs and waited for the guys to present us with lunch. We were on top of a mountain, so you could see over a lot of the city. It was amazing.

"Sasha, no wonder your ass didn't wanna leave. You think TJ got a place like this too?"

"Simone, I don't know what that man got. Would you stop asking me about him?"

"All I know is that I'm not messing up with this man. This could be my future husband if I play my card right."

Just then, my cell phone rang. It was Tray.

"Sasha, who is it?"

"Tray."

"You better not answer it from here."

"I know. I don't have anything to say to him anyway. He probably went to the house and saw that I took some of my shit."

"You didn't tell him you were leaving?"

"No, he ain't my father. I don't have to tell him every move I make. Shit, he better be worried about his baby mama."

"Sasha, you're his baby mama too."

"Don't remind me. You'll spoil the mood." I turned my phone off.

"Girl, let me turn mine off too. I don't want any interruptions."

"OK, ladies," Nick said, bringing out a serving tray with pasta in one dish and the sauce in another. TJ was right behind him with the bread all cut up and a bottle of wine in a chilled silver vase thing. We got up from the lawn chairs and joined them at the patio table.

"Smells good," I said to Nick.

"Yeah, really good," Simone said, looking at TJ. She was such a flirt.

"Would you like some wine, Simone?" TJ said, grinning at my cousin.

"Sure," Simone said gracefully. I'd never seen this side of her before. She actually had manners. It made me wonder about what she said earlier. I wonder if the guys are really like this, or are they acting too?

"I'll have some too," I said, grinning at Nick.

"That goes for me too," Nick said to TJ.

TJ poured us all a glass. "Here's to new beginnings," TJ said, looking at Simone.

"Cheers."

The food was wonderful, and I don't know if it was because we were going on our second bottle of wine, but it got very hot. I have to take off my jacket to reveal the back-out shirt I borrowed from my cuz.

"Yeah, it is a little hot out here," Simone said, taking her jacket off to reveal her braless nipple protruding from her wife beater T-shirt.

"Oh my, it is hot out here," TJ said, staring at Simone's perfectly round breast. I caught Nick taking a glimpse too. She was very well built. She had been that way since we were children. She never gained an ounce anywhere but her butt. That was a family trait: big butts and little waistlines. Even as big as Mel was, she still had a good shape.

When we were all done, the guys cleared the table. "We'll be right back," TJ said to Simone.

"Ooh, girl, he's got that look in his eyes."

"Simone, don't forget you have a man."

"You are not gonna blame me for this later, like when you were going out with Jeffrey and met Tray's friend, Mark. You blamed that whole night on me, and I wasn't even with you."

"Girl, that's when we were kids. I was, like what, eighteen then."

"Come on now. You still remember that."

"Hell, yes, I do, Moni."

"When Jeff left you, you cried for, like, a week and told everybody it was my fault."

"Well, this is different. This motherfucker's got money, and he's finer than any man I've ever seen up close."

"You're sure right about that. If I was into dark-skinned men, he'd be a good one."

"Shit, Nick ain't that light. He's a whole lot lighter than TJ."

"Well, I like chocolate. It's sweet, and it melts in your mouth."

"Simone, you're a nasty ass." We both started laughing.

"You know what, Sasha, I'm gonna go upstairs and change. You wanna come keep me company?"

"Well, I didn't wanna leave, Simone."

"Oh, don't worry about Simone," TJ interrupted. "I was wondering if she wanted to take a ride to my house so I could change. I don't live far. Just a few blocks from here."

"Oh, sure, TJ, I'd love to go for the ride."

"Oh, all right then."

Nick and I went into the house and upstairs to his room. "I wanted to get out of this stuffy suit and put on something more comfortable," he said to me while going up the stairs.

When we got to his bedroom door, he threw me up against the wall and started kissing me. He rubbed his hands up and down over my breast and then over my butt. "Oh, damn, you feel so good in my arms." We stood there in the hallway, kissing for about ten minutes before he actually opened the bedroom door.

When we went in, he had changed the sheets and the blanket. "Nick, do you have a cleaning person?"

"Yeah, an older lady comes in for about four hours and straightens up the house. She normally comes from Monday through Friday mornings at about nine. Why?"

"I just wondered because this place is so big and you're so busy. I just wondered when you would find the time."

"Yeah, it is a lot. I like her too. She reminds me a lot of my mother."

"Oh, OK."

He said from his walk-in closet, "OK, now let's go." Nick came out in a phat red sweat suit with a black T-shirt.

"Cute. We're matching."

"I thought you'd think that was cute."

"Funny thing is, I just bought this sweat suit the day before I met you."

"I guess we like the same colors too, huh?" he said, smiling at me. He took my hand and went back downstairs to the living room where we sat on the couch. "Now where is Mr. Grant?"

"Oh, is that what his last name is?"

"Yep, Terrance Jermaine Grant III"

"A name with a lot of history, huh?"

"Yeah, he lives in his great-grandfather's house too. It was left to his father, and his father left it to him when he passed away."

"Oh, his father passed away? So did Simone's."

"Boy, seems like we're all connected together in some way."

"I suppose so. This is so weird."

"What's so weird about destiny? When you meet the person you're destined to be with, everything else somehow falls into place."

"Nick," I said, feeling guilty about not telling him about the car, "I have something to tell you."

"What, Sasha? Is it something I might need a drink for?"

"No, I just wanted you to know that that wasn't my car."

"Oh, I know that. I rented that car before. If you were trying to hide it, you should have taken the Baller logo off the key chain." We both laughed. "Is that all, Ms. Longston?"

"Yes, that's it."

"Well, shall we continue where we left off upstairs?" Nick leaned into me and put his hand in the small of my back and started kissing all over my neck. "You make me crazy, you know that?"

"OK, break it up," TJ said, coming in the side door.

"Oh, now you come back," Nick said, looking disappointed to see them.

Simone had a cheesy big grin on her face. TJ had on a white sweat suit, with a black T-shirt and black sneakers. "What is this? We're all matching," TJ said out loud.

"You know how we roll," Nick said, laughing.

"OK, ladies, I was thinking about going to the movies and then maybe a boat ride or something."

"Whatever you guys have planned is fine with me," Simone said. Her hair seemed to be a little messed up. I just looked at her, shook my head slightly, and grinned. We went all the way out to Windsor to go to the movies. That was fine with me because I really didn't want to stay local. It was also better for Simone, seeing that this lunch turned into a date really quick.

"Let's take two cars," Nick said. We got in Nick's Hummer, and to my surprise, TJ was driving the hunter green Jag that was parked out front when we pulled up. I know Simone must be thrilled to be getting in that. She was so materialistic.

"Nick."

"Yes, baby?"

"Do you think there comes a time in a person's life when everything changes all at once?"

"Sometimes, Sasha," he answered as he helped me into the car. "It just all depends on where your head is," he said, shutting my door. When he got in the car, he said, "If you want things to change when you put the ball in motion, you can sometimes get outstanding results. Things that you didn't think needed to be changed will automatically change. You know God takes care of us all, and when you work your faith, he does the rest."

I couldn't believe what he had just said. Here I was, running from religion, and he was somehow embracing it. Too funny. Aunt Trudy always tried to get me to go to church with her, and I would make up all kinds of excuses why I couldn't go.

"I better call the movie theater and find out what's showing. Do you have anything in mind?"

"No, you can pick," I said, still thinking about what he said.

"You know what, maybe we'll just go down there and see what's playing and what time they start, then we'll work it out from there. Sound good?"

"Sounds good to me," I said. "Nick, do you go to church?"

"Sometimes. I went a lot more when my grandparents were here. They sang in the choir. I loved seeing them up there onstage just singing their hearts out."

"Sounds like you really love them."

"Oh man, my grandparents were the best people in the world. They're the reason why I'm so successful in my life today. They persuaded me to go for the law thing when I thought it would be too much for me. See, TJ had been in law school a year before I started. It was something that we both wanted to do, but he had more guts than I did at the time—and better grades. Man, that cat was brilliant. I didn't think I could do it because I wasn't so good with the books like him. He would study so hard, and when I watch him, it made me wanna do something else. I guess I just didn't have any confidence in myself. My grandparents would yell at me and tell me that TJ was no better than I was, and the only difference between him and me is that he was determined to succeed. They drilled it in my head the whole year I did construction until I just went for it. I mean, we had the financial support and all. I just didn't have the courage to pursue it back then. When I started to take my life seriously, I couldn't believe what happened. I started school, and within that first year, I was the head of the class. Amazing how a little support from loved ones can help you to achieve."

"That's a great story, Nick. I would never have pegged you for someone without confidence."

"Oh, yeah, Sasha, we all come from somewhere before we get to where we're going. You know what I mean."

"Yeah, I suppose I do." I knew he was talking about me and my art; he just didn't want to say so.

"So, Sasha, when are you going to paint something for me? I would really like to have some of your art in my home. It would brighten up the place and maybe give it a more family feel."

"Oh, Nick, you know damn well you need none of my art in your house. Your house is too much for my little work."

"Oh, but, Sasha, you're wrong. I know you have a lot to offer with your talent. You just need to start believing it. Maybe that's what's stopping you from going as far as you really want to. You got to tap into your power, Sasha. If I can see it, I know that all you have to do is believe in yourself, and you'll see what this world has in store for you. The universe is just waiting for you to rise to the challenge. Believe me, I know. I had to rise, or I would have fallen on my face. Shoot, instead of living in my house, I may have been the one building. That would have been so far from what I wanted to do with my life, and I would have had to settle for it, 'cause I wouldn't have believed I could do anything else."

"Nick, how'd you get so smart?"

"Girl, I'll tell you one thing. The more I learn, the more I know I don't know anything."

Did he just call me girl? He is kinda ghetto. Hmm. "Nick, have you ever gone out with a straight-up gangster chick?"

"Sasha, what makes you ask me something like that?"

"I don't know. Just making conversation."

"Yeah, I suppose I have. Back when I was a young man. I think I dated a girl named Laquisha."

"And what was she like?"

"She was nice, but I was scared of hanging out with her. She had a lot of fights all the time. I remember we went to the mall, and these two girls tried to jump her. I had to break it up, and the police came and everything. It was just a little too much for me. I couldn't handle that scene. I mean, that was just too much commotion for me."

"I know what you mean. I'm really not into the whole ghetto, fabulous scene myself. I like things very quiet and serene. Nick, have you ever smoked weed?"

"Yeah. Why? Have you?"

"I still do sometimes," I said bravely.

"You do? Now that's something I wouldn't have thought you would do."

"Why?" I said, a little sorry I admitted it.

"I don't know. You just don't seem like the type that would smoke. Well, Sasha, you know what, I do sometimes myself. Mostly with my boys. It's not an everyday thing."

"No, not for me either," I said quickly, making sure he didn't think I was a pothead or something.

"See, we do have a lot in common, despite what you might think."

"I didn't say we didn't have things in common, Nick."

"I'm just making sure you know how well we fit, baby," he said, rubbing my leg.

This guy was something else. When we got to the theater, the guys went in and checked out the shows. Simone got in the Hummer with me. "Damn, Sasha. I've never been in one of these before. This shit is wild."

"I know right. So how's it going in that Jag?"

"Girl, don't play. I'm in love. When we got to his house, which, by the way, is bad as hell. He told me to look around his house while he was changing. Girl, he writes poetry, and he draws. I like him."

"So did y'all finally kiss?" I said, being nosy.

"Kiss? He damn near stripped me. I thought I was gonna lose my mind. He's so rough."

"Rough?"

"Yeah, Sasha, you know I love it when a man just takes what he wants. Especially when he looks and smells like TJ. Shit, he could do whatever he wants to me."

"So does he have a girlfriend?"

"He said he got friends that he talks to, but nothing serious. He's been focused on his career. He said there was one girl he really liked, but she got a job somewhere down south and moved away. She wanted him to propose, and when he didn't, she decided to leave. Sasha, I don't need a proposal. I just want him to wine me and dine me. And by the way, shit, he's acting more ghetto than me. I can't believe the way he talks. 'He gone' and 'you bes.' I think maybe he thinks that's what I wanna hear."

"I don't know." I didn't wanna tell Simone that if he thought that, it wasn't a good thing. I just left her to her fantasy. "Simone, guess what? Do you know Nick smokes weed?"

"So does TJ. We talked about a lot of things on the way over here. He drinks more than just wine too. He also likes strip clubs. You know I like those types of men. Love a man that can just be his damn self. Shit, I like strip clubs too. I don't mind watching them women dancing on the poles. Any fool knows the best place to see some horny men is in a strip club, so why not let them get all excited and then come on home to Mama? I make them forget the strippers really quick."

"Simone, you know you ain't right."

"Oh, here they come," she said, excited. "Damn, he looks good."

"OK," Nick said, "the movie doesn't start until four twenty, so we have about an hour to kill. What would you ladies like to do?"

"There's a mall not too far from here. We could go hang out in there for a while," Simone said.

"I was thinking more along the lines of a walk," I said. "There's a trail back at the last exit."

"Does that sound all right with you guys?" Nick said to Simone and TJ.

"Or we could split up and meet back here in an hour," TJ said. "I'll take Simone to the mall, and y'all can go for your nature walk."

"OK, we'll see you back here at about four or so."

Simone got out of the car and got in the Jag. She didn't even wait for TJ to open the door for her. I don't think he minded either. He didn't seem like that type of person naturally. I hate to say it, but it seemed like those two were meant for each other.

We went up to the trails and parked. He came around to my side and helped me down out of the car. "Nick, you're such a gentleman," I said, smiling.

"My grandmother was a stickler for opening doors and pulling out chairs for a woman. She told me that if you treat a woman like a queen, they'll treat you like a king. I've lived by that motto my whole life, and you know, I like the way it feels. It makes me feel like I'm somehow doing something special for them, no matter how little it is. I enjoy making you feel special though. I enjoy you. Your company had changed so many things for me, you just don't know, Sasha. I've been sleeping better, and I think I've even been doing better in my meetings."

"How could I possibly have anything to do with that?"

"You just wouldn't understand. The company of a good woman can do wonders for a man. Why do you think God didn't leave Adam by himself? He would have gone crazy out there with them damn animals. There's nothing like a sweet woman to fulfill your life."

"Yes, sir."

"Nothing like it," he said, holding my hand as we walked into the wooded trail.

"Ooh, look at the birds, Nick. Are they kissing?"

"It sure looks like it. They got the right idea." Nick leaned up against a tree and pulled me into him. His lips were so soft, and I loved the way he held me, with his hand pressed into the small of my back. It made me feel so small. "Sasha, I know that it's only been a couple of days, but I gotta know something. Do you think you could fall in love with a brother like me?"

"Why do you ask that, Nick?"

"'Cause I . . . I think I'm in love with you. This is the first time in a very long time I've felt this way with a woman. You make my palms sweaty, and my heart beats so fast when you're near me. Damn, it makes me feel crazy inside. I just can't wait to see you when you're gone."

He was starting to scare me. "Hold on, Nick. Hold on. Slow down."

"Why, Sasha? I love you. Do you hear what I'm saying to you?"

I backed up from him a little. "How can you love me after only knowing me for four days?"

"I told you I just know. Things like this don't happen every day, and if you don't go for it, you may let the best thing in your life escape." He held me closer.

I backed up from him again. "This is all moving so fast for me. I'm not even divorced yet," I said, confused.

"Don't worry about all that. I'll help you work that out. I know I don't sound like a rational man, Sasha. But I'm very serious about this. I know you're my soul mate. I can feel it. If I let you go, I may never get a chance to know real love again. They say there's only one soul mate out there for you per lifetime."

"Nick, what are you doing to me? I didn't know it would go this far this fast. I mean, what about my son? What about him? You haven't even met him yet—or the rest of my family, for that matter."

"What do they have to do with the way I feel about you? I don't plan on being married to them."

"Married? Now wait a minute."

"Sasha, I thought that's what you would want. I thought you liked me too."

"I do like you, Nick. I just don't know if I love you. I mean, I know that when we're together, it feels nice and all, but I don't even know you."

"What do you wanna know, Sasha? You can ask me anything you want."

"Look, Nick, I can't just fall in love with you all of a sudden. These things take time, and you have to remember I just came out of a relationship. Remember I told you, you weren't a rebound."

"Yes, I remember that. But I thought you meant you wanted something more with me."

"I do, Nick. Don't get me wrong. It's just that I want to take my time and get to know you and your family."

"OK, Sasha, I hear you."

"Nick, please understand me. I am flattered that you love me."

"Yeah, you just can't return the love right now. Is that what you're saying?"

"No, that's not what I'm saying." Looking into his eyes, I could see the hurt I was causing. "Nick, I do love you. I just didn't want to admit it, OK? I don't wanna get hurt again."

"Sasha, I would and could never hurt you. You're too sweet. Do you think all this is fake, Sasha? You think I bring girls to my house all the time and make meals for them? TJ has never even met any of the women I have dated before you, unless he was there when I met them. I just don't operate like that. The only reason he wanted to meet someone in your family is because I spoke so highly of you."

"I thought you told me you hadn't dated in a while."

"Sasha, be serious. I've gone out on dates with women—but not to fancy restaurants or to my house. I know you don't believe me, but there are a lot of stalkers out there. When women find out you got a little something going on for yourself, they immediately wanna cash in. You're not like that. I have the feeling you would have still liked me even if I had nothing at all."

"How do you know that about me, Nick? How do you know that I'm not just a gold digger in disguise?"

"Are you, Sasha?"

"Well, no, but I could be lying."

"Listen, we are both too old to be playing games. I don't have time to try to figure out why I feel the way I do about you. If you feel the same way I do, let's just take it from there. If not, we can just be friends, and I'll go back to my boring life of work and casual dating."

"Nick, I don't want you to do that, but I just want to take it a little slower."

"OK, Sasha, so I guess you wouldn't wanna hold on to this then." Nick unzipped his sweat suit pocket to reveal a princess-cut diamond ring that had to be about five karats.

"Nick! What is this?"

"Sasha, I want you to hold on to this until your divorce is final, and then we can take it from there. Can you do that?"

"Nick, I can't. I can't take this," I said as I allowed him to put it on my finger.

"See? Look at that. I didn't even know what size your finger was, but it fits perfectly. What do you think that means?"

"I think it means you're crazy, Nick."

"You know what, Sasha? I'm gonna go back to the truck and leave you here for a moment. You come when you're ready. If you still have that ring on your finger, I'll know where we stand, and if you don't, I'll be disappointed, but I'll understand that too."

I stood there next to the tree and watched Nick walk back down the trail to the truck. I looked at the ring and thought about what it represented. This could be the beginning of a new life. But I just didn't know if I was ready to leave the old one behind. This was crazy. What man do you know meets a woman in a rib shack, dates her for four days, and gives her a five-carat diamond? Not to mention the fact that I was still married to someone else. He's either really in love or a fuckin' psychopath. I just didn't know what to do. I decided to do something very unlike me. I called Aunt Trudy.

"Hello."

"Hey, Auntie."

"Sasha, where are you? You ain't running errands yet?"

"Auntie, I have something very serious to ask you."

"OK, baby. What is it?"

"Auntie, when you met Uncle Mason, you know how you told us that when y'all met, you just knew right away that you would be with him for the rest of your life. How'd you know that?"

"Well, child, sometimes you just know. You get a warm feeling inside, and when you're with him, you forget about everything else in the world. Oh, and when you're apart, your heart aches. I remember when they called him off to that job in South Carolina for the weekend. I thought I would die the first time he left. I wasn't jealous or anything. I just wanted to be in his arms."

"Auntie, do you believe in love at first sight?"

"Child, God works in mysterious ways. I believe you can just look at a person and know. Same as how you can look at a person and know they just ain't the one for you. What is it, child? What's going on with you?"

"Auntie, I met someone, and he just proposed to me."

"What? Why, you're not even divorced yet. Does he know that?"

"Yes, I told him everything, and he said he would wait. He said he was giving me this ring to make sure I knew how serious he was."

"Well, how do you feel about him?"

"Auntie, everything you just said is how I feel, but—"

"But what, child? Now, Sasha, you know I've never approved of a lot of the choices you've chosen. Especially when you married Tray. But I didn't argue with you. Now I'm telling you, if this man knows everything about you and he's willing to wait for you, then sounds to me like you've got a winner."

"You think so, Auntie?"

"I could be wrong, baby. I'm not perfect. But that's what it sounds like to me."

I didn't realize I had tears in my eyes. I hung up the phone and just stood there for a moment. When I turned around, I wiped my eyes. Nick was coming back up the trail.

"Sasha, I'm sorry."

"Nick, I do love you," I said, interrupting him. "And I do want to be with you, and I'm sorry for everything I said."

"No, Sasha, I'm sorry for rushing you into this whole thing. I should have put more thought into where you were coming from in all this. Sometimes, I can be very impulsive."

I put my finger over his lips before he could say another word. "Shh. Nick, I do love you." I kissed him with all the passion I could find throughout my very being.

"Sasha, are you sure? You're sure I'm not putting too much pressure on you? I just don't know what I would do if I let this chance slip out of my hands. I know I'd regret it for the rest of my life."

"I'm sure, Nick. I'm more sure now than ever."

"You don't know how happy you've just made me," Nick said as he picked me up and carried me back to the car. He put me down in front of my door and kissed me again. "Oh, Sasha, I do love you."

"I love you too, Nick. I just didn't want to admit it." He helped me into the car and then went around to the driver's side with a big smile on his face. I watched him in amazement. Was this going to be my husband? Could he really make me happy? I guess I was going to find out. I couldn't believe it. This man just changed my entire life.

When we got to the movie theater, Simone and TJ were nowhere to be found. Nick called TJ's cell phone and got no answer. "His voice mail came on," he said, looking a little confused.

"I'll try Simone." She always answers her cell phone, but I got her voice mail too. Nick decided to call TJ's house. There was no answer there either. I started to worry. I hope nothing happened to them.

"Don't worry about them, Sasha. Simone is in good hands. TJ would never do anything to hurt her."

"I didn't say he would, but suppose something happened."

"Then they would have called us, wouldn't they?"

"I suppose you're right," I said, feeling a bit worried.

"Let's go in and enjoy the show. I'm sure wherever they are, they are enjoying themselves."

When we got in the movie theater, we turned off our cell phones and sat back and relaxed. Nick put his arm around me, and I rested my head on his shoulder. This all felt like a dream I didn't want to wake up from. During the movie, I kept looking down at my finger to make sure the ring was still there. Nick caught me once. He smiled and kissed me on my forehead.

When we left the movie theater, we both had messages on our cell phones. Simone told me that she was in love and that she would talk to me later. I think she was in lust. How could she possibly be in love with a man she just met? Nick said that TJ left a message saying that he was sorry he couldn't meet us at the movies but that something came up. I knew that probably wasn't the real message. He was just trying to be nice.

"Well," Nick said, "I suppose we've made some sort of a love connection." On the way back to Nick's house, he had a couple of questions for me. "So, Sasha, when are you gonna bring back that rental car?"

"The rental? Um, I have it for one more week." I couldn't believe he was asking me about the car. "Why do you ask?"

"'Cause I know that is an expensive car to rent, and if you need something to drive, I have a Mercedes in the garage you could use."

"Oh. Well, I do have a car, but it's not running so well right now."

"Does it need to go in the shop, or is it already there?"

"No, actually, it needs to be junked."

"Then why don't you get rid of it?"

"Nick, I don't want to drive your Mercedes."

"OK, how about I make it yours then? I'll put it in both our names. Would you like that?"

"Um . . . I guess."

"What do you mean you guess? Would you or wouldn't you?"

"I would, Nick. You'll have to excuse me. This is all so new to me."

"What is?"

"Having someone that really cares about me."

"Well, I guess a lot of things I do will be new to you. I told you, Sasha, I love you, and when I love, I love hard."

"Should I be scared of that statement?"

"Not unless you can't return the love."

"Nick, what are you looking for out of the relationship?"

"All I want is someone that will have my back, love me the way I love them, and be loyal to me and only me."

"Nick, why did you and your wife break up?"

"I knew you were gonna ask that question sooner or later. Well, you see, I had just worked at this new law firm, and it required me to be away from home a lot. Although I called Yvette all the time, she always thought I was out with another woman. You see, she had a lot of insecurities after seeing her parents' divorce, because her father was cheating with another woman. It made it really hard for her to see me for who I was. And that's it. Sasha, I'm just a black man trying to live a full life and, if I'm lucky, pursue some of my dreams. Three of them have already come true. At least I hope so."

"And what are they?"

"First was to be a successful lawyer. Two was to, one day, own the house I live in now, and three was to find the woman of my dreams and make her as happy as she could possibly be. Now I have some other goals too. But I don't think I'm doing too bad."

"No, I don't think so either."

"What are some of your dreams, Sasha?"

"I think you've fulfilled one of the big ones already. I don't know yet. I have to see. Another is to become a famous artist. I know that one, and another is to take a trip around the world."

"Hey, that's one of mine too," Nick said, smiling. "I knew we were right for each other. Now on a more serious note, Sasha, what do you think your son is gonna say about all this? I mean, he didn't exactly have a say in any of this."

"My son is with his father, and that's where he wants to be."

"How do you feel about that?"

"I didn't like it at first, but the more I think about it, the more sense it makes. I mean, I'm not exactly a stable person right now. Tray is much more stable emotionally than I am. He seems to be able to do all the bullshit he's doing and still keep being levelheaded about himself. I, on the other hand, cannot deal. You know what, Nick? I think it's time for my son to see what life is really like without me. I mean, after all, he did pick his father over me."

"What's your husband's name anyway?"

"Tramaine."

"Oh, good. I don't know any Tramaine."

"I'm glad you don't. Anyway, Nick, let's talk about something else."

"Like what?"

"Let's see, do I have any more questions for you? Ah, where were you born?"

"Ooh, good one. You'll never guess."

"I don't wanna guess. Just tell me."

"No, guess."

"Down south somewhere?"

"No. I was born in a Las Vegas hotel room with a midwife."

"A Las Vegas hotel room?"

"Yes, my mother went there with my father. He had a business trip out there, and she didn't want him to miss the birth, so they set up things here and there just in case. Well, I came two days early."

"That's a good story, Nick."

"Yeah, my mother used to say she knew I would make a lot of money 'cause I was born in the hotel at the casino. Where were you born?"

"I was born in Hartford Hospital. Very normal. No great stories to tell."

"That's all right."

"So what is your favorite food?"

"My favorite is barbecue beef ribs."

"Nick, that's so typical."

"Well, that's what I like. I love anything on the grill."

"Oh, yeah, I forgot that was your specialty."

"Well, what's your favorite?"

"I don't really have a favorite food. I just like to eat, as you can see."

"What are you talking about? You look perfect. I like a woman thick in the thighs. You have what they call a Coca-Cola bottle shape."

"Yeah, but the bottle needs to be a little smaller."

"Well, I like it just fine."

"Well, I'm glad you do, Mr. Abraham."

"Sasha, how do you think it sounds?"

"How what sounds, Nick?"

"Mrs. Sasha Abraham."

"Hey, what's your middle name?"

"It's Cossandra, with an O."

"Yep. That's different."

"Yeah, you can thank my mom for that. She knew a woman named Cossandra. She was so beautiful, she said. She looked like a movie star. Sasha Cossandra Abraham. Sounds good to me."

I couldn't believe we were having this conversation. How is it possible that someone I just met last Friday is talking this way? I really think I'm dreaming. It was about six thirty by the time we got back to his place.

"Well, we're home."

Listen to him. *We're home.* He's funny.

"So what plans do you have for tonight, Sasha?"

"Well, I really do need to go and check in with my aunt."

"Now this aunt is Simone's mother, right?"

"Yeah, Simone is the youngest of four."

"So who's the oldest?"

"Nathan. Then there's Tiffany, Melony, and then the spoiled brat, Simone."

"I'd like to meet them all one day."

"Maybe you will. I may just go to the Halloween party my cousin, Melony, always throws. Her oldest was born on that day. She'll be nineteen."

"Yeah, your cousin has a child that old?"

"She started early. It's a long story. I'll tell you about it sometime."

"So, Sasha, when are you gonna bring back that rental? I'll follow you in the Mercedes, and you can drop me off, if you want."

"I've already paid for the Beemer for the week, so I might as well keep it."

"OK, well, just let me know when you're ready for it. Sasha, I don't want you to be scared to ask me for anything. Remember, I'm your man now. You don't need to ask anyone for anything ever again. I'll provide all your needs."

I can't believe this fine-ass man is telling me all this. This has got to be a dream. We pulled up into the driveway and I got out of his car and into mine. Nick held the door open and gave me a big hug and a kiss.

"Remember what I said, Sasha. Don't forget, and if you do, just look at the ring finger on your left hand."

I looked down and saw the big diamond winking at me. I couldn't believe I was leaving his house with this. I wonder if he told TJ he was gonna do this. "Bye, baby," I said, closing the door and letting down the window.

"I love you, Sasha."

"I love you too, Nick." I pulled off and looked back in my rearview mirror. He was still standing there, looking at me drive away. I can't believe this. I can't believe he proposed to me. Shit, I can't believe I accepted his proposal. I really need to get a divorce—and quick.

When I got down the street, I tried to call Simone's cell phone. I got no answer. Where the hell is she? I know she wasn't still with TJ all this time. I know she didn't sleep with him. Oh, do I? I know how she can be. Maybe they just went somewhere or something. Anyway, I really do have my own stuff to think about. I'm engaged.

When I got to Aunt Trudy's house, I called for her but didn't see her. I went and looked out the back window, and there she was, sitting in the backyard with Mr. Carter. He was grilling, and she was drinking what looked like liquor. I just know that I wasn't seeing right. Aunt Trudy doesn't drink.

When I walked out the back sliding door, she put the drink by her side. She was drinking. "Hi, Mr. Carter. Hi, Auntie. What are you guys doing back here?"

"Oh, you're back early, Sasha. I thought you would be out for a while after the conversation we had earlier. So did everything go well?" she said, looking down at my hand.

"Yes, everything went better than well," I said, smiling at her.

"Well, I see. That's wonderful. Johnny, I'll be back in just a moment. Let me talk to this child for a quick minute." Aunt Trudy grabbed my left hand and went inside. When she closed the back door, she screamed. "Child, that rock could blind you! Who is this man?"

"He's a lawyer, Auntie."

"Now that's what I'm talking about, child. See the difference in care? I told y'all to marry somebody with some sense. So what did he say about you and Tray?"

"He's gonna get in touch with one of the divorce attorneys he knows to handle the case. But you know what, Auntie? Originally, I wanted half of everything that Tray had, but this man is rich. He has one of them mini mansions in Simsbury and everything."

"He does? Oh, baby, you hit the jackpot. So what did he say? And tell me everything."

I could smell the liquor on Aunt Trudy's breath. "Auntie, were you drinking?"

"Oh, I just had a little sip. Now you keep that to yourself now. Mr. Carter likes me to drink with him once in a while. We don't do it all the time."

Yeah, no wonder she liked being here all by herself. I forgot about Mr. Carter. Her and Whiskers. Yeah, right. She's probably in here, making all sorts of noise. I know Auntie used to be a freak back in the days.

"So tell me, child, and don't leave out anything."

"Well, he was married before, but he wife was too insecure. He said she used to follow him everywhere he went."

"Yeah, I know those types of women."

"And he doesn't have any children."

"No children, child? Oh my. You really hit the goal, didn't you? And what else, child?"

"And he said he loves me and wants to take care of me."

"What did he say about TJ?"

"He wants to meet him and all of you too. I don't think TJ is gonna wanna meet him though. He's so mad with me right now. I don't know what to do."

"Oh, baby, he's just hurt. He'll get over it. You need to call and tell him you love him. You know what I mean?"

"Yes, Auntie, I will."

"Well, well, child, you've finally caught a big fish. Ooh, your mother would be so proud. She always wanted you to marry well."

"Auntie, he wants to give me his Mercedes to drive. I told him my car wasn't working, and that was why I had the rental car."

"I wondered whose car that was you were driving. What's wrong with your car, child?"

"Nothing. It's just old, and plus, Tray bought me that car. I don't ever wanna see it again. Not since I found out his baby mama is driving something much nicer. He just made me feel like crap."

"Well, you never mind him or her. You're getting a chance at a new life. Now don't mess it up. You better call that man and tell him you made it home all right. And use the house phone, just in case he has caller ID. He can see where you're calling him from. You wanna keep them rich men sure in the beginning. You don't want him to think you're playing him in any way. Now let me go on back out here with Mr. Carter. I don't want to be rude to my guest."

Yeah, right. He probably stays here most of the time. When she went outside, I went upstairs and called Nick from the house phone like she said.

"Hello."

"Hey, I just wanted to let you know I made it here OK."

"Oh, I was wondering who Trudence Taylor was." He said referring to his caller ID.

"Yeah, it's my Auntie Trudy's phone. If you want me, you can call me here. Oh, and, Nick, I love you."

"I love you too, baby."

I hung up feeling like a young girl in love all over again. The only difference is that young girls don't get five-carat rocks from their boyfriends.

I tried to call TJ at the house, but there was no answer. I called Tray's cell phone, and he answered. "Hey, Sasha, so you're over at your aunt's house. I see you packed up some of your stuff. You're really not coming back home, huh?"

"What makes you say that?"

"'Cause you never go to your aunt's house. Nathan's house is always the pit stop. So I bet you told your aunt everything, didn't you?"

"Yes."

"Yeah, I bet she's hatin' on a brother right now."

"My aunt never did care for you. She only liked you 'cause she had no choice. We were married. And speaking of being married, I'm filing papers in the morning."

"You're serious about all this?"

"Yes, I am, Tray. Did you think you were gonna play me like this and I would just forgive you? Not this time. You've crossed the line this time. There's no turning back. Anyway, I didn't call to talk to you. Where's my son?"

"Right here."

"Can I speak to him, please?"

"Sure. TJ, it's your mother."

"Hello."

"Hi, baby. How are you?"

"I'm fine. How are you?"

"I'm fine, baby. I just called to tell you that I love you."

"I love you too, Ma."

"Ma, you're really not coming back home?"

"No, baby, I can't live there anymore. Do you really wanna live with your father?"

"Yes, I don't wanna leave my friends and my school and start all over again."

"OK, baby, but just know that if you ever change your mind, you can always stay at wherever I am."

"Where are you anyway?"

"I'm over at your Aunt Trudy's."

"You are? But you hate Aunt Trudy."

"Baby, that's not true. We don't always see eye to eye, but things have changed between us."

"So you're really gonna stay there?"

"Yeah, until I get myself together, this is where I'll be. If you need me, call my cell phone, OK, baby?"

"OK, Ma. And, Ma, I really do love you."

"I know you do, baby." I hung up the phone feeling a little better about the whole thing. Here I was thinking he was mad at me, and he wasn't. He really did love his mother. Boy, it sure does make things easier.

Chapter 9

I didn't talk to anyone but Nick last night. He called me about three times, and we fell asleep talking on the phone, like schoolkids. He wanted me to come over and sleep with him. But I just didn't want to. I have so much on my mind. He just doesn't understand the toll all this has taken on me. There's a lot of good going on but a lot of bad too—like the fact that I haven't figured out what I'm gonna do about this job situation yet, and I feel really bad about what I did to Tiffany now. I shouldn't have gotten Maritza involved in that. I should call her pregnant ass and find out if she got in touch with that damn boy.

Let's see what time it is. Shit, I really need to call the job first and let them know something. I don't wanna be there anymore, and I'm still under contract. I hope they don't give me a hard time. I guess I'll just call the administrator and let her know what is going on. Maybe she will understand. I hope she does.

Oh, shit, who's at the door this early in the morning? I don't even know if Aunt Trudy is awake yet. Damn, it's only, like, eight thirty. I went downstairs in my robe. "Who is it?"

"It's Melony."

Shit, I didn't want her to know I was here. I wish I didn't answer it. I had to open the door now.

When I opened the door, her face dropped. "Sasha, what are you doing here?"

"Oh, nothing," I said, slipping my ring off into my robe pocket. "I spent the night last night."

"Why? What's going on? Why didn't you sleep at your house? Where's TJ? Is he with his father? Whose BMW is that in the driveway?"

"Damn, Mel, can I answer at least one of those questions before you ask any more?"

"Well, Sasha, what's going on?"

"Tray and I broke up."

"Oh, that again."

"No, this time, it's for real. He did some really foul shit."

"What did he do?"

"I can't even go into it right now. All I know is, he hurt me in a way he ain't never done before."

"Girl, no way. Tray loves you. Y'all just having a fight. It'll be over soon."

"You say what you wanna say, Mel. If we just had a fight, I would be over at Nathan's house, right?"

"Well, yeah, that's true. That is your normal routine."

"Well, damn, Melony, does everybody know my business?"

"Oh, please, Sasha. Your ass is so predictable. How could we not know it? You always go to Nathan's house when you and Tray have an argument, and TJ goes to Lee's. We all know the routine. So what happened, and how did you come to stay here?"

"Mel, do you need to know all that?"

"Yes, you know I need all the details."

"All you need to know is that I don't go with Tray anymore and that TJ is staying with him."

"What? You've really given up on your son?"

"Good morning, ladies," Aunt Trudy said, coming out of her room and closing the door behind her.

"Good morning, Ma," Mel said to her mother. "How are you this morning?"

"Oh, I'm just fine, baby. I need some coffee. You're here awfully early this morning, Melony."

"Ma, what are you talking about? We are supposed to go to the social security office this morning. Remember I took the day off work and everything."

"Oh, baby, why didn't you call me last night? I completely forgot everything about it."

"Ma, what's gotten into you lately? You've been forgetting everything."

She should ask her who's gotten into her.

"Well, baby, I'm sorry, but I'm not gonna be able to go with you today. I've made other plans, and I need to go to the doctor."

"What? But, Mommy, I took the day off work."

"Well, if you leave now, you can still make it. I just can't go."

"Ooh, this is the last time I'm taking the day off for you. That makes three times in a row now you've done this to me."

"Auntie, why do you need Mel to take time off work? I'll go with you."

"I don't need her to go, baby. She just wanna know how much they're gonna give me, that's all."

"Um, hello, I'm standing right here. I am still in the room, you know."

"Oh, I'm sorry, Melony, but you know it's the damn truth. I didn't ask you to go with me. When I told you about it, you offered to go with me. Said you had some days you needed to take off work because you were gonna waste the time and it doesn't lapse into the next year. Remember, baby?"

"Well, I did say that, but I was trying to be nice."

"Well, that's very nice of you, but I can't go. Now you run along, and maybe you can still make it to work. I need to get some coffee in me. Sasha, baby, you want some coffee?"

Melony grabbed her pocketbook off the kitchen table and stormed out.

"Ooh, I'm so glad she's gone. She's been watching me like a hawk. Now I got to make Mr. Carter some breakfast. You want some?"

"Auntie, Mr. Carter is still here?"

"Yes, baby. He stayed to keep me company."

"Ooh, Auntie. You're sleeping with Mr. Carter."

"Shh, child, before you wake him up." She laughed.

Who would have ever known the prude that Aunt Trudy tries to portray is all a lie. She's a hoe. No wonder Simone acts like that.

"Now don't you go telling your nosy-ass cousin anything. Melony will have my business all out in the streets if I let her know. I had to take her key in the beginning of the year. Why, she used to walk up in here like she owned the place, and I couldn't have that. She might catch me and Mr. Carter running around here naked."

"Auntie . . ."

"Auntie, what? You're old enough now. You ain't a little girl anymore, and I sure ain't too old to get my freak on."

"You've changed."

"Yeah, well, a good man can do that, baby. He can change you inside out. Ha ha ha!" Aunt Trudy laughed as she turned over the eggs she had cooking on the stove. "Now put some toast in that toaster for me, while I pour this man some orange juice."

"Buttercup, you out there?" Mr. Carter yelled out from the bedroom, which was on the first floor.

"I'm coming, baby. I'm making you some breakfast."

"Buttercup? How corny."

"Now you just hush, child. Don't you have something to do with yourself, like go to work or something? Run along now. I have things to do."

I ran upstairs, laughing. Aunt Trudy is a little hoe. I can't believe it.

I called my job and asked for the administrator. "Hello, is Ann Tate available?"

"Who may I say is calling?"

"This is Sasha Longston."

"Oh, Sasha, I have a message for you. Ann wants you to come in and have a meeting with her and the counselor about your position."

"What kind of discussion?"

"Sasha, you know I can't tell you that. Are you trying to get me fired?"

"Susan, just tell me."

"You know they're gonna fire you."

"Good. That's what I want them to do. That way, they can't say I quit and broke my contract."

"Oh, girl, you got the right idea. You know if you break the contract, they would never hire you back here ever again."

"I don't plan on coming back. I don't even live out there anymore."

"What?"

"Sue, there's a lot going on. Just tell Ann I can't make it because there's a lot going on. When they tell you that I'm fired, tell them I called back and asked for my check to be mailed to me. Mail it to 2255 Andover Street, Hartford, CT 06123. Can you do that for me, Sue?"

"Sure, Sasha. I'm sorry to hear things aren't going so well. Good luck. Keep in touch, will ya?"

"I'll try, Sue. Have a good day, OK? And thanks again." OK, that wasn't so bad. Now I need to call this damn girl and find out if she got in touch with Ramón.

"Hello."

"Hi, Maritza."

"Hey, Sasha, what's up? I've been waiting for you to call me."

"Yeah, I've been very busy. What's going on?"

"Well, you know, I talked to Ramón. I told him to go over to Jade's house yesterday for the party. I haven't talked to him again since. I don't know what happened."

"Well, you know what, Maritza, I'm kinda sorry I asked you to do that. I shouldn't have done that to my cousin."

"Why'd you do it like that anyway? I mean, I know you were trying to get back at Jade, but I thought you didn't wanna hurt your cuz. Ain't that why you didn't let the cat out of the bag in the first place?"

"Yes, but the more I thought about it, the more I thought it was time for Jade to get hers."

"Well, I don't know what happened."

"So how's everything going anyway? Have you talked to your mother?"

"Oh, that's what I called to tell you the other day. I told my mother everything, and she and her sister wanna buy the condo from Tray. My mother said she understood what happened and that since I didn't know from the beginning, she ain't mad with me. Oh, and she wanna meet you."

"Meet me? Why does she wanna meet me?"

"She said you must be a pretty nice lady to stand by me through all this and that she feels so bad for you and your son."

"Well, you tell your mother I'm just fine. I've got a whole lot going on right now, and I will be just fine. Trust me."

"I know you, Sasha. You're a strong woman. So I guess that means you're not going back to Tray?"

"Oh, hell no. If you want him, you can have him."

"You know what, Sasha? The more I thought about it, the more I know I don't need him in my life. He called my mother and told her that she needed to take over the condo payments and that he was gonna take the cars. He told her that her daughter was a cheap ho and that he didn't wanna have anything to do with her. My mother cussed him out and told him that we didn't need him. And you know what else, since she got a new man, she done started working full-time and part-time, and she is really changing. She said she would take care of me and that I didn't have anything to worry about."

"So what's gonna happen to the shop?"

"Now that, I don't know. I still go to work every day and make my little money for now. I haven't heard from Tray at all. I keep trying to call him to work out something, but he doesn't call me back."

"Well, maybe I can work something out for you. I'll see what I can do, OK?"

"Thanks, Sasha. Thanks for trying to help me."

"You're welcome. Well, I gotta go take care of some business. I'll talk to you soon. If you hear from Ramón, let me know, all right?"

"Will do. Bye."

OK, now what am I going to do about this divorce? Let me call my man. Ha ha ha! That sounds so funny. Oh, shit, let me put my ring back on before I lose it. I can't afford to lose that . . . Who the hell is that now? I went to the front room and looked out the window. It was Simone. Ooh, let me see where this heffa has been. I ran downstairs to the door. "I got it, Auntie."

"OK, baby," she answered from her bedroom.

"Girl, get in here." I dragged her upstairs. "Where have you been?"

"And good morning to you too, Sasha."

"Bitch, don't even try it. Where have you been?"

"I've been with my man. Shit, don't question me. I'm grown-up."

"Your man? TJ?"

"That's right, girl. I've been with him since yesterday. I just got home this morning."

"What? You nasty ho."

"Oh, look who's talking, Sasha."

"So what about Richie?"

"Shit, fuck Richie. That bitch's gonna go to jail sooner or later. I got myself a real man now. Girl, you should see this motherfucker's crib. That shit is laid. He got it going on. Shit, that motherfucker got a Jacuzzi in his bedroom. Shit, Richie? Who's that? I have the best time. He took me shopping. Girl, he bought me, like, five outfits. Then he said we needed to go back to his place so I could model them for him. I was, like, hell yeah. Shit. I ain't stupid. That bitch is fine. Damn. He got no kids and has never been married either. Oh, I ain't letting him go. He got a girl though, but I'mma take that over. He said it ain't really serious or anything. That's all I needed to know. If it was, his ass wouldn't have eaten my pussy the way he was all night long. Shit, he damn near fell asleep in it. Girl, that mother fucker got game. Shit, we ain't even fuck yet. He said all he wanted to do was get an appetizer and save the main course for the next time we saw each other. He told me that I had forty-eight hours to get rid of that player I was dealing with and get back to him. Shit, Richie was good as gone when we got back from the mall. He was the first man I've ever been with that actually picked out the clothes and the shoes with me. He didn't go off somewhere else or go sit down outside the store. He was all in it. I love that shit."

"Simone, damn, I can't believe what you're saying to me."

"So, Ms. Sasha, how was your night?"

"My night? I slept here last night."

"Why? Why the fuck didn't you sleep over there with Nick?"

"Simone, my shit is a whole lot more complicated than yours. I got a lot to think about, and Nick just added to it."

"What do you mean?"

"Look," I said, pulling my hand out of my robe pocket.

"Bitch, no, he didn't."

"Yes, he did, Simone."

"That motherfucker proposed to you?"

"He sure did."

"How the fuck are you gonna get married and you still married to Tray?"

"He knows that, Simone. He said he wanted to make sure I knew he was serious and that all he was waiting on was me."

"Let me see this motherfucker. That shit is, like what, six, seven carats."

"No, crazy ass. It's only five."

"Only five! That shit is hot. Let me see it." Simone took it off my finger and tried it on. "Damn, this motherfucker's big. Goddamn, Sasha. What the fuck, you got gold in your pussy."

"Shut up, stupid ass. I didn't want to take it. I had to call Aunt Trudy and ask her what I should do."

"You called my mother? You must be crazy. Why the fuck did you call her?"

"Simone, I don't know what made me call her, but when I got the ring, I was so confused I didn't know what to do."

"So what did she say when you called her?"

"Simone, your mother told me to go for it."

"She did what? No, she didn't. You're lying. Not my prudish mother."

"Oh, I don't think you know your mother."

"Where is she anyway?"

"She's in her room. She has company."

"Company? Who my mother got in her room?"

"Mr. Carter," I whispered.

"What? Mr. Carter and my mother are fucking? You're lying."

"No, I'm not. She came out and made him breakfast and everything."

"What is this world coming to?"

"Girl, I don't know, but your mother has changed. She's all laid-back now, and yesterday, she was drinking in the backyard while Mr. Carter was grilling."

"My mother was drinking?"

"Yes, girl. Your mother was drinking, and she was fucking."

"So that's why she hasn't been bothering me about school. She got her own shit going on."

"Mel came over here this morning. I guess she and Auntie were supposed to go somewhere together. Auntie ran her up outta here quicker than you would believe. She didn't want her to see Mr. Carter. You know she can talk. Mel left mad as hell."

"I bet she was. She's always trying to get into somebody's business."

"Well, you know she doesn't have a life of her own, Simone. She doesn't even know what's going on in her own house. Anyway, what time is it? I gotta call my boo."

"Girl, your boo? Go, Sasha, you got a boo."

"Shut up, Simone," I said, dialing Nick's number.

"Hello."

"Hi."

"Good morning, sexy. How are you this morning?"

"Oh, I'm fine. Sorry I fell asleep on you last night."

"You know what, I didn't even realize we had both fallen asleep. When I woke up this morning, the phone was in the bed with me, and it was dead."

"Oh, I got up to go to the bathroom at around four and saw the phone in bed with me too," I said, and we both laughed.

"So what do you have planned for the day, beautiful?"

"Well, I do want to get this divorce started," I said, looking at Simone, who was waving. "Simone says hi, Nick."

"Oh, she's there. She found her way back, huh?"

"Yeah, I guess so."

"Yeah, I bet TJ got a mouthful for me today when I get to work."

"See, men gossip just like women."

"Yeah, we do. I just don't tell it all. My sex life is private. That's where I draw the line."

"Yeah, I know what you mean. Anyway, I gotta get going, baby."

"I should have been there already. I have a lot to do today. I have at least three new cases to review."

"OK, baby. Don't forget to check on the divorce lawyer for me."

"Oh, believe me, I won't forget about that. I want you all to myself."

"Well, have a nice day, baby."

"You too, beautiful. Hey, I love you."

"I love you too," I said, looking at Simone, who was making faces at me.

"I love you, Nick," she said, teasing me. "I can't believe yall are saying that already. Didn't you just meet this brother last week?"

"Yeah, right. That's why it was so hard for me to comprehend a proposal. Auntie said I got a winner."

"You know you do, Sasha. What are you gonna do about TJ?"

"Girl, I talked to him yesterday. He said he wanna stay with his father."

"Is he mad with you?"

"No, he said he doesn't wanna leave his school and all his friends. He doesn't want to have to start over again." Well, how do you feel about that, Sasha?"

"Girl, right now, I think he needs to stay right where he is. I don't want him all caught up in this shit anyway."

"How are you gonna tell him about Nick?"

"I haven't thought that far ahead yet, Simone. Damn, you're making my stomach hurt. I don't even wanna talk about that anymore. Anyway, what have you and blacky got planned for today?"

"I know you ain't calling my man blacky. Shit, TJ looks good as hell, and he got a big dick."

"I thought yall didn't do anything yet?"

"We didn't, but we did take a shower together. His body looks so good next to mine. Chocolate and vanilla."

"Yeah, your ass is really light next to him, looking like a white girl."

"Don't go there, Sasha. I ain't that damn light, and he ain't that damn dark. You just don't like black men."

"Oh, please, Simone. I've gone out with dark-skinned men before."

"Oh, please. The darkest guy you went out with was Ralph in the eighth grade, and he was Dominican."

"He was dark."

"That nigga ain't dark. His ass was red."

"Ha ha ha ha!"

"Sasha, I'mma go downstairs and knock on Mommy's door and see what happens. You coming?"

"I don't want no part of that. She's gonna bust you in the head. You better leave her and her man alone. He probably got her ass up in the air."

"Yuck, I don't wanna think about that, Sasha. You're nasty." Simone went downstairs to do her dirt. I stayed upstairs in the bed and just gazed at my ring in awe. I was engaged to a lawyer. Wow. You just never know what life has in store for you. When you think you're at your lowest, somehow God seems to shine a light on you. Listen to me. I sound like my fiancé.

Chapter 10

It's been a week now, and I haven't heard back from the job or Maritza. I've called and left a message on her cell phone, but I haven't gotten a call back. I spent the weekend at Nick's house, and we talked a lot about the divorce and what I would need to do. He put me in touch with a divorce lawyer, whom I'm going to see today. We also took the rental back on Sunday, and now I'm driving his Mercedes truck.

Aunt Trudy left last weekend with Mr. Carter and hasn't been back since. She said she and Mr. Carter had some things to take care of and that she wouldn't be back for a couple of weeks. I wonder what's going on with them.

Simone's been staying over at TJ's house ever since last Thursday. Her ass is running from Richie. He came back in town on Friday and had been looking everywhere for her. Let me call her and tell her what's going on.

"Yes, Sasha?"

"Simone, you must be screening your calls. Girl, you know Richie's been looking for you."

"I know. That's why I'm over here. Did he come over there yet, Sasha?"

"No, but Tony called over here."

"What did you tell him, Sasha?"

"I told him that I haven't heard from you and that I think you and Aunt Trudy went somewhere together."

"Me and Mommy?"

"Girl, your mother's gone somewhere with Mr. Carter. She didn't even tell me she was going anywhere," I said, putting on my jeans. "I probably wouldn't know if I wasn't staying with her, Simone. She just got her bags together and left."

"What is going on with my mother?"

"Girl, she's been getting some. You know that shit makes you act different."

"Anyway, I don't know what to tell Richie, Sasha."

"All I know, Simone, is that I have to go and see this lawyer Nick hooked me up with. I have my own problems, Simone. I can't help you with yours. Where's TJ?"

"He went to work."

"He left you in there?"

"Girl, I've been here all week by myself. He goes wherever he has to go and comes and checks in on me or calls. Did you know he got one of them Lexus trucks? Shit is phat. That's what I wanna be driving. Shit, I don't want Richie to spot my car out on the road anywhere."

"Well, what are you gonna do, Simone? You gotta tell him something. You can't just let him keep looking for you. Here it is, Tuesday, and you've been running since, when, Friday. You know that ain't right."

"I'm scared of what he's gonna say."

"You know what I would do? I would tell Tony to talk to him."

"You know what, Sasha. That ain't a bad idea. Shit, I'll let my brother take care of it. Let me call him, and I'll call you back."

I don't know what she's gonna do, but I know if he comes knocking on this door, I ain't answering it. I don't have anything to do with this one. I didn't tell her to go fall for another man when she already had one. Even if he is a lawyer. She might need him when Richie busts her ass. Oh, shit, my cell phone is ringing. "Hello."

"Sasha, it's me."

"Maritza? Why do you sound like that?"

"'Cause, girl, you just don't know what's been going on. I couldn't call you 'cause Tray's been up my ass. He said he wants to know why I had to get in Tiffany and Jade's relationship. Girl, he hit me."

"He what? Did you call the cops?"

"No, 'cause he's still around. He's been up underneath me for almost a week now. I guess Jade went and told him that I sent Ramón to their house, and Tray is pissed. He said that he was gonna make sure I don't bother anybody else. I tried to lie and tell him that I didn't have anything to do with it, but he said he was gonna talk to Ramón and ask him who told him to go out there. I'm so scared. Oh, shit, girl, I gotta go." Maritza hung up, sounding really scared. I didn't know what to do except call Tray and let him know it was me that sent Ramón over there, before he gets a chance to talk to him. OK, let me call Tray.

"Yo."

"Oh, that's how you answer your phone now?"

"What the fuck do you want?"

"I just wanted to let you know I did some foul shit."

"You? Foul? Nah."

"I called Jade's boyfriend and told him where Jade lives in Rhode Island. See, I was mad with Tiffany, and I wanted to get back at her, so I told it."

"Bitch, you know what you did? You fucked up my shit. He took some shit from Jade that belongs to me. Now I gotta find this motherfucker and get it back."

"Some shit? Like what?"

"Don't worry about what shit it is. Just know you really fucked me up, Sasha. You really fucked up this time!" Tray hung up the phone. I had never heard him sound that mad. Just then, Simone called back on the house phone.

"Sasha, I told Tony, and he said he couldn't believe I was playing his boy like that. He said he didn't want to get in it 'cause he couldn't afford to get on Richie's bad side right now. He said he and Richie had a lot going on right now."

"Well, Simone, Maritza just called me and told me that Tray is up her ass because of some shit that went down with Tiffany. I didn't tell you before, but I told Tiffany about Jade and her boyfriend."

"Her boyfriend?"

"Oh, I didn't tell you about that either? She got a whole man."

"She does? So what happened?"

"I got Maritza to send that boy over to Tiff's house. I just called Tray to tell him that I set it up, and he said Ramón, that's the guy's name, took some shit from Jade that belonged to him. I didn't even know he was dealing like that."

"Girl, Tray got a lot of shit with him, doesn't he?"

"Yeah, he does, Simone. I'm so glad I'm getting away from him. All his shit is coming out of the woodworks."

"Sasha, now that you know this, are you still gonna leave TJ with him?"

"Girl, I didn't even think about that."

"Well, you better, before he gets your son mixed up in his shit. He'll be having him transporting shit soon."

"Simone, you really think Tray would do that to his own son?"

"Sasha, after all that's happened lately, I don't know what Tray would do. Do you?"

"You know, you're right about that."

"Yeah, I've been right about him from the start."

"Yeah, Simone, I guess you have. I just wanted to be in love with someone so bad I couldn't see what was right in front of my eyes. I just can't believe I gave that man fifteen years of my life before I opened my eyes."

"Who knows, Sasha, maybe if you stayed with Tray for as long as you did, you wouldn't have met Nick when you did. You know how Nathan's always talking about the order of things and how when you fuck with the order of one thing, you fuck up everything else. Maybe that's what would've happened if you didn't go with Tray for as long as you did."

"Whatever. All I know is, I want Tramaine Longston out of my life forever, if possible."

"Well, Sasha, I don't know about forever. Yall do have TJ, you know. You can't not speak to Tray. It just ain't gonna work that way. Yall bound together forever, whether you like it or not."

"Simone, I don't want to hear that right now. That just makes me feel worse about the whole thing. I'm just calling it like I see it. Simone, don't you have class today or something?"

"Oh, now you're trying to get rid of me. I ain't going anywhere. Richie's probably waiting at the school, for all I know."

"So what are you gonna do about him? Tony said he doesn't want any part of it, and I know you don't think you can hide forever. Just call him and tell him. Maybe you need to go out with him somewhere and let him know the deal."

"Girl, do you know how mad he's gonna be? He'll probably try to kill me."

"I think you're going too far now. I don't think he's gonna try to kill his boy's sister."

"Yeah, right. You don't know this man. All the money he done spent on me. He's gonna lose his mind when I tell him I don't wanna be with him anymore."

"Simone, hold on. Somebody is ringing the damn bell off. Let me look out the window and see who it is."

"All right, I hope it ain't Richie."

I looked out the window to see Mel's car. "Damn, it's Mel. I'll call you back."

"Sasha, you better take off that ring."

"Girl, I'm one step ahead of you." I put my ring in my robe pocket and went downstairs.

I opened the door. "Good—"

Before I could get anything else out, Mel interrupted me and said, "Sasha, I need to talk to you."

"About what, Melony?" I said. She looked very upset.

"Come upstairs. I have to jump in the shower right quick."

"What's going on?" I said, taking off my robe and jumping in the tub.

"Sasha, Alex left me," she said, starting to cry.

"What? What do you mean he left you?" I said, looking out from the shower curtain.

"Well, I thought maybe he had something to do on Saturday morning 'cause he left really early," she said while sitting on the toilet in the bathroom. "I woke up at seven thirty, and he was already gone. Now that I think about it, maybe he didn't even come home on Friday night. I don't know. I had a headache, and I went to bed early. Then I went to the bank to cash my check from my part-time job, and they told me I didn't have enough funds to cover the check and that maybe it would be a better idea if I went to the bank where the check was drawn, so I asked them to print me out a statement. I thought maybe I messed up with one of the bills or something. When they gave me the statement, it said my balance was zero. And the last withdrawal was Friday. I can't believe this."

"Melony, are you telling me that he cleaned out your whole account?"

"Yes, girl. The savings account and the checking account. He probably closed out all of them. My other accounts only have my name on them."

"Melony, what are you telling me?" I said, going upstairs.

"You haven't heard the worst of it, Sasha. I haven't seen Alezandria either. I think something may have happened to her. I can't take all this at once."

"When was the last time you saw her?"

"It was Friday morning. She told me that classes weren't going very well, and she was thinking about switching her major. Then I made her breakfast, and that was the last time I saw her. I called the cops on Sunday and put out a police report, but I haven't heard back from them."

"Why are you just telling anyone this now? Melony, maybe someone could have helped you look."

"I came to tell Mommy."

"Mel, your mother's not here. She left this weekend and said she would be out of town for a while."

"Out of town? Where did she go?"

"I don't know."

"Why is everyone disappearing?"

I didn't want to tell her that her mother left with Mr. Carter.

"I can't find my sister either. I haven't seen or heard from Simone since Friday too. Have you heard from her?"

"Uh, no, I haven't."

"Aren't you worried about Simone?"

"No, Simone's a big girl. She can handle herself. And besides, it's not the first time she's disappeared. You know she and Richie like to take off sometimes."

"Yeah, well, Richie's been by my house, and he hasn't seen her either. Has this family lost its mind? First, you, and now this."

"What do you mean first me? What do I have to do with all this?"

"Sasha, don't let me start on you, 'cause I still can't believe you left that boy with his father. He is your responsibility."

"Melony, I didn't have TJ by myself, you know. There are a lot of kids that live with their fathers instead of the traditional father. You know what, I don't have to justify my actions to you. You can't even find your child."

"That was some mean shit to say, Sasha."

"Oh, bitch, don't act like you don't say shit when you're ready. I've been wanting to give you a piece of my mind for a long time."

"What do you have to say to me, Sasha?"

"First of all, I am sick and tired of your ass living in your little dream world. You should have known something like this was gonna happen. Where do you think is your daughter?"

"I don't know, Sasha. Why don't you tell me?"

"She's with your husband. Haven't you noticed the way they look at each other?"

"What are you talking about, Sasha? You're talking stupid."

"Melony, Alezandria has been messing with your husband ever since she got titties. Don't act like you didn't notice this all these years."

"Well, they're all really close, and she does still sit on his lap. But, Sasha, that's his daughter."

"Melony, that is not his real daughter, and he never treated her like a daughter. What father buys tight jeans and back-out shirts for their eighteen-year-old daughter? None. He would be trying to cover her up, not expose her. Open your eyes. I mean, damn, Mel, I know I've been naive about some things, but not things going on in my own house. You are too wrapped up in your own world. Sometimes, you have to stop and check out what's going on around you."

"What about you, Sasha? Why are you and Tray getting a divorce? I heard the rumors about Tray having another girl and all that. Why didn't you see it?"

"Because he was good at covering up his tracks, and OK, maybe I was consumed with myself too, but at least he wasn't kissing her up and shit right in front of my face. You know what, Melony, this isn't getting us anywhere. Basically, we're both in a bad way right now, and instead of arguing, we should be trying to console each other."

"Yeah, Sasha, you're right. Regardless of whatever's going on, we are still family, and it's times like these that we need to stand by one another."

"So, Mel, what are you going to do?"

"Well, I guess the first thing I should do is see an attorney and find out what I can do about all this. Sasha, you really think he ran off with my daughter?"

"Mel, trust me on this one. You know what, Mel? I know a good divorce attorney you could talk to."

"Divorce? Do you think I should be thinking like that already?"

"Melony, it's time you came out of the dark and into the light. There is so much going on that you have no idea about."

"Like?"

"Like the fact that your Diana has a boyfriend and has been having sex for the last two years."

"How do you know that?"

"'Cause your girls tell me things they just won't tell you, and besides, AleZandria took her to get birth control last year, 'cause she was scared to ask you."

"But she's only fifteen."

"Yeah, I know that. But did you know she's been talking about having sex since she was thirteen?"

"What? Why didn't anyone tell me all this?"

"We knew you wouldn't believe it, and you would do what you always do."

"And what's that, Sasha?"

"Tell us that we're just jealous of your girls."

"Yeah, I guess I do say that a lot."

"Yeah, you do. And all this time, you guys were laughing in my face. That just ain't right."

"Well, you weren't right either. All those comments you used to make about how TJ is skinny and that I wasn't feeding him. You don't think the shit you say hurts me, but it does. I just don't react the way you do. If I say something to you, you tell everyone in the family and have them treating me like some kinda trader or something. Then you start to pull out all my flaws and try to get back at me for what I've said to you. But I don't do that. You've always been a big baby about things, Melony. I've wanted to tell you that for years. It's time to grow up and come out of your perfect little world. If you would only open your eyes, you would see that there's a lot going on right in front of your eyes."

"Yeah, well, I guess I do need to take a closer look at things."

"Start with Diana. If you just sit down and talk to her, you would see she's a lot more grown-up than you think. And she is very sneaky. She may not talk to you, but at least you know you tried."

"You're right, Sasha. How'd you get so smart?"

"I'm not so smart. If I was, I would have known that my husband was cheating on me and got somebody else pregnant."

"What? Get out of here. What? He got somebody pregnant? That's going too far now, Sasha. You do need to leave him. I always said that the only thing that could make me leave Alex is if he got someone else pregnant. I didn't think he would ever sleep with one of my children."

"That's just sick. He's a sick man, Melony. Alezandria told Simone that she found pictures of naked college girls in his lunch bag one day when you told her to clean it out for him. She said you wouldn't believe her if she told you, so there was no point in trying."

"What? Oh my god, Sasha, I don't wanna hear anymore. This is all just too much for me right now."

"Oh, damn, what time is it? I gotta go," I said, picking up the house phone to transfer it to my cell phone.

"Where are you going?"

"I have to go and meet with the lawyer."

"Sasha, you're really going through with it?"

"You're damn right I am. Do I look stupid to you?" I ran out of the house with my pocketbook and cell phone in hand.

"I guess I'll leave with you."

"All right. If you need anything, just call me." *I probably shouldn't put my ring back on,* I thought, getting into the truck. I wouldn't want the lawyer to think I wanted this divorce just because I met someone else. I wonder how much Nick told him about what's going on. I did tell him quite a bit about my marriage last weekend. Maybe I should call him and find out. "Hello, Nick."

"Hey, baby, on your way to see the lawyer?"

"Yeah. What time are you supposed to be there?"

"At eleven. It's only ten fifteen. I have a little time to get there. It's good that you're going early."

"I have a question for you, Nick. What did you tell Attorney Peterson about the case? Did you tell him any details of the marriage or the breakup?"

"No, Sasha, that's not my place to do that. That's for you to sit down and talk to him about."

"Oh, OK. I'm so nervous."

"All I told him is that I have a friend that is looking for a good attorney. He told me he would do your case pro bono since he needed to get one under his belt. I've only known him for a couple of years, you know, but we've worked hand in hand on a lot of cases together. Yeah, I've spent a lot of long nights deliberating with that man over pots of coffee. He's a good man, Sasha. You don't have anything to worry about. He'll take good care of you. Don't you know I would only send my girl to the best?"

"Yeah, baby, I know."

"Anyway, I have to go now. I need to get some work done."

"Yeah, I need to get off this phone too, baby. There's a cop driving at the back of me. I don't want him to see me on the phone. I love you, Nick, and thank you."

"I love you too, Sasha. Have a good day."

When I got to the lawyer's office, I was surprised to see that Attorney Peterson was an old white man. I thought for sure he was a brother. We had a long talk about everything involved in the case, and he said that if I could prove the baby Maritza was carrying was Tray's, it would make my case even stronger. He said he needed to get an investigator to research him and find out what other assets he may have that I know nothing about. I figured if I was going to go for it, I may as well know exactly who I'm dealing with. Tray was very secretive. You know how those Virgos are. You would never know anything is going on with them until they get caught. And even then, they deny it or try to defend it by saying it was somehow your fault that they did whatever it was they did.

I called Simone when I got back in my car. I wanted to go to TJ's house and see how she was doing—and also to be nosy. I wonder what his place looks like. Simone didn't answer her phone, but she did call me right back. "Why didn't you answer your phone?"

"Girl, I was in the shower. I didn't hear it until it stopped ringing. What's up?"

"I just got back from the lawyer. I was in there for, like, two-and-a-half hours."

"You talked to him that long?"

"Well, I had to wait till he was done talking to somebody else first."

"What did he say?"

"He told me I had a pretty good chance of taking him for everything he had if I could prove that girl was carrying his baby."

"So you know what that means, girl? You need to go and see her and try to get her to talk him into taking a test."

"I'm tired of the tricks, Simone. I'm just gonna let the chips fall where they may. I don't wanna get myself in deeper shit with Tray than I'm in right now. He already wanna kill me."

"Sasha, he's just mad right now. That's all. You know as soon as he calms down, he'll be calling you again, begging you to come home."

"I don't think so this time. He was serious. I've never heard him sound like that, not in the almost-twenty years that I've known him. So, Simone, where does this brother live? I wanna come and check out his house."

"Oh, you're not coming to see me? You're just coming to be nosy?"

"Yeah, something like that. I mean, I am coming to check on you too."

"Yeah, right. You see, when you get to Nick's house, all you have to do is go three streets past his house, make a right, and it's the seventh house on the left. It's in 89 Trailway Drive. The one with all the trees at the driveway and the rooster mailbox."

"A rooster mailbox? What's that all about, Simone?"

"Girl, I don't know. I guess he likes the manly look of the rooster." We both laughed.

"OK, well, I'll be there in a little while. Do you need anything?"

"No, I'm good. I have everything I need."

"I'm sure you do." I hung up, thinking how sudden everything was happening: the man, the divorce, me living with Aunt Trudy, me talking things out with Mel. This is all very strange, but I suppose change is good. It's bringing me to a new chapter in my life.

As I was pulling into the driveway, my phone rang. Unknown number. "Who is this?" I answered the phone, pleasantly surprised. "Hello. Who is this? Who is this?"

"It's Maggie."

"Maggie? Hi, it's Sasha."

"Didn't I call Mommy's house?"

"Yeah, I transferred the phone to my cell phone."

"Oh, OK, are you staying there now?"

"Oh, girl, yeah, there's a lot going on right now."

"What happened to Tray and TJ?"

"They still live in East Lyme."

"What? What the hell is going on out there?"

"Well, you know, Maggie, something is always going on out here. Isn't that why you left? To get away from all of us? I haven't heard from you in, what, seven years. You better be glad Auntie never changed her house phone number, or else you would have to come out here."

"Sasha, don't make things sound that horrible. I've been going through a lot out here."

"What's going on?"

"I just got out of the hospital. They said I need to take a break from dancing, if I could take a break from the fast-paced life of New York."

"What happened to you?"

"I had a nervous breakdown, and I'm having problems eating."

"You always did have a problem eating. Are you still skinny as a rail?"

"No, I look all right. I could probably lose a pound or two. I need to come home, Sasha." She started crying. "I need to make amends with my family and try to do something different. It's killing me."

"Well, your mother is gone for a couple of weeks. She went out of town."

"Where?"

"Girl, don't start me to lying. I don't have the slightest idea. All I know is, she left me in charge of the house. All the bills are paid, and the freezer is full with food."

"Well, Sasha, I'm taking the bus out there. Do you think you could meet me at the bus station?"

"What time are you coming?"

"I'll be there at about five."

"OK. Just call me."

"All right. Thanks, cuz. And . . . I love you."

"I love you too, Maggie. See you later."

I called Simone.

"Sasha, why are you calling me again? Would you just come on already?"

"Simone, guess who just called me."

"Who? Richie?"

"No, you will never guess."

"Just tell me, Sasha. I don't know who. It could be anybody."

"Maggie."

"My sister, Maggie?"

"Yep. She's on her way out here. Says she's sick or something. She said she just got out of the hospital, and they told her that she needed to leave the big city for a while."

"Serves her ass right. That's what she gets for running to New York by her damn self in the first place. Talking 'bout she wanna be a dancer. I mean, don't get me wrong, Sasha. I'm not knocking out the girl's dream. But she could've at least called her mother."

"She thought she was too good to call any of us, Simone. Well, now she needs us, and you know we can't turn our backs on her. She's just a baby."

"Just a baby? What is she now? Twenty-five? She ain't a baby. She's a grown woman. She's gonna have to explain to me why she thought she was too good to . . ."

"OK, Simone, you said it's which house now?"

"Oh, you're on the street. It's the seventh house. Number 89. It's on that rooster mailbox. I'll go outside. See you in a minute."

I pulled up into the long driveway. The house was on the top of a hill like all the houses in this neighborhood. Shit, the town of Simsbury was on a hill.

Simone was sitting outside on a cement bench that was attached to the house by the doorway. "Hey, girl, park on the side over there." She directed me to an open space of pavement next to the Lex. "Oh, bitch, what did you do? Trade the BMW in for this?"

"No, girlfriend, this is my man's car," I said, getting out of the Mercedes.

"You didn't even tell me. See how you can keep a secret."

"Ooh, Simone, this house is nice," I said, changing the subject.

"Ain't it though? He's got a lot more land in the front than Nick."

"Yeah, but not in the back."

"He has his on the side. You see that shit?" she said, showing me the side of the house. "He has a full-length basketball court, with a fence going around it."

"Damn."

"Girl, he got a Jacuzzi in his bedroom and a sauna off the back of the kitchen. You know what else? He got an indoor swimming pool. It ain't really big like Nick's, but it's long. You know, like, them ones you practice laps in. Come inside."

When I went in, he had mirrors all over the place by the front door, with a big fish tank like Nick's. His took up one whole wall. Then he had a sunken living room, and his pool was in a room off the living room, with a full gym. "Nice," I said, looking around. "This brother's got style."

"Come in the kitchen," Simone said, leading the way like she was a realtor. His whole kitchen was done in black porcelain, and the floor was that black-and-white tile. This all so phat. Everything in Nick's place was wood. It was beautiful, but this was ghetto fabulous. I guess Simone was right. He was ghetto. We sat down at the kitchen table, with a big-ass rooster on it.

"Simone, what is up with your man and roosters?"

"Girl, I told you, he got a thing for them. You know what? So anyway, Sasha, what were you saying about my trifling little sister now?"

"Nothing. She wants me to pick her up at the bus station at five."

"Why did she call you, and how did she get your number?"

"I transferred Auntie's phone to my cell."

"Oh. OK. I was gonna say."

"Simone, stop being jealous."

"So what do you think, Sasha? Does this life look me?"

"Sure does, Moni. Ghetto fabulous."

"Right. I told you he and I were a lot alike."

"I can't believe it. You're talking about all this shit. Did you decide how you were gonna tell Richie it was over between yall?"

"Girl, I've been thinking about this shit all morning. I don't know what to do. I'm so scared of what he's gonna say."

"You just gotta tell him. It really doesn't make any sense in waiting. The more time that goes by, the worse it's gonna be."

"I know, right? I just don't know how to break it to him."

"Just tell him you need some time to yourself. Tell him you've been thinking about y'all getting married, and you don't really think you're ready for all that. Where's your ring anyway?"

"Girl, I ain't 'bout to wear that ring in front of TJ. I do not want him to know all that. Shit, I'm trying to get one from him."

"Well, don't count on it."

"I'm not. I'm just playing this thing one day at a time. The more time I spend with him, the more I'm realizing that I almost settle for less than I deserve. I don't deserve to be going with some man that sells drugs for a living and only spends time with me when he ain't got anything else to do. Shit, he doesn't even take me out anywhere. All he does is give me money and disappear again. I thought that was enough for me, but it's not. I want more than that. Shit, TJ and I watch movies together. He cooks for me. He gives me massages. Shit I only dreamed of a man who would do that for me, and I don't even ask him to. He's just like that."

"Has his phone rung?"

"No, I think he transferred his calls to his cell phone or something, 'cause that shit hasn't rung once since I've been here."

"So what does that mean?"

"It means he doesn't want me talking to anybody that might call his house. I mean, he done already told me about the girl and, shit, how she left."

"Oh, shit, Simone, speaking of 'left,' Alex done left Melony."

"Get out!"

"No, sir!"

"What?"

"He left, and guess who he left with?"

"Who? Alezandria?"

"Yep. See, I told Mel she was the only person that didn't see that coming. She said she never noticed the way they looked at each other."

"Shit, Sasha, she should've known that as soon as he started buying her them sexy clothes. He wasn't even buying for his damn wife."

"That's what I'm saying."

"Well, what is she gonna do?"

"I told her she needed to get an attorney."

"Yeah, you're just promoting attorneys now."

"No, for real. He cleaned out their joint accounts and everything."

"What? You're lying, Sasha! He did that? Oh, damn. He did her dirty. Where do you think they went?"

"Girl, you're asking me. Ain't no telling with his crazy ass. You know he ain't wrapped tight. Running away with a nineteen-year-old. Simone, now you know that's sick."

"Well, Sasha, Mel did have her when she was, what, fifteen. It's like he grew up with the two of them."

"That's what I was thinking, and you know, he never treated her like she was his. See, I told you, Simone, you should've been trying to talk that girl out of all that stuff she used to tell you about him. How he used to watch her take a shower and how she caught him jerking off to one of her pictures."

"What could I do, Sasha? I tried to get her to go away to college, but he wouldn't let her go, and you know Mel was on his side. I couldn't do anything else about it."

"You should've told Mel."

"You know she wouldn't believe anything I was telling her. She already thinks I talk bad about how she raises her kids. She wouldn't ever listen to anything I say. Plus, I'm younger. According to her, I don't know shit."

"Well, she's still your sister, and you should try to be there for her."

"Be there for her? What the fuck done got into you, Sasha?"

"Nothing. I just had a good talk with Melony, and we came to an understanding about a couple of things."

"Oh, yall did, did yall?"

"Yes, we did, and you know what? None of us is perfect, and we all could learn a thing or two from each other if we would just stick together and stop tearing each other down."

"Whatever, Dr. Sasha. All of a sudden, you know so much. I guess that lawyer sperm done got to your brain."

"Simone, you're so damn nasty."

"So? TJ likes it."

"Speaking of TJ, what time is he coming home?"

"Shit, I gotta put that roast in the oven."

"What roast?"

"Sasha, I was cooking for him."

"Shit, I might as well die here. Who would've thought I would see the day when Simone turns into a happy homemaker?"

"Fuck you, bitch. Who would see the day when I had a man worth cooking for? Richie's ass sure wasn't worth it, and he sure didn't come to my house enough for anything but a movie and some pussy. In that order."

"Simone, you really need to brush up on your vocabulary. Does every word you use have to be a cussword?"

"Whatever, Ms. Proper Diction. Sasha, I wonder what my mother's gonna say when she comes back and sees Maggie here. Her ass will probably be happy."

"Oh, you think so, Simone? You don't know your mother is living her life. She ain't got time for anybody and their problems. Trust me, she's in her own little world. If I know your mother, she ain't gonna be happy about having to help Maggie get on her feet and interrupting her flow."

"Her flow?"

"Yeah, I'm trying to tell you, she and Mr. Carter are getting it on. For real."

"I thought I told you I didn't wanna hear that shit."

"Doesn't anybody wanna hear about Mommy and her lover getting it on?"

"That shit is just plain nasty. Old asses rolling around in the bed. Yuck."

"I don't know why you think it's so nasty. Aunt Trudy got a right to get her freak on too."

"Sasha, just shut up with that shit. I done told you already, I don't wanna hear that."

"What time is it?"

"It's, like, three thirty."

"You know what, Simone, I need to find out what I'm gonna do for work. I can't just live off Aunt Trudy or Nick. I don't want him saying I ain't worth anything, and I definitely don't want him to think I don't have a mind of my own."

"Well, what do you wanna do with yourself?"

"I was thinking about painting or maybe writing that book I talked about, like, ten years ago. I still have the thoughts in my head."

"You're still talking about writing a book? You're so white. Black girls do not write books."

"Whatever, Simone, you're so damn ghetto. I know a lot of black authors. What about Deana Nelson? She's a black author, and she comes from out here."

"She wasn't born here though. She was born in New York."

"Yeah, but she still lives out here now."

"Yeah, whatever, Sasha. You write your damn book then."

"Or maybe I'll open a museum and get some local artwork together. You never know. Shit, my man got money. As long as he sees potential, he might wanna help me."

"All I know, Sasha, is that I'm 'bout to make sure I get a couple of trips out of this brother. Shit, you never know when he's gonna get tired and give me the boot. At least I could say I went to Japan or Hawaii or something. I'm going somewhere, even if I gotta go by my damn self. He's gonna send me. I ain't no fool. Shit, he hasn't given me a ring."

"Maybe if you act like you got some damn sense, he would, Simone."

"Look, I ain't sitting around, playing the phony role to get a ring. I know damn well I can't keep that shit up long. This is me, and if he doesn't like me the way I am, then oh well. I guess that will just be the end of us."

"Is that how you really feel, Simone? You really think he's just taking you for a ride?"

"I don't know, but what I do know is, I only have one life to live, and if I don't try to live it to the fullest, I'll die with tons of regrets."

"So if you think TJ is taking you for a ride, why would you break up with Richie?"

"To be honest with you, Sasha, I've been trying to break up with Richie for the longest. I just didn't know how to do it, and I never had a good enough reason."

"Oh, now you have a reason?"

"Well, yes and no. If nothing comes out of this relationship with TJ, I can always fly solo. Shit, there's a lot of men that are coming on to me, and I don't wanna talk to them 'cause I'm scared they might know Richie. I'm tired of living like that."

"Oh my god, Simone, I didn't know you were like that. Here I am, thinking you really like this guy, and all along, you're just using him to get away from another guy. You are sick in your head. You need to just be a woman and tell them all where they can go shit. What are they gonna do? You ain't married to any of them. The worst that can happen is that you have to get serious with your life, finish school, and get a real job. When was the last time you went to class?"

"I'll pick up back where I left off next semester."

"You say that 'every semester,' and every semester keeps going by, and you still ain't finished. It's only a four-year college, you know. Not a twenty-year."

"Yeah, yeah, now you sound like my mother. I don't wanna hear that from you too. Ain't it five yet? Don't you need to go and get Maggie?"

"You're not gonna come with me?"

"No. I'm cooking. I ain't going anywhere."

"Let me get out of here and go get this chick."

When I was getting in the truck, my phone rang. "Hello."

"I'm here."

"Oh, you're early?"

"Yeah, I took the express bus."

"I'm on my way right now." Simone looked out the door at me. "She's here. I'll talk to you later."

"Yeah, all right, ho. Catch you later."

I wonder how Maggie is gonna look now. When she left, she was so damn skinny. She had to be about 110 pounds. Now she said she put on weight, which is not that hard to do, being in this family. We all have to try really hard not to gain. Shit, if I look at food, I gain weight. With my big ass. I heard my phone ringing again. It's Nick.

"Hey, baby."

"Hi."

"How did your meeting with the lawyer go?"

"It went OK. Nick, you didn't tell me Attorney Peterson was gonna be an old white man."

"You didn't ask. Does it matter?"

"No, I was just expecting to see a brother."

"No, there's only three brothers. Me, TJ, and Andrew. He's the newest one on board. I think he just got out of school or something. I don't know the whole story, but everyone else there is white."

"Andrew? Andrew what?"

"Why? Do you know someone named Andrew?"

"My cousin used to date someone named Andrew a while back."

"Who? Simone?"

"No, Tiffany."

"But I thought you said your cousin was gay."

"Yeah, but she wasn't always gay."

"Well, I don't think it's this guy. He's really young."

"Oh. He is?"

"Anyway, what are you doing now?"

"I have to go and get my cousin from the bus stop."

"Another cousin?"

"Yes, this is the one I didn't tell you about because she moved to New York right out of high school. She never kept in touch with anybody, so we don't really talk about her."

"Oh, Sasha, that's sad. I don't care how bad my family is. I would never disown them."

"Yeah, especially since now she needs us, being as how she's sick and all."

"Sick? What's wrong with her?"

"I'm not exactly sure. All I know is that she is stressed out or something, and she hasn't been eating right. A doctor told her that she needed to get away from the big city for a while, and that's the only reason why she's coming home."

"Well, you never know what wind blows you back in the right direction. I mean, hey, look at us."

"Yeah, I guess you're right."

"Anyway, baby, I got to go now. I got a lot of work to do. I won't be home until later on tonight. I'll give you a call before I leave the office."

"OK, sweetie, see you later."

"Hey, Sasha."

"Yes, Nick."

"I love you, beautiful."

"I love you. Talk to you later. Bye." Oh, man, I'm really falling for this man.

When I pulled up at the bus stop, I didn't see Maggie anywhere in sight. I couldn't call her back because she didn't leave a number. I think she called from a pay phone or something. I don't know. I parked the car and had to go into the station. There she was, sitting on the bench, looking pitiful. I can't believe how emaciated she is. She couldn't be more than ninety pounds. And she said she gained weight. I'd sure like to see what she looked like before.

"Hi, Sasha," she said, picking up her bag and flinging her fake hair that was down to her butt behind her.

"Hi, Maggie. Long time no see."

"Yeah, I know it has been a long time."

"Well, let's get you home. Are you hungry?"

"No, not really."

"Well, you look like you could eat something. I'll stop and get something on the way. I haven't eaten anything all day anyway."

Maggie looked really bad. She didn't look like one of Aunt Trudy's kids at all. Her face was skin and bones. I couldn't imagine ever looking like that. I mean, here she was, five foot seven and ninety pounds. That just didn't look right at all. And I think she sees herself fat. She did tell me she could stand to lose a few pounds. I'm gonna have to keep a close eye on her. On the way, we stopped at Mickey D's. She didn't want anything but some diet soda. "You better eat, girl. Do you know you look smaller than when you left?"

"No, I'm not."

"Yes, you are, Maggie. You're a lot smaller. You don't even look like Simone anymore. I remember when everyone thought you and Simone were twins. Do you remember that? Now you're half of her, and she's already skinny."

"Whatever, Sasha. You always had something to say about my weight. Why can't you understand? I can't be a fat dancer."

"Shit, you can't be a dead dancer either."

"I'm not going to die."

"No, you're not 'cause I'm not gonna let you." I pulled up into the driveway of Aunt Trudy's house. "Wait until your mother sees you. She is gonna be so mad that you haven't been taking care of yourself."

"I take care of myself, Sasha. Just because I don't eat a whole bunch of food, yall always saying I'm not taking care of myself. Well, I am. Better than you know too."

"Yeah, I bet. How? With drugs? You look like you've been doing some."

"Now I remembered why I left. Damn, can I get a break? Why are you sweatin' me? I came home to make my life better, not worse. I don't wanna hear shit from you."

"From me? Wait till the rest of the family sees you. Don't worry, you won't have to take shit from just me."

"You make me wanna get right back on the next bus outta here."

"Go ahead, and you'll die right there in New York in some hospital room. You don't like to hear the truth, Maggie, but I'mma tell you anyway. The truth is, you never wanted to listen to anyone. You've always wanted to do things your way. Your way has never seemed to amount to much. You went all the way to New York to be a dancer and ended up being a secretary in some law office. You said that that damn boy in New York loved you so much, and he left and went to Hollywood with that damn hippie girl at the drop of a dime. We know all about what's been going on with you out there. You don't have to call and tell anyone."

"Yeah, I know, Sasha, 'cause all yall do is sit around and talk about my life all day."

"Girl, do you see that I'm driving? Do I look like I've been sitting around focused on your successes and failures? Please don't flatter yourself. I have my own life to worry about, and it doesn't include every crisis that takes shape in yours. So if you think you wanna get on that bus and go back where you came from, just let me know. Otherwise, I'll drop you off at your momma's house 'cause I got things to do."

"Sasha, I'm sorry. I didn't mean it like that. It's just that I feel a lot of pressure to be this perfect person all the time from this family."

"You're not the only one that feels that. You're just the only one that ran away. I hear shit all the time, but I don't give a damn. I'mma do whatever the hell I wanna do whenever the hell I wanna do it, and if anybody in this family or any other family doesn't like it, oh well, too bad. I'm not running away from anything. I may make the necessary changes in my life to survive, but I ain't running from anybody. Family or not. You got to be strong, Maggie, I know it ain't easy being a part of this family, but it's the only family you got, so you can either take it or die alone."

"Well, I'm here, aren't I?"

"Yeah, you're here, but do you hear what I'm saying to you? You look sick, and we better fatten you up some before your mother sees you. Shit, she's gonna have a heart attack."

"Sasha, I just don't know what to do."

"Let's talk more when we get in the house," I said, pulling into the driveway and getting out of the car.

"Oh lord," Maggie said, sitting there for a moment. "This is really hard for me to do."

"What is? Maggie, come on."

"Sasha, a lot of things happened in this house that I don't care to remember."

"Like what?"

"I don't want to talk about it right now. Maybe one day."

"Well, whenever you're ready to talk about anything, I'm here to listen. You may find that the others are not as receptive to you at first. They're still mad with you. I know Simone and Tony are, for sure. Maybe Mel won't feel that way. She's going through a lot right now. Maybe you're just what she needs."

"Yeah, you think so? I'll have to call her when I get my stuff situated."

"Yeah, Maggie, why don't you do that?"

Maggie had moved back into her old room. There were five bedrooms in the house: four upstairs and one on the first floor. Aunt Trudy had the girls upstairs and the boys in the basement, which was finished. She thought it was best to separate all the girls and let the guys share the basement, since it was split off into three rooms anyway. Then when I came along, hung around with Simone so much anyway, I shared a room with her. I guess that's why we're the closest now. All the rest of the sisters are split up, doing their own thing. Aunt Trudy's second husband paid off the house before he died, so now all Aunt Trudy has to pay is the taxes and utilities. Pretty good deal, I'd say. Now she has Mr. Carter. I'm sure she doesn't have to pay for anything now. Long as she treats Mr. Carter right, he's the type of Jamaican that will take care of a woman. I just know I'mma find myself somebody just like him, even if he's not Jamaican.

"Well, I really do have to go now," I said, looking at my watch. "Call me if you need anything."

"Sasha, thanks, and I am sorry for the way I came off on you."

"Like I said, Maggie, I know it's tough being in this family. Just hang in there and stop running away from everything. Sometimes, you just have to face things in order for them to get better." On that note, I went out the door. I need to call my man and find out what's going on with him. It was almost seven o'clock. "Hey, Nick."

"Hey, beautiful. I was just getting out. Where are you?"

"I'm just leaving my aunt's house. I had to drop my cousin off."

"Meet me at the house. I have someone I'd like you to meet."

"Who?"

"Just come to the house. Oh, by the way, TJ and Simone will be there. I told Simone to meet us over there. TJ is just getting off too."

"Oh, OK. I didn't know you had something all planned out. That's nice. Well, I guess I'll see you there in a little while, right?"

"Yes, baby, I'll see you in a little while."

This man always has something up his sleeve. I never know what to expect from him. It feels so good to have a man that is always thinking about how to surprise me. Tray never did anything like that. He was always too focused on his own damn shit to be interested in me.

I tried to call Simone on my way over to Nick's house, but I got no answer. Her voice mail didn't even come on. I wonder what's going on. When I got to Nick's house, there was a silver Cadillac in the driveway along with Nick's and TJ's cars. *Whose car is that?* I thought to myself. I went in the side door since that was the door I had a key to now. Everyone was in the living room. When I walked in, I always shit on myself. It was Andrew. The Andrew that Tiffany had been with so long ago. I knew he was younger than her, and I had a feeling that's why I was asking so many questions. I just didn't want to pursue it. I might have made Nick feel like something had gone on with me and him. Simone looked at me and opened her eyes really wide as if to say, "Girl, do you see who's sitting here?" I tried to ignore her.

"Well, Sasha, nice to see you again," Andrew said when I entered the room. Nick sat on the love seat, just looking at me and waiting for my response.

"Hi, Andrew. How've you been?"

"Oh, I've been fine. Boy, this sure is a small world," he said, sipping on his drink.

"It sure is," Simone said, crossing her legs from one side to the other.

"So, Simone, how's your sister been?"

"Who? You mean Tiffany?"

"You know I mean Tiffany. Who else would I be talking about?"

"Oh, ah, she's fine. She lives in Rhode Island now. Has a house out there and everything."

"Does she now? I'd love to see her again," he said, sounding ultra-feminine. Now I see why they got along. He was the girl, and Tiff was the man. They made the perfect couple, until he moved away to go to law school.

"So I heard you just finished law school. I thought you have finished a long time ago," Simone said, looking his soft ass up and down.

"I went out there to Texas and got sidetracked. You know how that goes." Andrew sat with his leg crossed over the other one, drink in hand, with his elbow resting on his knee. How much more gay could he look? I wonder if he is.

"So, Sasha, how long have you and Andrew known each other?"

"Oh, we met as teenagers, during the time he was dating my cousin."

"Your cousin, Tiffany?"

"Yes, Nick," I said, giving him the look as if to say, "Don't let the cat out of the bag."

"Um. So when was the last time you saw Tiffany, Andrew?" TJ asked.

"Oh, it's been almost seven years now. When I left to go to Texas, I lost track of her. She didn't seem to want to keep up the relationship. You know it's hard to love long-distance."

"Yeah, I can only imagine," Nick said. "I'm so glad my lady is here with me. I don't know if I could stand commuting to go and see her."

"So how long have you two been together," Andrew asked, leaning forward.

"Oh, it's been a while now, right, Sasha?" Nick said, smiling at me.

"Yeah, I can't keep track."

"Oh, that good. Oh, I see, and how long have yall been together, Simone?"

"Oh, we just met a couple of weeks ago."

"Oh, for real? Yall mighty tight. Looks like yall made a love connection. Look good together and everything."

"Yeah, sometimes you get lucky and find that special one when you're not even looking," TJ said, looking at Simone. She must have really laid it on him good 'cause he was whooped. Just as whooped as Nick was. I wondered if this was all some sort of game the two of them were playing. It made me think. We're both staying at their houses, driving their cars, all in a matter of weeks. I wanted to believe it was all good, but something just didn't feel right. Now they bring this gay-ass man over here that they work with, and Nick doesn't even bother to mention to me that he's gay or appears to be anyway. What the hell is going on? "Can you excuse me for a minute? I have to use the little girls' room," I said, getting up to leave the room.

"Yeah, me too," Simone said, following me. "You know ladies travel in pairs."

When we got in the bathroom, I turned on the water and started laughing. "Girl, is he as gay as he wanna be, or am I just imagining the tattooed eyebrows and the bend in his pinky finger?"

"Sasha, that motherfucker is as gay as he wanna be. I can't believe the guys would even keep company with him. You know that shit doesn't look good. See, that's the difference between rich niggas and ghetto ones. I know Richie wouldn't be caught dead with anybody like him, and you know Tray wouldn't either."

We both went back into the living room.

"I took the liberty of ordering some Chinese food for all of us. I got a variety of items to choose from. Something, I'm sure, for everyone. It would be nice to have dinner out on the patio. Got to try and soak up whatever hot days we have left. You know what I mean?" Nick said, leading us out to the back by the pool. "I'll be out there in just a moment. Sasha, could you come into the kitchen with me?"

I went into the kitchen and saw what looked like enough food to feed everyone at one of our family picnics. "Nick, why did you get so much food?"

"It's not a lot. Just a couple of boxes for each thing. I got some boneless ribs, garlic chicken, some fried chicken, fried fish, curry shrimp, fried rice, plain rice, with pork and with shrimp. Oh, and there are some egg rolls in that box over there. What should we serve with it? Soda or juice?"

"Why don't you just bring out all four kinds of soda you got here and that fruit punch we got last weekend? That should be more than enough."

"OK, you get the plates, forks, and glasses, and I'll bring out all the food. Is that OK?"

"Sure, when you go out there with the food, call Simone to come and help me with the glasses."

"All right, baby."

When Simone came into the kitchen, she was looking at me the same way I had looked at the counter when I first came into the kitchen. "Girl, that's enough food to feed a small army."

"I know that's right, Simone. He really went all out."

"Yeah, and I made that damn man dinner back at his house. He's gonna tell me we can eat it tomorrow. You don't know how burnt I was."

"Oh, oh, is this the first time he pissed you off?"

"Yeah, and from the looks of things, I'm sure it's not the last. It seems like whenever Nick says jump, TJ jumps."

"You really think that's the case?"

"I don't know if it is, but if that's what's going on, girl, we gotta nip that in the butt. I can't have a punk for a man. Being pushed around by my cousin's man. That doesn't even sound right. I'm starting to think this shit wasn't such a good idea. You and me having men that know each other."

"Why, Simone? You can't stand the pressure?"

"It ain't pressure like what you think. I just don't wanna be competing for TJ for affection with Nick."

"With Nick? You talk like they're lovers or something."

"Girl, nowadays, I don't put it past any man. When a man spends more time with his boy than his girl, it's time to examine the situation."

"Oh, Simone, you're overreacting as usual. We better get back out there before they come in here and get us."

"Oh, shit, I forgot all about them niggas," Simone said, grabbing the plates and heading for the side door.

"Damn, ladies, I thought you forgot all about us," TJ said, grinning. "I'm hungry."

Yeah, you wouldn't be if you ate the food I cooked you, Simone thought to herself. She was really in a bad way over the whole cooking thing. I can understand where she's coming from though. See, even though Simone knows how to cook, it's a rare treat when she does. That was the good thing about her being with Richie. He did all the cooking, or they went out to eat most times. That's why her ass is so damn slim. If Richie doesn't feed her, she will live off fruits and sandwiches.

"So, Simone, what do you do now?" Andrew asked.

"Oh, I'm going to school now."

"What do you aspire to be?"

"I'd like to be a physical therapist."

"Oh, that's an admirable profession," Andrew said, sounding as gay as he wanna be.

"Well, I wanted to do something to help people, and I am not the blood type of girl, so I couldn't go into the medical field. You know, like become a doctor or even a nurse or something. So I decided on this one."

"You know, I didn't even know that about you," Nick said, looking amazed that Simone had a goal. Little did he know, she had been trying to obtain this degree for the last, what, ten years.

"So how much further do you have to go?" Andrew asked.

"Well, see, that's the thing. I had to go part-time because that's all I got a scholarship for, and I also work. It's taken a lot longer than I had originally anticipated."

Boy, Simone almost sounded intelligent there for a change.

"I know how that can be," Andrew said. "Remember back when I was dating your sister, I was going to school, and then I went to Texas. I got all sidetracked, and then when I came back up here, I had to start all over again. I never knew how hard it would be. I just knew that if I didn't make a decision to do something, I would be sleeping in an alley somewhere."

"Oh, Andrew, I doubt very seriously with your smarts, you would end up living in an alley," I said, thinking about how ridiculous that just sounded. The more I listened to him talk, the more I realized he was a drama queen. And a better one than even Melony was. She could complain like nobody's business. I can't believe Nick and TJ were sitting here, listening to this man talk about his life in the manner in which he was speaking. His voice totally repulsed me. I couldn't wait till this dinner was over.

"Mmm, these ribs are so good," TJ said, licking his fingers. "Where did you order this food from, Nick?"

"Just a little place in the center of Simsbury. I didn't think it was all that good, and one night, I ordered some egg foo yong. Man, you know how I love that. It was the best I had ever tasted, and you know, I've had Chinese food from everywhere you could think of." Nick and TJ looked at each other and laughed. Was that supposed to be some secret code or something? Simone was right; they were kinda weird. Almost as if Nick was the puppet master and TJ was the puppet. Laugh, puppet, laugh. Ha ha ha ha ha. I looked at Simone, and she raised her eyebrow. I knew exactly what she was thinking. Maybe I didn't know what I was getting myself into.

"Oh, the time is going fast," Andrew said, looking at his watch. "I was supposed to be somewhere. Well, I guess I have to be going now," he said, getting up from the couch. "Thank you so much for having me over. It was marvelous."

"Yeah, man, it was, really," TJ said.

"All right, we'll see you at work, man," Nick said, walking him to the front door.

"Bye," I said.

"Nice seeing you again, Simone."

"Talk to ya, man," TJ said.

After Nick closed the door, he came back into the living room where we were all sitting and burst out laughing. "Damn, TJ, he is really a fruitcake, isn't he?"

"Man, I told you."

"Oh," Simone said, "so you guys thought so too?"

"Hell yeah," TJ said, looking at Simone. "What, you think we're stupid? I knew he was a little soft around the edges at work, but to see him out of the work environment is a whole different story. He is too damn soft."

"Yeah, he must be the girl," Nick said, laughing. "Oh, sorry, Sasha," Nick said, looking at Sasha's reaction.

"Oh, I think something's wrong with the brother too. Any man that can cross his legs better than I can is funny," Simone said, laughing.

"Well, ladies, it's only nine o'clock. What do you suggest we do with the rest of our evening together?" Nick said, looking at me and grinning.

"Well, man," TJ said, standing up, "I gotta go. I need to catch up on some sleep."

"Oh, yeah, me too," Simone said, looking at TJ. "I really need to go and check on my cousin. See if there's anything she needs."

"Why don't you just call her, Sasha?" Nick said, looking at me with lust in his eyes. I know what he wanted, but I really wasn't in the mood for it.

"I'll talk to you later, man," TJ said, grabbing Simone's hand and heading for the door.

"Later, guys. Thanks for dinner and the entertainment," Simone said, laughing on her way walking out.

I went up out to the car and got my cell phone. I never bring it in the house with me. I hate to be interrupted when I'm with Nick. I had two messages on my phone: one from Maggie and one from Maritza. Maggie wanted to know what time I was coming back to the house, and Maritza sounded like she was crying again. I am getting tired of babysitting this woman. Just think about it. Here she is, pregnant with my soon-to-be ex-husband's baby, and she's looking for me to protect her from the world. Shouldn't it be the other way around? She got herself into this shit. I have a good mind to let her rough it on her own. As a matter of fact, I'm not even calling her back right now.

I called the house, and Maggie answered the phone, sounding really pitiful. "Hello."

"Maggie, what's going on?"

"Nothing, Sasha. I am so bored here, and Melony called, looking for you. I told her to call you on your cell phone, but she sounded like she wanted you right then or not at all, and Tray called here for you too. He said something about you getting yours or something. I'm not really sure what he was talking about, to be honest with you. All I know is, he sounded really mad. Oh, and some guy named Ramón called for you too. He said you and him had some shit to talk about. He asked for your cell phone number, but I told him I didn't have it. I think he knew I was lying, 'cause he was like, 'Yeah, right.'"

"Well, I'm gonna have to call him when I have some time. Did TJ call me?"

"No."

I really didn't expect him to anyway. I still didn't tell Maggie what was going on with me and Tray. All she knew is that I was staying at Aunt Trudy's for a while. I never tell all my business to people. They always try to use it against you. Especially family. They're the worst. They'll have your business all out in the street quicker than you can get it out of your mouth. I know you know what I'm talking about.

Anyway, I don't know what to do with this man. I am really not in the mood to get my freak on. I wonder if I can get out of it. Maybe I suddenly developed a headache, or worse, I got my period. No, I can't say that, 'cause when I really get it, he won't believe me. I'll just tell him I have a headache. When I went back in the house, he was on the phone upstairs. I could hear laughter. He's probably talking to his little flunky, TJ.

"Nick!" I shouted up the stairs.

"I gotta go," I heard him whisper. "Here I come, baby."

"Who was that?" I asked him as he came down the stairs.

"Oh, that was TJ. He was letting me in on a joke. I guess after they left, Andrew called him and asked him what he was doing later. TJ told him he was gonna be bumping and grinding with his woman. I don't think Andrew took it well. He said, 'Whatever,' and hung up."

"What? Are you telling me Andrew just tried to come on to TJ?"

"Baby, I don't know what's going on over there. All I know is what's about to go on over here."

"Well, you know, Nick, I really have a bad headache, and I do need to go home and check on my cousin. She just got in today, and she's all by herself. I feel bad. I need to spend some time with her."

"OK, baby, I understand. How about a rain check then? Sure you don't need a rain check? You got the keys to the house."

I loved it when he talked to me like that.

"Why don't you go take two aspirin, check on your cousin, and come back and put me to sleep later?"

Oh, this damn man just won't get it through his head. *I'm not in the mood!* I screamed to myself. "OK, baby, I'll call you before I come back over." I'll just have to fake it. Lord knows I didn't wanna do him like that, but he asked for it. Besides, I am driving his truck. I should reward him somehow. I kissed him on the cheek and ran for the door.

"Oh, um, Sasha, what was that? I know you can do better than that."

"I'm sorry, baby," I said, puckering up for a big wet one. He grabbed me, pressing me into him with the palm of his hand, and tongued me down. I melted in his arms; he was such a good kisser.

Chapter 11

I woke up at one o'clock in his bed. I couldn't believe he conned me into staying—or, should I say, seduced me.

"Good morning, baby," Nick said, rolling over. "What time is it?"

"It's almost eight o'clock."

"I gotta get to the office. I got a lot of research to do for an upcoming case. This lady killed her husband."

"What? Nick, how can you deal with those types of people all day? That is so crazy to me."

"I think she did it in self-defense. Anyway, I have to make sure I have all the evidence together. I also need to research if she's been married before and if this has ever happened in her life before. You can't be too careful these days. I don't want any surprises in the courtroom."

"I hear you. Is TJ working on the case with you?"

"We don't really work on a lot of cases together. Just in the same office is all."

"Oh. Well, I'll go downstairs and make some coffee," I said, sliding off his silk sheets.

"It's already made, baby. I set it for seven forty-five. Come here. I have something for you." Nick pulled me back in the bed by my waist and lay on top of me. He slid his head down the front of my robe and began kissing my stomach. With each kiss, his lips went farther and farther down until his head disappeared between my legs. How could he do that first thing in the morning? He is so damn horny.

"Mmm, you taste so sweet," he said, rubbing his fingers around my clit as he entered me with his tongue.

"Oh, damn," I said. It felt so good. He stroked my thighs as his tongue licked from one end of my vagina to the other.

"OK, now I'm up." He stopped, jumped up out of the bed, and headed for the bathroom. Now he didn't just get me all hot and bothered and leave me like this.

"You're done?" I said, feeling unsatisfied.

"Yeah, for now. You'll have to wait till later for part two."

"Later? I have to go all day feeling like this?"

"At least I'll know you're thinking about me."

"I guess so. Nick!" I screamed.

He just laughed and went into the shower. "I'll be out in a minute. Can you make the bed?"

There I lay, soaking wet, with my T-shirt up around my waist. I was so mad. I'll fix him. I went into the bathroom, took my T-shirt off, threw it on the ground, and got in the shower with him. I looked him straight in the eye, him standing there with his toothbrush hanging out of his mouth. I grabbed his sopping, wet dick, got on my knees, and licked and sucked all over it until it could stand on its own.

"Oh, shit, Sasha, turn around," he said, letting out a moan.

"No, you'll have to wait until later," I said, stepping out of the shower, laughing. That'll teach him to tease me.

"Sasha!" He screamed from the shower.

I just ignored him and closed the bathroom door and went downstairs. He can make his own damn bed. When he finally came downstairs, I had gotten dressed and was sipping on a cup of coffee at the kitchen bar counter.

"You little—"

"Little what, Nick? Serves you right. That'll teach ya," I said, taking another sip.

Nick just looked at me and grinned. "You wait until later. You're gonna get it."

"Yeah, yeah, promises, promises."

He got a cup of coffee and went into his office off the kitchen to get his briefcase.

"Nick, what time do you think you'll be here tonight?"

"I'm not sure. Before eight though."

"Well, I have a lot to do. I really need to find out what's going on with my son, and I also need to finally go and check up on my cousin. You may not hear from me until around four or five, OK?"

"All right, baby," Nick said, getting ready to go out the door. "Come give me some sugar."

Give him some sugar? He sounds like a dirty old man. Shit, the last time I kissed him, I spent the night. "Here I come," I said, getting up from the barstool. This felt so nice. I can't wait to get everything in order. I ran to the door and gave him a big wet kiss.

"I love you, baby."

"I love you too, Nick. Have a good day, and I'll call you later."

"OK, baby."

"Good luck with your case, by the way."

"Thanks, baby."

There he went out the door. My man. And what a good one he was. I can't wait to be Mrs. Abraham. I can't wait. I went upstairs and got into the shower. I had a few outfits here now. Two that he bought me and a couple that I brought over with me. I never know what type of mood I'm gonna be in. I feel like wearing a skirt today, the one I had on when I met him. I love that one. It's really short, and it shows off my pretty big legs. That's my family trademark: pretty big legs and a big old butt. Even Simone got one, as small as she is. She ain't made up of nothing but booty. Now Maggie, on the other hand, has lost her shape altogether. I swear, it doesn't even look like she's in this family anymore. I really need to go and check on her.

After I got out the shower and dressed, I headed to Aunt Trudy's house. I wonder when she was coming back. She didn't even give me a definite date as to when she would be home. I hope she's all right. What am I saying? I know she's fine, 'cause she's with her lover man, Mr. Carter.

I called the house as soon as I got in the car. I noticed I had a blocked number in my calls-received box. I wonder who that is. When I checked the messages, I was surprised to hear was that guy named Ramón. How'd he get my number? Probably Tray's trifling ass. He would do something like that, seeing that he's supposed to be so mad at me. He's just sore 'cause I won't let him do whatever he wanna do with me. I ain't anybody's toy. I am a woman, and if he can't treat me like one, well, damn, I know a couple of fellows that can. I also got a call from Richie. I don't know how he got my number either. There was one call from Maritza and two from Mel. Why don't these damn people leave me alone? I really don't wanna be bothered by anybody but my son and maybe Simone.

When I got to the house, there was a Range Rover in the driveway. The music was blasting, and the windows were tinted, so I could not see who was in it. I parked on the street and then sat there for a minute. I called Maggie inside to see if she knew who it was.

"Hello."

"Maggie, do you know who's parked in the driveway?"

"That's that guy, Ramón, or whatever his name is. He's looking for you."

"I don't even know who gave him this address."

"I didn't."

"OK." I got out of the car and walked over to the truck. If he was gonna do something to me like shoot me, I don't think it would be in front of my house. As I walked up, the window came down.

"You're Sasha?"

"Who's asking?"

"I left you a message on your cell phone. I go with Jade. You know who I am."

"Yeah, so what can I do for you?"

"Yo, I need to get some shit straight with you. I don't appreciate that little shit you set up the other day."

"What are you talking about? I didn't set up anything."

"Yeah, all right. Well, one of y'all bitches is lying."

"Well, it ain't me, and I ain't a bitch. My bad, I'm saying though."

"Y'all could've gotten my ass shot out there in the damn boonies. There I was, thinking I was gonna check on my girl at some party, and y'all done set my ass up to meet some damn female she's fuckin'. That shit was really low."

"Well, I didn't have the pleasure of personally setting it up, but I knew about it, and it serves her ho-ish ass right. She deserves everything she gets. Ain't nobody got time for Jade and her fucking games? I guess you didn't know who you were dealing with."

"I'm saying that's beside the point. Why'd y'all have to get me caught up in your shit?"

"You were caught up the day you started messing with her."

"Damn, Sasha, you're kinda fine, yo."

"Yeah, whatever. Anything you came all the way over here to say to me?"

"I just wanna get it straight. Don't be putting me in shit. I ain't got time for the kid shit, and I'm trying to be a man about it. I could be whooping your ass right now, fine as you are. I'm trying to take it easy on you. Why the fuck does your man wanna cheat on you? What the fuck are you doing? Probably wilding out in the damn streets."

"No, I'm not like that. He was the one, so get your story straight."

"I'm saying, can we get together sometime?"

"I can't believe you came over here to cuss me out, and now you're trying to pick me up. I'm taken, Ramón."

"What's that got to do with us?"

"I'm in love."

"What's love got to do with me and you?"

"There is no me and you."

"Shit, you got a fat ass and them pretty-ass legs in that skirt. Sure would like to see what's up under there. Shit, you're almost as fine as my girl."

"Don't compare me to any of your hos. You'll never have a classy lady like me."

"Shit, why don't you be my classy lady?"

Ramón was begging with his fat ass. He looks like he weighs about 280 or so. And he doesn't look all that tall either. "Ramón, I have things to do, so if you're done, I have to go outside."

"All right now, you don't know what you're missing. I'll lick that pussy dry."

"Yuck, nasty pig. What is this? Pussy-licking day? First of all, you sound really nasty, and I don't mean that in a good way, and second of all, if you knew anything about a real lady, you would know that kind of talk doesn't turn me on. As a matter of fact, it disgusts me."

"Well, yo, you got my number. Holla at a brother sometimes." He just kept on talking like he didn't even hear what I was saying to him. I walked up the stairs, and I knew he was staring. "Goddamn," he said, pulling off. My ass does have that effect on niggas at times.

I turned the key and heard somebody run up the stairs. What the fuck is she running for? She must have thought I was crazy enough to bring that fool in the house. "Maggie?" I screamed in the house.

"I'm upstairs. Are you alone?"

"Yes, who would I be with?"

"I don't know. I thought maybe you brought that guy inside with you."

"You must be out of your damn mind." That little ghetto thug wannabe. Now I see how Jade could play both sides. He is real dumb acting. "Come downstairs."

"OK, let me get dressed." Maggie came downstairs in some baggy sweats that look like they could fit a ten-year-old better and a big sweat top. She looked pathetic.

"Are you all right, Maggie?"

"I'm fine. Why do you ask?"

"'Cause you don't look so good. You look kinda sick. You're feeling all right?"

"I just have a little cold or something."

"Did you eat?"

"No, not yet."

"Come and sit down in the kitchen and let me make something for you."

"I'm really not hungry."

"I know you heard what I said, Maggie. Come in the kitchen and sit down. You need to start eating, or you're gonna end up in the hospital for that next."

Shit, for all I know, she was probably lying to me. That's probably why she was there, to begin with. She was skin and bones, and she had brown spots under her eyes. My poor baby cousin. She looked like she was dying. I made her an egg sandwich and some tea. God knows she needed more than that, but her frail body didn't look like it could handle it.

"Here. Now eat," I said to her, watching her frown up her face as if I had given her poison.

I wanted to cry. Didn't she know that the longer she went on this way, the harder it was going to be for her body to accept it. She may even need to go into a treatment facility for anorexia. She didn't think she had a problem, and clearly, that was the first sign to prove that she did. I wanted to slap some sense into her. What the fuck was she doing in New York, living off bread and water? Shit, it didn't even look like she was living off bread, just some damn water.

"Maggie, what's gonna happen if you can't ever eat again? Do you know?"

"What are you talking about, Sasha? I'm fine."

"Maggie, you do know this is serious? You're not a little girl anymore. You can't play the naive game anymore. You gotta know that if you continue this way, you're gonna end up six feet under."

I couldn't bear to watch her eat. She sat there, taking rat-size bites out of the sandwich like her jaw was wired shut, and she couldn't do any better than that.

"Maggie, I have to go upstairs and make some phone calls. Please try and eat most of the sandwich and don't throw it away. Oh, and by the way, the garbage disposal is not working, and if you put it in the toilet down here, you'll clog it up."

Maggie just looked at me as if she wanted to say something but couldn't find the right words. I started for the steps and stopped on the third one to see if she would get up from the table. And just as I thought, about one minute later, she got up, and I heard the garbage rattle. I ran back down the stairs and caught her putting the sandwich underneath some of the other things that were already in the garbage.

"What are you doing? You're sick, you know that."

"Sasha, I just can't eat it. It's making me sick. I just can't." She threw the sandwich on the top of the garbage and ran upstairs crying. I didn't know what to do with her.

Why was this my responsibility? I felt like if I didn't try, I would be blamed for what she was doing to herself. I couldn't believe this was happening in my family. Black people don't have eating disorders; they have bad eating habits, but we don't have a problem eating at all. That's a white thing. Or so I thought.

My aunt raised us to think all kinds of stupid shit; now look what has happened. Everything she's said black people don't do, her kids have somehow ended up doing. I suppose that's what happens when you think things in the world can't affect you personally. It finds a way to infect your very being.

I decide to go upstairs and have a serious conversation with Maggie.

"Maggie!" I shouted from behind the closed door. I wanted to know when it got this bad and how. I really needed to know if there was anything I could do to help her with this. "Maggie! Can I talk to you?"

"What? What do you wanna talk to me about, Sasha? There's nothing to discuss. Why do you care about me anyway? You never did before. All of a sudden, you care? Nobody in this family ever really cared anything about me. I grew up all alone. No one ever came to any of my plays or recitals or anything else for that matter. And after what Uncle Peety did to me, why should I ever trust anyone in this house?"

"Uncle Peety? Maggie, what are you talking about? Will you just open the damn door so we can stop screaming back and forth?"

When Maggie opened the door, both of her wrists were bleeding.

"Maggie! What did you do?" I ran into the bathroom and grabbed two washcloths.

Maggie collapsed in the doorway while I was calling 911. When the ambulance came, they rushed her to the hospital. I heard them calling her a suicide case and that she would need a psychiatric evaluation after they got her stable. They said if she had cut her wrist straight down instead of straight across, she wouldn't have made it.

I couldn't believe what was happening. I followed the ambulance to the hospital. I called Simone to meet me there.

"She did what?"

"You heard me. Maggie slit her wrist. She kept muttering something about what Uncle Peety did to her and that she couldn't trust anyone in this house and how none of us cared about her."

"Uncle Peety? What does he have to do with this?"

"Girl, you're asking me. I need to call Mel. You call Tony and tell him to meet us there."

"He doesn't even know she's here."

"I'm sure Mel told him."

I dialed Mel's number once I got to the hospital.

"Mel, it's Sasha. Maggie is in the hospital. St. Francis. Come quick."

"What happened?"

"She tried to kill herself."

"Tried to what?"

"Just come down here."

I couldn't get in touch with Lee since he was at work, but I left a message on his voice mail. Hopefully, he'll check. I called Nathan, and he was the first one at the hospital even though he was the last one I called.

"Sasha, what's going on with Maggie, and why didn't anybody tell me she was here?"

"I didn't get around to it, and I thought maybe she would call everyone on her own. She thinks we all hate her."

"Nobody hates her."

"She hates us, as far as I know. It was her that ran away to New York, and if I didn't try to keep in contact with her every time I went down there, I wouldn't even know she was still alive. I'm just telling you what she said."

Just then, Melony and Simone came into the waiting room. "What happened?"

"I don't know. She just started rambling on about how we all hate her and that Uncle Peety had done something to her."

"Here comes Tony," Simone said.

"What's up? When did Maggie come back, and why is she here?"

"She tried to kill herself, Tony."

"What? What's going on?"

"She said we all hate her," Mel said to him. "She also said that Uncle Peety did something to her."

"Peety? What the fuck did he do to her?"

"Sorry, Nathan, man. You know you're a nice man. Everything's kinda hectic right now."

"So what happened, Sasha? Tell us," Simone said.

"I made her a sandwich, and she wouldn't eat it. Oh, by the way, guys, Maggie is suffering from anorexia. She's only about ninety pounds, so when you see her, don't react."

"I'm gonna go find out what's going on with her," Mel said, going to the information desk.

"Ninety pounds," Tony said, sighing. "My sister?"

"I gotta see her," Simone said.

"I need to know what's going on," Tony said.

"We'll find out in good time," Nathan said.

"Anybody know where Mommy is?" Tony asked.

"She went out of town with Mr. Carter."

"Mr. Carter?" Mel said, coming back from the desk.

"What did they say?" Tony asked first.

"They said she will have to stay and that she's in the back. They said we can go back and see her now."

We all went into the back of the emergency where all the patients were still waiting to be seen. When we got to room 5, there Maggie was, lying in that bed, looking pale and frail. Everyone stopped cold in their tracks.

"Maggie?" Tony said in disbelief.

"Maggie? Is that you?" Simone said, looking at her sister with tears in her eyes.

"What happened to you?" Mel said, bursting out into tears.

Nathan just opened his Bible and started praying, "The Lord is my shepherd. I shall not want . . ."

We all surrounded Maggie's bed. It was the first time we had been in the same room since we were little.

"Hey, guys, I got your message," Lee said, coming into the room. "Oh, Maggie," he said, looking at his little sister just lying there.

She hadn't opened her mouth yet and said a word. She just looked around at all of us and smiled, with tears in her eyes. "So this is what it takes to get us all in the same room," she said, looking at us. "If I had known, I would have done it sooner."

"Don't play, Maggie," Melony said, shaken.

"This is really serious. We're all gonna have to take care of you now," Tony said.

"We're gonna make sure you're all right," Nathan said.

"Maggie, what happened?" Lee said, gently holding her hand.

"I just couldn't let it go, Lee. I couldn't. I tried and tried."

"Lee, what is she talking about?" Simone asked, confused.

"I think I should let Magdalena tell yall that for herself."

Just then, Tiffany walked into the room. "What's going on?"

"Maggie is sick, and she has something she needs to tell us all."

This must be serious because Lee never called Maggie by her real name. She hated it.

"Close the door," Maggie said. "When I was sixteen . . ." Maggie began to cry. Lee held her hand.

"It's all right, Maggie, we're here for you," I said.

"When I was sixteen, I was home alone, and I was taking a shower. Uncle Peety came upstairs, and he was high on crack, I think. He came into the bathroom and held me down and raped me. I called Lee because I was so scared to tell anybody else. That's why Uncle Peety moved into that crack house. Lee took me to the hospital, and I made him swear never to tell a living soul, not even Mommy."

"What?" Tony said with a fury in his voice. "That motherfucker did what?" he said, beginning to pace back and forth in a little space by the door.

"Oh my god," Simone said. "That's why you were acting so funny."

"My god, that's why you left home and never called anyone. Why didn't you tell us?" I said, crying.

"Why didn't you share it with us?" Simone said, getting mad.

"We're supposed to be family, Maggie!" Mel said, crying and screaming out loud.

"I couldn't. I just couldn't. I felt like it was my fault. I felt like if I hadn't been walking around in those little shorts in front of him all the time, maybe it wouldn't have happened."

"Oh, Maggie, baby, I could never have imagined anything worse happening to anyone," Mel said, looking at her.

Tiffany just leaned against the wall and kinda zoned out for a minute. The whole room got quiet.

"I gotta go," Tony said.

"Tony!" Maggie said. "No, don't! I know what you're gonna do. Don't!"

"What do you mean 'don't'? That fuckin' crackhead destroyed your life and ours too. Because of him, we all grew up apart and were always wondering what one did to another. Shit, I went my own way when I saw everybody else doing their own thing. Maybe I would've been a doctor or something like Mommy wanted instead of owning a fuckin' strip club."

"Tony, it doesn't make sense for you to go get yourself in trouble over him. You know he ain't good, and God will deal with him."

"God, Nathan? God? God is the one that allowed this to happen to my little sister in the first place."

"No, Tony! God is the one that allowed Maggie to live through it. Bad things are gonna always happen, but God helps us to deal with it. You gotta understand the power of the Almighty. He gives man free will. So man sometimes can do some wickedness. But the Almighty give you the strength to get through it."

"I have a question," Mel said. "Did God intend for my husband to walk out on me with my daughter?"

"Mel, what?" Simone said. "What are you talking about?"

"I don't wanna play this secret game anymore. Alex left me last week and took AleZandria with him. I don't know where they are, but the two of them left and closed out my bank account."

"Well, since we're all coming clean about things," I said, "Tray and I have been apart for almost two months now. And if yall really want to know the truth, we've been apart living together for the last three years. Oh, and I'm seeing someone else."

"You're what?" Melony said.

"Yeah," I said, taking my hand out of my pocket to reveal the big five-carat diamond. Oh, shit, this cat must be balling.

"That shit looks real," Tony said, grabbing my hand.

"He's a lawyer," I said, boasting.

"A lawyer?" Tony said. "Well, if you can't be what Mommy wants you to be, why not marry into it?" We all laughed, even Maggie.

"I got to tell yall something," Tony said. "Emily is pregnant. She's, like, around five months now."

"Five months?" Simone said.

"And you weren't gonna tell us?" Melony said.

"No, I didn't wanna ruin my bad-boy image."

"Go ahead with that mess, Tony," Lee said, laughing. "Well, I have something to say. I got remarried about three months ago."

"Lee, you didn't?" Mel said. "To who?"

"Yall don't know her. She doesn't live here. I met her when I went to DC on for the business trip."

"That was some business trip," Tony said.

"Yeah, he has taken care of business, all right," I said.

"She's Indian," Tony said, looking like he remembered something he didn't wanna share.

"Indian?" I said.

"Go, Lee, with your Kama Sutra lover," Simone said, laughing.

"It was love at first sight," he said, gazing off in the sky.

"Well, we're all glad for you, Lee," I said. "It's been a long time since you had a good woman in your life."

"Yeah, man, I agree with that one," Tony said, giving him dap. "You're gonna be eatin' a whole bunch of hot-ass food now."

"All right," Tiffany said, "I guess since everyone is coming clean, I . . . uhm . . . I'm a . . . I have something to say. I'm uh . . . I'm . . ."

"Would you spit it out already," Tony said.

"I'm gay."

"You're what?" Mel said, shocked to hear there was some information she didn't know first.

"I've been living with a woman for the past six years."

"Who? Jade?" Tony said. "Her fine ass is gay? Damn, what a waste."

"Yeah, Jade. She was my girlfriend."

"Was?" I said, looking at her.

"Yeah, I put her skanky ass out. She had a whole nother life going on, and I couldn't be bothered with it." Tiffany just looked at me and grinned.

"OK, my turn. I met someone too," Simone said. "I am officially dating a lawyer named TJ. I haven't told Richie yet 'cause I'm scared he's gonna whoop my ass."

Tony looked at Maggie. "Ain't anybody hurting any of my sisters anymore. What about you, Nathan? Don't you have anything to say?" he asked, looking over at him.

"Nah, man, mi nice. I don't have anything to say other than probably, it's time for us all to go to church together when Maggie gets better."

"Oh lord, can you imagine that. I'll go," I said first.

"Yeah, I'll go too. I got to pray that Richie doesn't kill me when I break up with him."

"Yeah, man, count me in," Lee said without hesitation.

"Damn, can I go and still own the club?" Tony said. "I don't want the church to come down on my head."

"God accepts all his children," Nathan said.

"You sure now."

"I'll go. I need an outlet to deal with this whole divorce I'm about to go through," Mel said, looking at me.

"I don't think I better go," Tiffany said.

"Why not?" Simone said. "If we can all let go with all the stuff we done did, why can't you?"

"Yeah, I guess you're right."

"Maggie, are you gonna come?" I asked.

"Of course, I wouldn't miss it for the world," she said, looking at all of us.

Chapter 12

It's been six months since Maggie was in the emergency room. Everyone pitched in and helped her recover. The doctor said she will always be prone to anorexia, but if she eats properly and takes her vitamins, she should be all right. They gave her a counselor to discuss her past issues with Uncle Peety. And that seems to be going well. She was up to 120 pounds and looking like her old self. Simone and I called Uncle Peety and told him we knew what he had done to Maggie, and no one has seen or heard from him since. We never told Aunt Trudy. We didn't think she would be able to handle it.

She was very surprised and thrilled to death when she came back home to see that Maggie had come back from New York and that we had all camped out at the house for a couple of days to help out. She surprised us and came back married to Mr. Carter.

Melony filed for divorce, and it'll be final in a couple of weeks, along with mine. She's going back to school this fall to study law. She really enjoyed watching the process of her divorce firsthand. Alex tried to come back to her, and she turned him down flat. She told him she was too good for him and always was. Her girls were so impressed with her strength that they helped her get rid of all his belongings. Alezandria calls every now and then, but she's too ashamed to show her face. She will never understand the true concept of family.

Tony finally told Richie that Simone didn't wanna be with him anymore. He was so hurt he left for a couple of months and just resurfaced when he heard Tony was looking for a buyer for the club. He sold it to him for almost half the worth out of sheer sympathy. Tony bought a house in Farmington with his girlfriend, Emily, and their new baby girl, Magdalena. He said it was time he settled down with one woman. He opened a clothing store in downtown Hartford.

We all got to meet Lee's new wife, Naldi, who taught us girls some things for the bedroom I can't even share with you.

Nathan opened a little shop on the avenue where he sells candles and incense. He also has poetry and dance there at night. He put Maggie in charge of running the shows.

Simone and I thought it would be a good idea to hook Tiffany back up with Andrew since he said she was one of the best sex partners he ever had. We figured with her being so masculine and him being so feminine, they'd do just fine. There's someone out there for everyone.

Simone moved in with TJ and is his full-time woman, and she finally started going to school full-time too. She has three semesters to go.

Maritza had her baby, and Tray left her again, since she chose to name the baby Sasha. She said that I had been a blessing in her life and that if her baby came out with half of the heart I had, she would have a beautiful beginning for a good life. She's going back to school, and her mother helped her open another beauty salon with the older lady, Trina, from the old shop, since she was the only one with a cosmetology license.

I don't know where Tray is and don't care. He disappeared after he lost the house in the battle, and TJ decided to live with me and Nick. I don't hate him though. I feel sorry for him. I was the best woman he ever had.

Now as for me, I'm working on renovating the building Nick bought me for Valentine's Day. He wanted to give me a jump start on my future in the world of art. I'm planning to open a museum that will carry both adults' and children's art. TJ's gonna run the children's department for me. Oh, and did I mention all my cousins are helping me plan my wedding? They all say they want it to be the biggest, baddest wedding Hartford has ever seen. My son, TJ, offered to give me away. It's about time we put Hartford on the map.